GIRL
WITH
BRUSH
AND
CANVAS

Alfred Stieglitz's photograph of Georgia O'Keeffe
in her early thirties

GIRL
WITH
BRUSH
AND
CANVAS

Georgia O'Keeffe,
American Artist

A NOVEL

CAROLYN MEYER

CALKINS CREEK
AN IMPRINT OF HIGHLIGHTS
Honesdale, Pennsylvania

Calkins Creek
An Imprint of Highlights
815 Church Street
Honesdale, Pennsylvania 18431
calkinscreekbooks.com
Printed in the United States of America
ISBN: 978-1-62979-934-6 (hc)
ISBN: 978-1-68437-627-8 (eBook)
Library of Congress Control Number: 2018955595

First edition
10 9 8 7 6 5 4 3 2 1

Design by Anahid Hamparian
The text is set in Neutraface Text.
The titles are set in Neutraface Text and Folio.

For Deborah Blanche, actor

Taos, New Mexico—Summer 1929

"MISS O'KEEFFE, SLOW DOWN, PLEASE. YOU ARE going to kill us." Tony spoke calmly, as though he didn't mind dying.

I was flying down a rutted dirt road outside of Taos behind the wheel of a shiny black Buick roadster. I ignored Tony and pulled the throttle. The roadster shot forward. This was my second lesson, and I already knew that I loved driving fast. I wasn't going to slow down just because this man told me I should.

"Mabel will be mad if you wreck her auto. She loves it, maybe more than she loves me."

The Buick belonged to Mabel, Tony's wife. Mabel was very rich, and she could buy another automobile if anything happened to this one. She'd come to New Mexico from New York. At her house, Los Gallos—"The

Roosters"—she made herself the center of attention, surrounding herself with artists and other interesting people. My friend Beck and I were staying in a little guest *casita* on her property. Tony Lujan, the tall, handsome, broad-chested Taos Indian in the passenger seat beside me, was Mabel's fourth husband. He was holding my box of watercolors and a sketchpad on his lap. He didn't talk much.

"Bridge ahead," Tony said.

I'd been across that bridge—no railings, just some wooden planks laid end to end and a pair of posts—on my first lesson. "So narrow only an angel can fly over it," I'd told Beck afterward.

"Watch this!" I said, aiming straight for the bridge. "I'm going to thread the needle!"

Tony sucked in his breath but didn't say a word. We hurtled across, the wooden planks rattling, with only inches to spare on either side. I let out an exultant whoop.

But on the far end I misjudged somehow, and the Buick clipped a post with its right fender. There was a loud crunch, the Buick spun around, and next thing I knew, we were facing back the way we came. One of the rear wheels was lodged in a ditch.

My heart was pumping fast. I looked at Tony. "Not good," he said.

We climbed out to inspect the damage. The right fender was as crumpled as an old rag, and the bumper hung at a rakish angle. Tony sighed and shook his head. "Mabel is going to be mad."

"She's in Buffalo for a month, isn't she? I'll have it fixed before she gets back. She doesn't have to know." I tried to sound calm, reasonable.

"You were not paying attention, and you were going too fast," Tony said.

"I know it was my fault." I walked around the auto again. "What do we do now?"

"We wait."

We sat beside the Buick. Tony was silent. It was very pleasant, sitting there by the side of the road. The air was cool and fresh. The sun was sinking, bathing majestic Taos Mountain, still snowcapped, in a rosy glow. I retrieved my watercolors from the auto and began a painting, working quickly before the light faded.

I showed it to Tony. "Sacred Mountain," he said. "Mó-ha-loh in our language. Very powerful. If you stay here, it is because the Mountain has allowed it."

Eventually somebody from the pueblo came along on horseback. The two men discussed the situation in their language. Then they tied one end of a rope to the saddle horn, the other end to the front bumper. They got behind the auto and pushed, I urged the horse to pull, and the roadster was eased up out of the ditch.

I was more cautious driving back to Los Gallos, my confidence shaken.

Tony said nothing until we pulled up near the shed in back of the Big House. "That was your last lesson," he said.

"I don't need any more instruction?"

He shook his head. "You drive very bad. I will not go with you again."

He walked away. I didn't know whether to laugh or throw something at him. Beck came out of her studio—Beck was a painter, too. "How did the lesson go?"

"Tony quit. You're my new teacher."

"*Me?* What happened?"

I shrugged. "Just a little problem. I won't be driving Mabel's Buick anymore. I'm going to buy my own auto."

I wondered if what Tony had said was true—that I could stay here if the Sacred Mountain allowed it.

Part I

"I'm going to be an artist."

1

Sun Prairie, Wisconsin—
Summer 1900

THE FIRST TIME I TOLD ANYONE THAT I WAS GOING to be an artist, Lena and I were hanging wet sheets on a clothesline. Linen is heavy when it's wet, and it took two of us to make sure the sheets didn't drag on the ground. Lena's mother was our washerwoman, and Lena was my best friend. I was twelve years old, and she was thirteen and taller than me and had a bosom.

We heaved another sheet over the line. "What are you going to be when you grow up?" I asked. The question just popped out.

Lena's dark eyes flickered over me. "A grown-up lady, I guess." She squared up the corners of the sheet. I passed her a couple of wooden clothespins from a cloth bag, and she clamped the sheet to the line. "Like your ma, and mine, looking after a husband and a whole lot of children." I had six brothers and sisters; Lena had eight. Lena shrugged, her skinny shoulders going up and down. "You planning on being something different?"

"Yes," I said. "I am going to be an artist."

I felt very sure about that, although I'd only just arrived at that decision. It was like stepping off a train in a town I'd never been to before.

Lena's face always showed exactly what she was feeling. She shook her head and frowned. "An artist? What d'you mean, Georgie? What kind of artist you planning on being?"

I hadn't thought about that part. Were there different kinds? "I want to paint pictures," I said.

Lena snatched a pillow slip from the basket and flapped it hard. "Pictures of what? Cows? Plenty of them around here, for sure."

Ours was a dairy farm with tobacco as the main cash crop, like most other farms in this part of Wisconsin. She was right—there were plenty of cows.

"Pictures of people, but not just anybody. Only people who are good-looking." Gloomy portraits of Mama's ancestors glared down from the walls in our parlor. I didn't want to paint anything like those.

Lena's face, round and plain as a custard pie, collapsed into a pout. "Of me?" she asked in a pinched voice, and I understood that she was afraid she wasn't good-looking enough for me to paint her picture.

"Of course, Lena! A very nice one of you!"

Her pout faded, a smile broke across her face, and for that minute she *was* good-looking. Almost. Her eyes were too close together, and there was no help for *that*.

We threw the last sheet over the clothesline. Lena propped up the sagging rope with a wooden pole. A breeze came up, and the sheets billowed like sails.

I stepped back to admire a drift of clouds piling up along the western horizon. The clouds had taken on a violet tint that was deepening to purple. "Look at that sky, Lena," I said. "Pretty, isn't it?"

"Nuh-uh. Gonna rain, for sure," she grumbled, "and we'll just have to take everything down and then hang it all up after it's done."

Lena was right again. We'd just climbed up the narrow, twisty stairs to my tower room when the sky turned the color of wet slate and daggers of lightning slashed through the clouds. We rushed down to rescue the bed linens before the rain broke loose, but we weren't quick enough to avoid getting soaking wet ourselves.

I was the next-to-oldest O'Keeffe, after Francis; then came four sisters with another brother in between. Our mother said that each of us had been given a different talent, and some of us more than others. My sister Ida, two years younger, was the one Mama decided had the most artistic talent. Every time Ida drew a pretty picture, Mama made a fuss about it. I kept it to myself that I did not have in mind just drawing pretty pictures—I was going to be an *artist*. There was a difference, and I knew that, even then.

On long winter evenings we gathered in the parlor, and Mama read to us, working her way through all five books of James Fenimore Cooper's Leatherstocking Tales. Sometimes she played the piano and we sang. Mama had taught me to read music and started me on scales and arpeggios, but I wanted to learn to play the violin, because Papa did—he called it a fiddle. He loved to dance, too, and taught us jigs and reels. "It's the Irish in me," he said, and I believed I was like my father and had plenty of the Irish in me, too. When I was about seven, Mama found a music teacher in Sun Prairie who taught both violin and piano and gave me lessons for a year. I was quite passionate about both instruments but not about practicing—I either played for hours each day or not at all for days. After the teacher moved away, I kept on with my exercise book for a while and then I stopped.

All but the youngest of us O'Keeffe children trooped down the dirt road to Town Hall School at the edge of our property. Three dozen or so students from neighboring farms attended the dark and dismal one-room schoolhouse. It was old: our parents had gone there as children. Lena and I had shared a desk since the first day of first grade, when I was five and she was six. The teacher, Mrs. Edison, boarded with us during the week.

I was in school because I had to be. I disliked it, but I was well-behaved, so as not to disappoint Mama.

A few years later Mama hired Mrs. Edison's sister, Miss Belle, to come out from Sun Prairie once a week to give art lessons to Ida and my second sister, Anita (who we called Nita), and me. Miss Belle showed us a book of drawings of balls and pyramids and cylinders, and we practiced copying those shapes. Everybody in Sun Prairie agreed that Miss Belle had natural artistic talent. Just like Ida, I guess. I was about ten and I tried hard, but my drawings didn't receive much praise. Not like Ida's.

It didn't take long for Miss Belle to run out of inspiration. "I've taught the girls all I know, Mrs. O'Keeffe," she said, as if apologizing for not knowing more.

The next year, when I was eleven, Mama found someone in the village with a larger supply of artistic ideas. Twice a month Papa hitched Danny Boy, our best draft horse, to our new John Deere wagon—we always called it "the John Deere"—and drove Ida and Nita and me to Mrs. Sarah Mann's home in Sun Prairie for lessons.

The walls of Mrs. Mann's house were white; the furniture was plain, and there wasn't much of it. This was not like our house, where the parlor was stuffed with velvet settees and carved chests, the walls were papered with floral designs, and crocheted shawls and antimacassars were draped on everything. I liked the plainness, but I did wonder if Mrs. Mann was unable to afford the nice things my mother favored.

She had us sit on benches at an unpainted wood table, gave each of us a box of watercolors, a cup of water, clean brushes, and a sheet or two of paper, and passed around art books with colorful pictures she called "chromos" that we were supposed to copy.

I turned the pages carefully, studying the pictures and trying to understand how the artist could look at a bunch of real flowers or a real tree or a real horse and then figure out how to show its likeness on a sheet of paper. I chose a chromo of a bowl of red roses and tried to copy it, but my roses didn't look like the ones in the picture. They did not look like real roses either.

We took our little paintings home and showed them to our mother. "Lovely colors, Ida," she said. "You've captured the horse quite well, Nita." Then she glanced at mine and frowned. "Rather unusual, Georgie." Mama doled out praise as if her supply was limited.

Nevertheless, she put my painting of the roses in a carved wooden frame and hung it in the parlor next to a painting that Grandmother Totto—Mama's mother—had done of two plums and one by Grandmother O'Keeffe of moss roses. While they were alive, my grandmothers had painted bright pictures of flowers and fruit and outdoor scenes. Both of them had died when I was younger, but their ghosts hung around everywhere, like their pictures.

"Strong ladies, those two," Papa used to say. "You're a lot like them, Georgie."

Mama and Papa were married because of those two strong ladies. The O'Keeffe and Totto families had once owned farms next to each other. Papa was only ten when his father died, but he left school to help his brothers run the O'Keeffe farm. After a few years he grew restless and struck out for the West. Meanwhile, down the road, George Totto, a Hungarian count with four daughters and two sons, went back to Hungary to collect money he believed was owed him. My grandmother had to figure out how to survive while the family waited for him to return. The two boys were too young to be much help, and it cost too much to hire extra farmhands. After the longest time Grandfather Totto still hadn't come back, and no one knew what had happened to him. The two women put their heads together and arranged for a Totto daughter, twenty-year-old Ida, to marry an O'Keeffe son, Frank, who was thirty-one by then, merging the two families and the two farms and solving their problems.

It always bothered me that my parents named me Georgia Totto O'Keeffe for a man who'd deserted his family. But I never asked why he hadn't come back or why they'd given me his name, and they never explained.

Grandmother Totto's sister Jennie had come to help with her fatherless nieces and nephews. After my parents married and their first baby, Francis, was born, Jennie moved in with them, and she stayed on as one after another of us arrived. I was next, followed by Ida, Anita, Alexius, Catherine, and Claudia. Auntie played with us and did all the things that Mama was too busy to do, like letting us ride her handsome carriage horse, Penelope. We called the little mare "Penny-lope."

Auntie taught me to sew outfits for my family of dolls, and even when I was very young I knew how to cut the cloth and make small, neat stitches. But more important than what she taught me to do was how she made me feel. I believed I was Auntie's favorite, and that mattered because I knew that Francis was Mama's favorite: he was a boy and the oldest. Francis, of all of us, was most like our mother, tall and thin with Mama's delicate features, dark eyes, and long, thick eyelashes. Quiet and studious like her, too. Our father was burly and broad-chested, outgoing and hearty. "A doer, not a thinker," Mama said.

Anything Francis could do, I was determined to do as well as he did, or even better. I raced him on the way to school and taunted him when I won, which I often did. And I wouldn't stop bragging when I got better marks than his, which I often did too. Francis was short-sighted, and I teased him by pretending to see things that weren't really there.

"Look at that bird, Francis!" I'd say, squinting up into the empty sky. "A raptor, and what's that he's got in his claws?" Nothing, of course. There was no raptor either. When my brother figured out that I'd fooled him, he'd clamp his jaw so tight that he'd turn red in the face and refuse to talk to me for two or three days until I apologized. Then, as soon as I could, I'd do something like it again, just to get his goat, and it always worked.

"You mustn't be jealous of Francis," Auntie chided me. "He's a boy and the oldest, so of course he gets the lion's share of attention."

"I'm not jealous!" I insisted. "I don't mind at all." But that wasn't true. I *did* mind. What about the *lioness's* share? Nobody ever talked about that!

The truth was, I pitied Francis for his short-sightedness. How awful it must be, I thought, not to be able to see the world clearly, always blurred. But pity didn't keep me from tormenting him.

My sisters claimed that I was the spoiled one. I insisted on doing things my own way, which had to be not like what my sisters were doing. When they braided their hair, I let mine fly loose. When they wore ribbons, I refused. If they wore black stockings, mine had to be white.

"That Georgie!" they said, making sour faces. "Always has to be different—her and her crazy notions!"

In a big family like ours, if you wanted something you had to figure out a way to get it on your own. Papa had built a tower onto one corner of our farmhouse—I guess he, too, liked things that were different—and I wanted the room at the top with the big windows that faced north and west. You could see sunsets and storms coming in and stars blinking on. I declared that I must have it all to myself because *I deserved it*. Ida and Nita, who had to share a room, insisted that it was not fair—Ida loudly, Nita quietly but persistently—and that we should take turns. Auntie tried to keep the peace, but I raised such a fuss that they gave in, although they never entirely stopped complaining. Auntie squeezed in with the two littlest ones, Catherine and Claudia, called Claudie, who were too young to protest. No one was allowed to come up to my tower room unless I granted permission. Boots, our black and white cat, spent most of his time with me there. I never wanted to leave it.

The art lessons with Mrs. Mann had come to an end, but alone in my tower room, like a queen in her castle, I filled page after page of a sketchbook with pencil drawings: flowers and trees and cows, the big cow barn, the springhouse, and the barn where bundles of tobacco leaves strung on wooden laths were hung to cure. None of those sketches satisfied me. I tried watercolors, too, but they turned out no better. I crumpled most of my pictures into balls and tossed them away, and sometimes for days I didn't paint or draw anything.

Lena had seven brothers. Two of the older ones—silent, hulking boys who hardly ever said a word to me—worked as hired hands for Papa. When Lena wasn't helping her mother wash our clothes, she stayed at home to take care of her baby brother. Buddy was thin and pale and couldn't walk, though he was old enough that he should have. Something was wrong with him, but they didn't know what.

One day Lena came by with Buddy on her hip and let him crawl around my tower room while Lena and I sat and talked. Pinned to the easel Papa had built for me was a picture I'd been working on, a watercolor of a woman hanging a sheet on a clothesline while a man in a cap watched. One end of the rope was tied to a tree, because I thought there ought to be a tree somewhere in the picture, but I hadn't decided what the other end of the rope should be tied to. The woman wore a red cloth around her head, because I wanted something red at exactly that spot.

Lena stared at it. "What's this supposed to be a picture of?" she asked finally.

"A lady hanging up laundry," I said.

"Is that supposed to be you with the red scarf? Or me? Because it doesn't look like either one of us."

"It's not *supposed* to be anything except an interesting picture with some people in it."

"All right." She shrugged, and it was plain that she didn't much care for it.

Buddy tried to grab Boots's tail, but the cat wouldn't allow it, and Buddy wailed until Lena picked him up and carried him downstairs. I stayed in my tower room and worked a little more on the watercolor, but it didn't improve much. Once you did a watercolor, it was done, and you couldn't do it over.

I turned thirteen that fall. The months went by without much happening, except for the usual freezing-cold winter that Papa hated, until spring planting season came around again. The next September Francis got ready to start his second year at the little country high school in Sun Prairie. I assumed I'd go to the same high school, and Lena would too, and we'd see each other every day, as we always did. Maybe we'd even share a desk again, although Francis said in high school everybody had a separate desk.

"I want to go," Lena said, "but my pa says I've had enough schooling. I'm needed at home, what with Buddy being so sickly. You can tell me what you're learning," Lena added wistfully. I promised I would, though I was disappointed.

But then everything changed for me, too. I wouldn't be going to the high school in Sun Prairie after all.

"I have enrolled you at Sacred Heart Academy," Mama informed me. She'd come up to my room where I was making a sketch of Boots. "It's a Catholic boarding school for young ladies in Madison."

I could hardly believe it. I was being sent away! Away from the farm, away from my family! I stared at Mama. "But why?"

"The nuns are excellent teachers, and you'll learn more from them. We are paying an extra twenty dollars for you to take art lessons, and I'm sure you'll enjoy that," she said. "I wish we could afford to pay for watercolor lessons, too, but that's not possible."

I didn't care about art lessons! I could paint and draw all I wanted right here! "I'm not Catholic," I muttered, as though that made a difference. Mama wasn't Catholic either.

And I had to go all the way to Madison? Madison was the state capital, twelve miles from Sun Prairie, an hour's drive in the John Deere. It might have been as distant as the Pacific Ocean. I'd never been away from home. It felt like a knife in my heart.

Why must I do this? I wanted to call after her, but Mama had already gone back downstairs. I crumpled the drawing into a ball and threw it across the room as hard as I could, but it wasn't hard enough to make me feel any better.

2

Madison, Wisconsin—Fall 1901

BOARDING SCHOOL WAS MAMA'S IDEA. PAPA would not have wanted to send me away—I was sure of that. He liked having his girls around, especially me, although he never said so. He didn't have to say it; I just knew. Mama was different. She was determined for me to get a better education than I could in Sun Prairie, and whatever it was, Mama usually had things her way.

I told myself that art lessons might make this new school tolerable. Maybe watercolor lessons would have made it better, but I understood that I could have some things but not everything, and it was useless to wish for what I didn't have.

The Mother Superior at Sacred Heart had sent a list of the things I needed to take with me: a certain kind of underclothes, two white shirtwaists and two blue woolen jumpers for everyday, two sets of bedsheets, two towels and two washcloths, and a knife, fork, and spoon. I would also need a black dress that came down to my ankles, "without trimming or any trace of white or color," according to the list, and a veil of black silk net exactly one yard square and edged in narrow black lace. This was what I was required to wear to Mass every Sunday.

I helped Auntie sew the clothes; I had been a good seamstress since she taught me how to stitch outfits for my dollies. Auntie knew I wasn't happy about leaving, and while we sewed she tried to cheer me up with the story of how she, Jennie Wyckoff, just seventeen, had married Ezra Varney, and the two had headed west to California to make their fortune in the Gold Rush. But soon Ezra fell sick and died, carried off by consumption. Brave Jennie was only nineteen and a widow when she booked passage on a schooner that sailed from California to the tip of South America, where storms and raging seas threatened to dash them all to their deaths on the rocks. The ship sailed up the east coast of the Americas and arrived in Boston six months after the voyage began. Auntie's hair was gray now, but her eyes sparkled the way they must have when she was a young girl setting out as Ezra Varney's bride.

I tried not to think too much about leaving home. Ida and Nita were being especially nice. I suspected they'd be sneaking into the tower room while I was gone. Claudie was just a baby, and Catherine, only five, didn't really grasp that I wouldn't be around for a while.

Francis, as usual, ignored my existence, or pretended to, but dear eight-year-old Alexius rushed up to hug me whenever he had the chance. Francis might have been Mama's favorite, but Alexius was mine.

Papa laughed and slapped his knee when he found me trying on the black dress while Auntie pinned up the hem. "You look like a nun, Georgie!"

Papa was Catholic and knew about nuns. Mama was Episcopalian and didn't. They sometimes argued about which religion was better, each of them insisting the other's church made no sense. I didn't understand their arguments, but soon I would learn about nuns and what Catholics did.

In early September Mamie, our cook, fixed a farewell dinner of chicken fricassee and apple pie, and the next day Mama drove me to Madison in Auntie's buggy—a treat, because it was just the two of us, and we were hardly ever alone together. She reminded me again how important it was to get a good education, worth whatever sacrifices had to be made.

"Sister Mary Margaret is expecting you," she said. She told me—unnecessarily, it seemed to me—to be a good girl and patted me on the shoulder; she was not one to kiss her children, except when we were babies. She flicked the reins and Penelope trotted off, leaving me alone on the stone steps of Sacred Heart Academy.

I gazed up at the pointed arches, square turrets, and narrow windows with little colored glass panes. Papa would admire this building, I thought; it was like a small cathedral. I picked up my suitcase—Auntie's old leather one—and stepped into the entry hall. Only one dim lamp was burning. It was like entering a tunnel that would lead to someplace far away, maybe another country. I hardly ever cried when I was a child, and I didn't now, but I did feel something cold and hard buried inside my chest.

A nun with glinting glasses emerged from the shadows. "Welcome to Sacred Heart," she said. "My name is Sister Mary Margaret." As she led me through silent corridors to the dormitory, she explained the rules.

On the farm we'd all been expected to do our regular chores, but otherwise we did pretty much as we pleased and nobody said anything about "rules." Sacred Heart Academy was going to be a different story. There were rules for everything.

Attendance required at chapel every morning, evening prayers after supper, Mass on Sunday and on special holy days—Epiphany, Ascension, Assumption. I had no idea what she was talking about, but I nodded. Visitors, allowed only on Saturday afternoons, must be approved first. Visits home permitted only at Christmas and Easter. Letters to parents to be written once a week, and the letters read and corrected for spelling and punctuation errors by Sister Claire, who taught English. Letters addressed to us would be opened and read before they were given to us. "To prevent undesirable correspondence," Sister Mary Margaret explained, but she did not explain exactly what kind of correspondence was undesirable.

My head began to ache.

"And this is our dormitory," said the nun. Two long rows of white iron cots faced each other, each cot with a plain wooden cross nailed above it, each cot except one made up with a dark blue blanket. "You are the last student to arrive," she said, pointing to the unmade cot. "The other girls are having their daily exercise with Sister Clothilde. You may join them outdoors when you've unpacked."

I made up my cot, mitering the corners of the sheets and blanket the way Auntie had taught me, hung my jumpers and shirtwaists and black Sunday dress on a row of empty pegs, and went out to look for the other girls. I expected to find them playing ball or running races; instead, they were marching back and forth in pairs while a tall, skinny nun barked orders. That was Sister Clothilde, and I knew right off that I would not like her.

At the end of the first week I wrote the required letter home, not mentioning my dislike of nearly everything—not just the Exercise Nun. I was used to the privacy of my tower room, and now I had to share space with nineteen other girls.

I was also used to breakfasts of eggs from our chickens, bacon from a pig Papa had slaughtered the previous fall, bread baked by Auntie and spread with butter made with milk from our cows and strawberry jam that Mamie and her helper, Hannah, had put up during the summer. The first morning at Sacred Heart Academy we served ourselves bowls of cornmeal gruel. The second morning, the gruel was made with oatmeal; the third morning, rice gruel. Then the cycle began again. On Sundays we were each allowed a single boiled egg and toast that was cold when it came to the table. Noon and evening meals were equally monotonous. Not really awful—just awfully tiresome.

But before we ate any of it, we had to give thanks: *Bless us, O Lord, and these Thy gifts, which we are about to receive . . .*

When I told one of the older girls that I found the meals dull, she shrugged. "During Lent there won't be any butter on the gruel, or molasses either." I knew nothing about Lent. Papa had never mentioned it.

After I submitted my first letter home, Sister Claire called me to her office. There was a problem with my spelling, and my punctuation was untidy—too many dashes, she said. I was instructed to copy the letter over with corrections. After two more tries I got it right.

Sixty girls were enrolled at Sacred Heart—no rowdy, disruptive boys—and divided into four levels. I hadn't been much of a student at Town Hall School and hadn't learned anything of importance. Mrs. Edison's time was spent keeping track of forty boys and girls of different ages and all levels of learning, and being ignored had suited me. This was different. Algebra, ancient history, composition, geography, and geology were my required classes. Every one of them was a lot harder than anything I'd studied before, but I managed to keep up.

There were seven of us in the art class taught by Sister Angelique. One was a thin, nervous second-year student named Agnes; the rest were third-year students.

Tall windows looked out onto trees, gardens, and a lawn reaching all the way down to the lake, but our stools were placed at a long table facing the front of the light-filled studio, so that we sat with our backs to the view.

Sister Angelique's skin was very pale, with no lines or wrinkles. Her hands were graceful as doves. She placed a white plaster cast of a baby's hand on a pedestal. "Young ladies," she said in a fluty voice, "this is your first exercise: draw what you see here."

I bent over my sketchpad and set to work with a stick of charcoal. Sister Angelique lurked behind us, peering over our shoulders. One of her shoes squeaked a little, *skeek . . . skeek*, a warning that she was close by. The squeaking stopped near my stool. I glanced down at the polished black shoes standing beside me.

"That is much too small, Miss O'Keeffe," said the nun. "And much too black. Why have you made the infant's hand so small and black? It looks like a lump of coal."

Her words stung. I was not used to having my work criticized. No one had ever, *ever*, said anything like that about my drawings. Miss Belle had praised them; Mrs. Mann said my work was excellent; Mama framed my pictures and hung them in the parlor. But Sister Angelique said my drawing looked like a lump of coal.

I tried to explain why I'd drawn the tiny hand the way I had—*because it was tiny!*—but the nun was not interested.

"You must strive for delicacy, Miss O'Keeffe!" she said. "For lightness! And for goodness' sake, do make it large enough to engage the viewer. One must experience the tenderness of each little finger, each dimple on the back of the infant's knuckles!"

Sister Angelique moved on to her next pupil, *skeek . . . skeek,* long skirt swishing, rosary beads clicking. I swallowed hard. Had she not seen that my drawing of the baby's hand was well proportioned and accurate?

I turned to a clean page in my sketchbook and began again, vowing that never again would I make a drawing that was *too small!*

As we left the classroom, Agnes sidled up to me and whispered, "She's mean! She didn't like what I drew either." She opened her sketchbook to show me her drawing of an object that looked more like a potato than a baby's hand.

I didn't know what to say, so I patted her arm and said, "Maybe she won't always be so mean."

Agnes nodded, biting her lip. "I hope you're right," she said, and slumped away.

The next time our class met, Sister Angelique brought out a collection of wooden spheres, pyramids, cubes, cylinders, and twelve-sided figures, arranged them on the pedestal, and instructed us to draw them singly and then in groups. They were like the geometric shapes in Miss Belle's drawing book, but those had been two-dimensional, and these were three. Week after week, more complicated casts appeared (she kept a closetful)—a nose, an ear, a pair of lips, a head. I struggled to draw a curly-haired Venus and a craggy-faced Beethoven.

After the shock of Sister Angelique's harsh words, I began to understand that if I truly *intended* to become an artist—and not just *wished* to become an artist—I would have to learn to accept criticism. Not everything I did would be worthy of admiration, at least not in the beginning. But that was hard. I dreaded the sound of the squeaky shoe.

At first even mild criticism was like a painful cut, but I slowly got used to it, even expected it.

"Try this, Miss O'Keeffe." "Still not quite right, Miss O'Keeffe." "Ah yes, you see? Much better!"

My drawings did improve. They became lighter and more delicate. Better.

Life at Sacred Heart Academy was orderly and calm. The nuns swished through corridors and classrooms in long black robes, black veils worn over stiff white coifs. They looked elegant and dramatic, and I decided that someday I would dress in stark black and white.

But I wondered about the nuns' hair. I wore mine plaited in a single thick braid that hung down my back. Did the nuns have braids tucked under those coifs? Or was their hair pulled back into a knot, like Auntie's?

I asked Maureen, the green-eyed, freckle-faced girl assigned to the cot next to mine.

"They shave their heads," she said matter-of-factly. "They're bald as eggs."

Maureen had become my friend on the first day, when I discovered that she disliked Sister Clothilde nearly as much as I did. After weeks of daily exercise that was administered as if it were punishment, my dislike had grown even fiercer. Normally I would have looked forward to the freedom of being outdoors, but there was no freedom with the Exercise Nun. She shouted at us for most of the forty-five minutes we were allowed. I had always been a fast runner—faster than my brother—and I could throw a ball, climb a tree, or skate across a pond as well as any of the girls and some of the boys at Town Hall School, but Sister Clothilde found fault no matter how well we did. Poor Maureen was terrible at everything. The nun gave her no peace, and she often ended up in tears. "You really try," I'd said to her. "That's what counts."

"Bald as eggs?" I said now, laughing, not sure I could believe her explanation about the nuns' hair. "Can't you just picture Sister Clothilde without the coif and veil—her naked skull and that long horse face?"

"Georgie, you're just terrible!" Maureen said, smothering a giggle, and soon my comment had been repeated to all the girls in the first-year dormitory. We were united in our loathing of the Exercise Nun.

I was homesick when I first arrived at Sacred Heart. I missed my family, and I missed Mamie's delicious meals. But the homesickness melted away like a late spring snowfall. I loved the school's small chapel with the stained-glass window that glowed like the little rubies and sapphires in Mama's Totto family jewelry. The rumble of the priest's voice chanting Sunday Mass in Latin, and the nuns' soft voices singing the hymns and responses. The candles flickering on the altar. The mysterious smell of incense.

Each Sunday at the end of Mass the priest called for any girl who would observe her birthday that week to step forward and receive a blessing. Four days before my fourteenth birthday in November I knelt by the railing at the front of the chapel, and the priest laid his hand on my head. His hand was warm and smelled of lavender.

After Mass, we trooped over to the dining room for our Sunday dinner, liver and onions with custard for dessert. If I'd been at home, Auntie would have baked a cake—we each had our favorite; mine was devil's food—and my younger brother, Alexius, would have turned the crank on a freezer of ice cream made with cream from our cows. It was raining hard that day, too wet to go down to the lake, and we retreated to our dormitory room. Maureen gave me a bag of sugared almonds that her grandmother had brought her, and I shared it with the other girls. Agnes left a drawing of a four-footed animal on my pillow, one of our class assignments. I think it was a horse.

At Christmas we were allowed to go home for three days. I had not been back to the farm for more than three months. The house smelled of gingerbread that Mama always made from a recipe she'd learned from her mother, who'd learned it from *her* mother, who'd come to America from Holland long ago. There was the scent of the fir tree Francis and Papa had cut, and we decorated it with the homemade ornaments we'd made every year. I inhaled deeply, happy to be there again.

I had painted a tiny watercolor for each member of the family, and one for Lena, too. We hung ours on the branches of the tree. On Christmas Eve Lena and her mother came by with jars of grape jam, and I gave her the little painting. As we sat drinking mugs of hot apple cider, I happened to catch the look that passed between Lena and Francis. I saw his face turn deep pink and wondered about it.

The next morning we opened our gifts—knitted scarves and caps and matching mittens for each of us—and I was given the fine sable brushes I'd been wishing for. Mamie had stuffed and roasted a goose, and Auntie baked mince pies. Ida and Nita made little sugar pies with the leftover scraps of dough. Everything seemed just as it had always been, and yet I had missed all that had been going on in the family without me. Claudie was walking now, Catherine proudly showed me that she was learning to read, Alexius was trying—unsuccessfully—to teach Boots, my cat, to ride on his shoulder, and Francis had made a high score on a mathematics exam.

Two days after Christmas, Papa drove me to Madison in the John Deere. He tied Danny Boy to a hitching post and walked with me to the entrance of the "cathedral," hugged me tight, called me his dear little Georgie, and told me he'd be so glad when it was Easter and I'd come home again.

I waved goodbye and hurried inside, as happy to be back at Sacred Heart as I'd been to go home three days before.

Spring came. Sunny days gradually replaced the dark, cold ones, and the air lost its bitter bite and began to warm. One fine day Sister Angelique announced that she was taking our class down by the lake.

"Young ladies, today we are going to do *plein air* painting. That's French for 'open air.'" Painting out of doors was all the rage in Europe and among certain American artists, she explained. Winslow Homer was her favorite. She had a book of chromolithographs, "chromos," like those Mrs. Mann had shown us—not only the seascapes for which Homer was famous, but also his rural scenes.

Sister Angelique especially admired Homer's painting of two farm boys in a pasture. She pointed out the brightness of one boy's white shirt, and how the two are gazing at something beyond the edge of the painting. She liked to quote Homer: *I always prefer a picture composed and painted outdoors. The thing is done without your knowing it.*

"That is the reason we are going to the lake," she said.

With our sketchpads and charcoal sticks and pencils we followed Sister Angelique down to the shore of Lake Wingra. A weathered statue of the Virgin Mary contemplated the dark water, and someone had draped a wreath of flowers around her neck. Perched on a log with the sketchpad on my knees, I drew the statue from straight on. Then I moved around behind it and tried another angle. From a third angle the light slanted on the Virgin in a different way. By the end of the afternoon, as we were preparing to climb up the hill, I had done a whole series. Now I understood what Winslow Homer meant: *The thing is done without your knowing it.* Light changed everything, and you didn't even think about it—you *saw* it and *felt* it. I knew that someday I was going to paint in *plein air* whenever I could.

I'd studied hard, and that had earned me a place in advanced classes in the second term. Sister Angelique chose my drawing of a duck hunter with a gun, copied from a wood engraving, and it was published in the school catalogue. At the end of the school year I was awarded the prize in ancient history and a gold pin for improvement in illustration and drawing. I even won a medal for deportment!

Sister Angelique pinned up several of my drawings on the walls of the art studio. On each drawing she had written *G. O'Keeffe* in black pencil. I stared at those bold letters. I had always been Georgie, a farm girl from Sun Prairie. But when I saw my name on those drawings, I felt different—as though "G. O'Keeffe" was some other person, the artist I was on the way to becoming.

3

Sun Prairie, Wisconsin—

Summer 1902

BACK ON THE FARM THAT SUMMER I RETREATED TO my tower room whenever I could get away. Ida, going on thirteen and bossier than ever, and Nita, eleven and doing whatever Ida said, were thick as thieves, whispering conspiratorially whenever I was around. I suspected they had made free use of the tower room while I was away, but they claimed innocence. I was already looking forward to going back to Sacred Heart in September, to my art classes, to Sister Angelique's pale hands fluttering over my drawings and her fluty voice urging me to *do it this way, Miss O'Keeffe,* and *try that.*

Lena came to help out with the washing from time to time. I was always glad to see her, but something had changed.

"I'm sorry I didn't write to you like I promised," Lena said. "But you know how it is."

I said yes, I did know.

"I have a beau now," she confessed.

"A beau?" Lena's news surprised me. I'd never thought about having a beau, myself.

Lena nodded, her cheeks coloring as pink as a morning sky. "William."

"William? William Traxler?" He was the big, brawny fellow Papa had hired along with two of Lena's brothers to help with the farm work. We sold our milk to William's father, who owned a creamery and several other businesses in Sun Prairie.

William had hardly a word to say when I was around. *Dull*, I thought. I tried to imagine Lena keeping company with him.

I knew that Francis didn't think much of William either. "Traxler doesn't really have to work," he'd said sourly after a long day in the fields cutting tobacco. "His father always gives him everything he wants. He lets the rest of us take on most of the chores whenever he can get away with it."

"William wants us to get married as soon as he's saved up enough money," Lena said now. "He wants a farm of his own."

Married? I was shocked. Why on earth would she want to get married? "But you're only fifteen! You won't be sixteen until next winter!"

"William is almost eighteen," she said, as though that explained anything. "And I'll be seventeen when we actually marry. That's plenty old enough."

I couldn't imagine why Lena wanted to get married. I saw what my mother's life was like, even with Auntie helping out with the youngest children, Mamie and Hannah in the kitchen, Lena's mother doing the washing, plus a hired girl when extra help was needed. Mama had scarcely any time to call her own. Lena's mother's life must be even harder, with no daughters besides Lena to help out.

"Well, that's nice," I said, insincerely. I couldn't think what else to say.

Lena must have known what was in my mind, because she didn't mention it again.

But the next time Francis grumbled that William Traxler was as lazy as a lizard on a warm rock, I said, without thinking, "The mystery is that Lena's going to marry him."

"I know," he said. "Traxler's been bragging about it."

When I saw my brother's face, I remembered how he and Lena had looked at each other at Christmas. There must have been something between the two of them then, and now there was not. Now there was William. I wished I could take back what I'd just said.

I'd looked forward to those long, hot summer days on the farm. On the Fourth of July everybody in Sun Prairie turned out for the annual picnic at Town Hall School, Auntie and Mamie baked a half dozen pies, Papa played his fiddle, and we all had a good time—except, probably, Francis, because Lena was dancing with William. There were other girls who would have been glad of a partner, but my brother didn't seem interested.

But in August hornworms attacked the tomatoes and the tobacco, some of the milk went bad before it got to the Traxlers' creamery, and to make matters even worse, the complicated corn harvester Papa had bought a couple of years earlier broke down three times. The third time, Papa clenched his jaw tight and said the corn would have to be harvested by hand, and he didn't have enough help to do that. It seemed like just one piece of bad luck after another.

I pitched in with the chores along with Ida and Nita, but I also spent hours alone in my tower room, painting and drawing. Everything was a possible subject: vines of fat red tomatoes, regimented rows of corn, the cow barn and springhouse. A few sketches that I made of members of my family, especially one of Auntie, turned out nicely, but I didn't much like to draw or paint likenesses of people. It was the natural world that made me want to paint.

I loved the farm and thought I would never want to leave it, but as the time crept closer for me to go back to Sacred Heart Academy, I was glad. That's the way it was for me: wanting to be in both places at once.

Then, abruptly, I learned that I would not be going back. Francis and I were being sent to live with Mama's younger sister, our aunt Lola, in Madison, and we would attend the public high school there. Ida and Nita were going to Sacred Heart instead.

"I'm sorry, Georgie," Mama said. "I know you've come to like Sacred Heart, but there's not enough money to send all three of you. Your father and I believe you must each have the best education we can afford, and each of you must have a fair share. You've had yours, and now Ida and Nita must have theirs."

Ida would be given my black dress and my lace-trimmed black veil. The nuns had found a smaller dress for Nita from a girl who was leaving.

I struggled not to show how upset I was, not to be going back to Sacred Heart, not to be with my friends Maureen and Agnes, not to be ridiculing the Exercise Nun or listening for Sister Angelique's squeaking shoes and basking in her praise when she finally gave it.

I could not stay on the farm and attend the high school in Sun Prairie, and I could not go back to Sacred Heart. I was being sent to a new school where I would know no one in a strange city. I dreaded it.

4

Madison, Wisconsin—Fall 1902

I FLOUNDERED IN MADISON AS AWKWARDLY AS I had when our pond froze and I put on ice skates for the first time. Back in Sun Prairie, everybody knew I was Frank and Ida O'Keeffe's oldest daughter. Now a river of strangers pushed past me on the bustling sidewalks of the state capital. From a small girls' school where my life had been carefully supervised by nuns, I was plunged into a high school teeming with hundreds of students. At Sacred Heart I'd heard birds chirping and nuns singing their hymns. In Madison I endured the sound of clanging trolleys and Aunt Lola warbling her favorite Stephen Foster song, "Beautiful Dreamer."

It must not have bothered Francis, or if it did, he never said. But that was Francis.

Aunt Lola lived in the drafty old house where Grandmother Totto had moved with her and her older sisters, including our mother, after Grandfather Totto went back to Hungary. Lola was a spinster schoolteacher. Being a spinster—an old maid—was not the same as being a nun. The nuns at Sacred Heart were the brides of Christ, they'd told us, and that's why they'd never married. While Auntie was helping me pack, she'd confided that Aunt Lola's heart had been broken by a man who'd asked her to marry him and then changed his mind and married somebody else.

"Now she doesn't trust men," Auntie whispered. "Can't say as I blame her."

Aunt Lola was what Papa called "high-strung." Everything I did seemed to make her nervous, and Francis often drove her to distraction with his long, brooding silences. Her third-grade pupils must have been exceptionally well-behaved. She had a habit of talking to Francis and me as if we were third graders too.

Still, we had a place to stay that didn't cost our family anything except expenses for our board. Aunt Lola's food was plain and sometimes not cooked quite enough—half-raw chicken—or else cooked a little more than it should have been—mushy vegetables—but there was always plenty of everything. Especially the vegetables.

"Now, children," she said in a schoolteacher voice, "it is important for us to clean our plates. Francis, will you have more beets?"

My brother and I exchanged eye rolls. He detested beets.

I felt guilty for even thinking of complaining, so I never did. But it was hard not to, and I was thinner than ever.

On the first day of class, the art teacher, Miss Fellers, tripped into the classroom wearing yellow stockings and a hat with an untidy bunch of artificial violets drooping over the brim. She possessed none of the calm sensibility of Sister Angelique. The stockings and the outlandish hat together with her twittery voice made it impossible to take seriously anything she said.

"Firstly," she said, "you must learn to *look* at a plant or a flower if you wish to draw it or paint it. You must study it until you can truly see it." Miss Fellers motioned for us to gather around her as she held up a jack-in-the-pulpit. "Please take note of the elegant shape," she said, lifting the striped hood of the "pulpit" to reveal the "jack," the stamen. "Observe the colors, students! The remarkable colors!"

Jack-in-the-pulpits grew everywhere around the farm, but I'd never really looked at one before. And I'd never thought of painting a flower by looking at a real flower, not just copying a picture of a flower. It wasn't easy to create the delicate greens and rich purples with watercolors.

When I asked if we could paint in *plein air*, she dismissed the idea. "Oh dear dear *dear*, no! We don't paint outdoors here," she said. Miss Fellers was not an admirer of Winslow Homer's seascapes and landscapes. She preferred still lifes, and the more realistic, the better. Week after week she brought bunches of flowers, piles of fruits and vegetables, armloads of dried branches, boxes of shells and stones, candles, pewter pitchers, and brass candlesticks and arranged them on a table in the center of a circle of desks, so that we each had a different perspective. If I'd chosen to paint the violets on her hat, she probably would have approved.

One day she gave the class a new assignment. "Today you are to paint whatever you fancy, be it real or imagined. Let your inner eye see whatever it wishes to see."

By mid-October the temperature in Madison had dropped below freezing by nightfall, but my inner eye saw a lighthouse with foamy little waves cresting around it near a beach lined by palm trees. I'd never seen a real lighthouse or a palm tree, or walked upon a beach beside an ocean with waves breaking on the rocks, but I'd once seen a picture in a geography book, and that's what I painted.

Miss Fellers studied my invented scene. "You have a vivid imagination, Miss O'Keeffe, and you've rendered it well," she told me with a smile so warm that I forgave her the silly hat. The violently colored stockings, too.

In the evenings before Francis and I climbed up to our chilly bedrooms, Aunt Lola fixed us each a cup of hot cocoa. Francis was usually in a hurry to finish his cocoa and get back to his schoolwork—he was good with mathematics and didn't have to struggle with essays the way I did—but I liked to stay at the kitchen table, nursing my drink and warming my hands on the cup, listening to my aunt's family tales until we were too sleepy to stay awake any longer.

"Our father told our mother that he was going to Budapest to claim his lost inheritance," Aunt Lola recalled, as though it had just happened. "I was seven years old. I remember how we waited for him to come home and make everything right." Aunt Lola arranged three ginger cookies on a plate and set it on the table. "There were rumors that Father had taken part in a revolution when he was a young man, and perhaps after all those years he'd been arrested and thrown into prison. We didn't know if the rumors were true or not. Our mother never stopped hoping, but Father never came back."

I bit into a cookie. It was as hard as a rock.

"Our mother struggled," Aunt Lola continued. "She didn't have the least idea how to manage a farm. She rented the land to tenant farmers and used the money to buy this house. She wanted us all to get a good education and become successful. Or at least to marry well. But it was no easy thing to find successful husbands for all of us girls. Your mama was the lucky one. She married a handsome Irishman with a beautiful smile."

Francis glanced at me and winked. We knew that part of the story.

"I was *not* so lucky." Aunt Lola sighed and chased a crumb across the table. "One by one, the others moved away until I was left to rattle around alone in this old house. Then the two of you arrived!"

The story I was waiting to hear was about the man who'd broken her heart, but she didn't mention him.

"You know, don't you, that your mother wanted to study to be a doctor?" Aunt Lola asked.

Francis and I gaped at her. Here was something entirely new. "No," I said. "I never heard that."

"Girls can't be doctors," Francis declared flatly.

"Of course they can!" Aunt Lola snorted. "But not many are. Well, let me tell you, children, your mother was the smartest of all us Totto girls. A real intellectual! But she followed a different path. She decided to marry Frank O'Keeffe and become a farmer's wife. If she hadn't, you wouldn't be here, now would you?"

I shook my head, unable to think of a thing to say. Mama as a doctor! Imagine!

"Your mother didn't get the schooling she wanted—and should have had, in my opinion. That explains why she's determined to give her children a good education, the best she can afford. The world is your oyster—that's what your mother says." She leaned close, as if she was about to tell us a secret. "Ida O'Keeffe doesn't fit in well with the country people out in Sun Prairie. Some say she has too high an opinion of herself. I used to tell her she ought to move back to Madison. People here are more broad-minded. But no, Ida O'Keeffe is a stubborn woman. You're the ones she's counting on. You children will leave Sun Prairie some day—mark my words!"

Yes, I thought, I might leave some day. But Sun Prairie will always be part of me.

I wondered what Francis was thinking. I hardly ever knew what was going on inside his head, because he rarely talked about it, but I did know that he didn't like farming. I wondered if he thought about Lena. If he'd loved her, and maybe still did. If she had ever loved him, and what happened to make her choose lazy, spoiled, dull William Traxler.

We drank the last of our cocoa, cold now, and said good night. I took the oil lamp and went upstairs. I wrapped myself in a blanket and tried to warm my hands at the lamp. I knelt by the window and gazed out at a wet snow that had just fallen—the first that year—and clung to the bare branches of two large trees. A shiny coin of a moon had sliced through a bank of clouds and blazed a silver trail on the snow. My breath glazed the windowpane with frost, and I rubbed it away with my fist.

I wanted to paint that scene, but how was I to do that? The snow was white. The paper was white. Then I hit upon a solution: I wouldn't paint the snow, white on white—I'd paint the shadows that fell on the snow. I got out my watercolors and brushes, cracked the ice on my water pitcher, and stroked black and pale blue and a bit of lavender onto the paper, leaving swaths of white exposed.

That painting was much better—much truer—than palm trees on a beach beside an ocean with a lighthouse I'd seen only in a geography book. I was painting not just what I saw but what I *felt*, and that was something new for me.

It seemed odd: we were going to Sun Prairie for the weekend. We hadn't planned to go home until Christmas, and it wasn't yet November. Mama sent the message that Lena's brother Samuel would pick us up in the John Deere, after he'd collected Ida and Nita. That was odder still: permission was never granted for weekends away from Sacred Heart. The four of us speculated the whole twelve miles about the reason for it, but none of us could come up with an explanation.

As Danny Boy plodded toward Sun Prairie, Samuel filled us in on farm news, which cows had calved, how many young steers Papa was planning to sell at auction in Milwaukee.

"Plenty busy, like always," he volunteered. If something was wrong, some kind of problem we were needed for, he didn't mention it.

"How's Lena?" I asked, sneaking a glance at Francis, who stared straight ahead.

"Oh, she's good," Samuel said.

We arrived in time for supper, and we were gathered around the table when Papa broke the news. He'd been even more talkative than usual, and Mama kept looking down at her hands in her lap and then glancing over at him with a little smile. Maybe, I thought, she was expecting another baby. Claudie was almost three, so it would be about time for another O'Keeffe.

But that wasn't it at all. Our family would be leaving Wisconsin, Papa told us. "We are moving to Virginia!"

Leaving Sun Prairie? Why? I was stunned. I could tell we all were, but no one dared ask. We gaped and waited.

"One by one," Papa said, "my own father and my three brothers have died of consumption." I remembered when Bernard, the youngest of his brothers, had moved into our house a few years earlier. Mama had nursed him through his last months. "I don't want to be the next O'Keeffe to die and leave my family alone," Papa said.

He blamed their sickness and deaths on the harsh weather. Winters in Wisconsin were fiercely cold. The past February, while Francis and I were in Madison, the water froze in the well in Sun Prairie. Even the food stored in the root cellar froze.

"I can't tolerate any more worry like that," Papa said grimly.

No one spoke.

Terrible as the winters were, there was more to it, Papa went on. He had five O'Keeffe daughters—"Lovely girls, beautiful and talented, and I am proud of them," he always said—but only two sons, Francis, just seventeen, and Alexius, who was barely ten, to help with the work. Hired hands cost money, and even with Lena's two brothers and William Traxler, my father didn't have enough hands to take care of the cows, milking them twice a day, and to plant, hoe, and cut tobacco, and harvest the corn, and keep up with all the other farm chores.

"I'm sick to death of it," Papa was saying. "It saps a man's soul clean out of his body."

He pulled a well-worn pamphlet out of his pocket and spread it on the table. I was sitting next to him, and I could see the words spelled out in curlicue letters:

Williamsburg, the Garden Spot of Virginia

Papa read parts of the pamphlet aloud, his voice trembling with enthusiasm as he described the mild winters of Virginia, the beautiful landscape, the gracious homes, the friendly people. One statement in particular stood out: *Inflammatory diseases are very rare, and the absence of tubercular consumption is well authenticated.*

"Our land is worth a lot of money," he explained. "It's prime farmland, and it stretches for miles in every direction. I know I can get a good price for it. We'll have more than enough money from the sale to buy one of those beautiful old houses in Williamsburg, and we'll have all the room we could ever want." Then he added, "It will be good for the health of us all," and he slapped the table with the flat of both hands, as if that put an end to any questions we might have.

Mama was beaming and nodding, every bit as eager as Papa. "It will be a different kind of life, and I know you children are going to love it. It's sure to be the best thing in the world for all of us!"

I tried to visualize the map of the United States I had studied in geography and see Virginia on it. And what had I learned about the state in my history class? One of the original thirteen colonies. Tobacco, which we had plenty of in our part of Wisconsin, and Negroes, which we did not. I wasn't sure I was going to *like* it much, let alone love it. Not the way I loved Sun Prairie and the plains stretching all the way to the horizon, the clouds rolling in before a thunderstorm, the snow piling like a thick white blanket during those long winters that Papa said he hated. I loved the wildflowers that rioted everywhere all summer long in colors I didn't know yet how to mix.

I didn't want a different kind of life; I wanted to keep on having the life I already had. Even if Aunt Lola was sure Mama wished for a bigger world for me.

"We'll be near a river," Papa said, "and the ocean is very close."

I'd never seen an ocean, but I'd tried to paint as though I had actually walked beside it and watched the waves crash against the rocks. Would there be a lighthouse? That did seem like a new kind of experience.

"Well, I for one am surely ready for a journey to someplace new," Auntie declared. "I haven't done anything this exciting since Ezra and I traveled in a covered wagon all the way to California. Now, *that* was an adventure!"

Ida, Nita, and Alexius stared at their dinner plates while our parents discussed their plans for our new life. My sister Catherine and tiny Claudie, still too young to care, kept up a wordless conversation with each other.

Finally Francis spoke up. "When do we leave, Papa?" His voice sounded hoarse, as though he had a cold.

"Just as soon as I find a buyer ready to offer me the right price for the farm. I don't want to spend another winter here, if I can help it. By next summer I expect we'll be settled in our new home."

"You and Georgie will go back to Lola's, and Ida and Nita will finish the year at Sacred Heart," Mama said. "The four of you will join us in Virginia at the end of the school term in June," she continued. "And so, before you leave for Madison on Sunday, be sure to pack up whatever you absolutely must keep and take it with you. We're selling everything."

"*Everything?*" I gasped. I couldn't believe she meant it.

"Yes—land, house, furniture, animals. All but a few precious belongings, things that can't be replaced, like my family jewelry and Papa's violin. We'll buy whatever we need once we're there. Everything will be fresh and new."

But how could they do such a thing? Our whole lives were being thrown away, as though none of it mattered, nothing was worth saving!

Unable to look at my mother, I jumped up and began to help Hannah clear away the dishes. Mamie brought in a blackberry crumble and a pitcher of cream, but I don't think anybody except Papa and Mama and the youngest children ate even a bite of it.

The following day, Saturday, passed in a blur. O'Keeffe property stretched as far as I could see in every direction, horizon to horizon. I tramped around the boundaries, storing up pictures in my mind of every tree I'd climbed, every bush I'd stripped of berries, every field I'd watched turning from green to gold, every nickering draft horse and cow switching away flies with its tail, every cat that prowled the barn, mewing and hoping for a squirt of fresh milk. Those were the valuables we would not be taking to Virginia.

I was in the tower room sorting and packing when Lena came by with little Buddy. He was still pale and sickly, but he could finally say a few recognizable words. The rest was gibberish that only Lena understood.

"So you're leaving," Lena said while Buddy jabbered. "All of you? Even Francis?"

"Yes. Everybody seems happy about it except me, and maybe Francis."

Lena opened her mouth and closed it again, before whatever she might have said had a chance to come out. "You're not glad to be going, Georgie?" she asked finally.

"No, I'm not! This place—the prairie, the farm, the animals, all of it—it's part of me. It's in my blood. I can't imagine living anywhere else. You don't know how lucky you are, Lena. Staying here. Marrying William. Your life is all settled."

"Yes," she said, sighing. "That's the plan, anyway."

Buddy was stuffing something in his mouth, and Lena bent to take it away from him. The little boy started to howl, and Lena had to raise her voice to be heard above the racket. When she got up to take Buddy home, she threw her arms around me.

"Promise you'll come back someday," Lena pleaded. Tears glistened in her eyes, and I knew it wouldn't take much before we'd both be bawling, but maybe for different reasons.

"I will," I said. "I'll come back when I'm an artist. And I'll paint your picture when I do."

I meant it, too.

By Sunday afternoon my tower room was almost completely cleared out. I stood at the window and gazed out across the frozen fields, the sun already low in the western sky. When would I ever see this sky, this sunset, again? The cow barn, the tobacco barn, the springhouse, the farmhouse, my tower room?

Mamie, her eyes red and puffy from crying, had prepared a grand feast—roast chickens, corn pudding, the last of the tomatoes that had been wrapped green and stored—but I had no appetite for any of it. Neither did Francis, or Ida or Nita. Only Alexius and Catherine and Claudie, who had no experience of what it was like to be anywhere but Sun Prairie, seemed unbothered by the momentous changes ahead. But our parents were in a fine mood.

"It seems that I have a buyer, as of this morning," Papa announced. "Or at least a firm offer. Nothing has been signed yet, there are details to be worked out, but I'm confident it will go through."

"Who bought it?" Francis asked after a long silence. "Somebody from Sun Prairie?"

Papa helped himself to another drumstick. "Jacob Traxler. William will farm it. Live in the house someday, too, I imagine."

My eyes searched for Francis's, but he would not look at me.

"He's getting it for a good price," Papa added.

"*Too* good, I'll bet," Francis muttered. "You should have held out for a better offer."

"I'm satisfied," Papa said. "I'll make enough, and I need the cash to start our new life in Virginia."

Abruptly, Francis shoved back his chair and left the table. We all stared at the empty place. I was shocked. I'd never heard Francis contradict our father. Never heard him use that tone before.

"What about Penelope?" I asked, breaking the stunned silence.

"Oh, don't worry about her!" Auntie said cheerfully. "Where I go, my horse goes."

"And Boots?" Alexius asked, his voice trembling. After I left for Sacred Heart, the cat had transferred his affections to my little brother.

"Boots stays," Mama said. "He'll have a new friend now."

Alexius sobbed—he was emotional, like Papa—and Ida and Nita clung to each other, weeping quietly, until seven-year-old Catherine joined in, and then the weeping got noisier. Claudie was only three, but she felt the sadness and began wailing. I sat with my hands in my lap, knotting and unknotting my fingers, trying to be strong, but when I saw tears rolling down Auntie's face and even Mama dabbing at her eyes, my strength deserted me, and I started sobbing, too.

"Well, now!" Papa said, looking at us with a pained expression. "No need to take on so!"

Later, after all of us had more or less quit bawling, I wrapped a slice of apple crumb pie, Francis's favorite, in a napkin and went looking for him. I found him sitting on a split log by the springhouse, his head bowed and his hands dangling between his knees. I'd never seen him so upset. He took the pie and set it down beside him on the log.

"I don't think you should have said what you did," I told him. "About selling it to Mr. Traxler. Papa got the best price he could."

"You don't know anything about it," Francis said scornfully.

That was true, but I didn't want to admit it. I also thought Francis had a slanted opinion because he disliked William, and maybe because he still loved Lena.

"Jacob Traxler has no respect for our father," Francis said. "He's been spreading it around that Frank O'Keeffe is a poor farmer, that he took advantage of his Irish luck when he inherited land from his brothers and then married a girl with a lot of property, and he didn't deserve a lick of it because he's *incompetent*." He spit out the word like a bitter seed. "'An incompetent farmer if there ever was one.' Those were Jacob Traxler's exact words."

I saw him struggling to control anger that seethed just below the surface. I wanted to ask if his anger also had something to do with Lena, but I could not find the right words, and Francis would not volunteer such information. Instead, I asked, "How do you know all this?"

59

"William. We got into a fight. I lost. He's bigger than me. Heavier."

"A fight? When was this?" I couldn't imagine anyone less likely than Francis to get into a fight.

"We were at the high school. You were at Sacred Heart."

Francis stood up and plinked a pebble against a tree, and then another one. I stayed quiet, waiting for him to say more. The sun had set, and I wished I'd thought to wear my coat.

"So here's what's going to happen," Francis said. "This farm is one of the biggest in the county. Jacob Traxler will probably give the house and fifty acres or so to William and sell off the rest piece by piece. Doing it that way, he'll make a huge profit."

Bad enough that Papa had sold the farm. Worse, that he'd sold it to Jacob Traxler.

"Couldn't Papa have done the same thing? Sold it in pieces and gotten more money?"

"He could have. But you heard what he said," Francis said angrily. He shoved his hands in his pockets and started back to the house.

I hurried after him. "You've forgotten your pie!"

5

Madison, Wisconsin—Winter 1902

TEARS WERE POURING DOWN MY FACE WHEN I LEFT my tower room for the last time, and again when Papa drove the John Deere down the lane for the last time, taking stony-faced Francis and me and our sisters back to Madison—Nita and Ida to Sacred Heart, Francis and me to Aunt Lola's.

My classes were generally uninteresting. The only one that mattered to me and held my attention was Miss Fellers's art class; she let me draw or paint whatever I wanted. I'd made no real friends—friends like Maureen and Agnes. At Sacred Heart we'd lived together, eaten together, spent all our free time together after classes. But at Madison High School everyone scattered when the last bell rang, and I didn't see them again until the next day.

Francis focused entirely on his schoolwork and got high grades. He was sure to be a success someday. "I never wanted to be a farmer," he told me after that last trip to Sun Prairie, "but it's what Papa would have expected. So I'm glad he's sold the farm."

He still sounded angry. *Just not to Jacob Traxler*, I thought.

Papa had probably never wanted to be a farmer either, but he'd seen it as his duty, and he'd done it. It wasn't Irish luck that put so much responsibility in his hands—Jacob Traxler was wrong about that. It was *bad* luck that did it, when Papa's father and his three brothers died, one by one, of consumption. If we stayed in Sun Prairie, Papa might die of consumption, too, and then it would be up to Francis and Alexius to run the farm. Papa didn't want to pass that burden on to his sons. He was betting that the move to Virginia would change his luck, and theirs.

Mama never mentioned that she'd once dreamed of becoming a doctor. She was expected to marry, just as Papa was expected to take over the farm. It was her duty, and she did it without complaining. I knew she hoped I'd become an artist, and it was what I wanted to do. But Mama also made it clear that I was going to have to earn a living. Most likely I'd become a teacher, she said, like Aunt Lola. I thought of Miss Fellers and Sister Angelique, and tried to picture myself in front of a class, probably mostly girls, showing them chromos or plaster casts or real flowers and explaining how to make a picture.

That was what Mama had in mind for me, but it was not what I wanted. I was fifteen, and I knew I wanted to paint the pictures *I* wanted to paint and draw what *I* wanted to draw. But how was I going to do that? I had no idea.

One blustery day in early December, the whole family gathered at Aunt Lola's. Mama, Papa, Auntie, and the three youngest children—and Penelope!—were taking the night train from Madison to begin the journey to Virginia. This was a farewell supper and such an unusual occasion that nobody knew quite how to act. Mama took charge of the pot roast, rescuing it from Aunt Lola. Ida and Nita, who had permission to be absent from Sacred Heart for a few hours, were put to work slicing onions and carrots. Francis was responsible for peeling the potatoes and mashing them until not a single lump survived. I made tapioca pudding with coconut, Papa's favorite. Auntie and Catherine entertained Claudie. Everyone seemed subdued except Papa, who was exuberant and couldn't sit still. Mama kept chasing him out of the kitchen.

At last a big meal was laid out on the table, but nobody was hungry except Papa. I hardly touched my plateful. Alexius called the dessert "fish eyes," made a face, and pushed it away.

Then it was time to go to the railway station.

Our family had never been separated like this. Four of us had been sent away to school, but we always knew we could get home—Sun Prairie was only an hour away. Once in a while Papa had come to Madison on business, or Mama made a special trip to the city to shop or to visit a doctor. We'd grown used to the comings and goings, but this was different. We would not all be together again until summer, and summer was a long way off.

The travelers—especially Papa—were excited, looking forward to a new life, but those of us who would be left behind, even temporarily, were already feeling the loss. Alexius was the first one to begin sobbing and had to be pried out of Nita's arms. Then everyone was crying—except Francis, and even he was probably choked up.

The conductor shouted, "All aboard," there was one last round of embraces and promises to write, and the travelers hurried to climb onto the Pullman sleeping car. Papa had reserved a lower berth for himself and Mama and little Claudie, and an upper berth for Auntie and Catherine and Alexius. Penelope had already been led onto a special car fitted with horse stalls. The whistle blasted twice, smoke belched from the locomotive, and the train lurched forward. White handkerchiefs fluttered from the open windows as the train gathered speed. The rest of us stood on the station platform and waved until the last flicker of white had vanished.

At Christmas my brother and I collaborated on a greeting to send to the half of the family that was now in another part of the country. I begged a sheet of fine watercolor paper from Miss Fellers. Francis, who had a talent for elegant printing, copied the words of "Silent Night" in the center of the sheet—it was Mama's favorite carol, and Papa's, too. Around the borders I painted miniature scenes of the stable and the manger, the shepherds and the animals, the three Wise Men and the star. We packed our gift between sheets of cardboard and mailed it off to Virginia.

The nuns agreed to allow Ida and Nita to spend their three-day holiday with us at Aunt Lola's. Francis volunteered to give up his bed and sleep downstairs on a divan I knew would be too short for his long, lean frame. Aunt Lola ordered a turkey—goose seemed too much to undertake—and Francis would do his special mashed potatoes again, and I would attempt to bake a chocolate cake. We would ask Ida and Nita to help with the cranberry sauce and cauliflower, even though we all hated cauliflower and probably no one would eat it.

Everything was planned when my sisters sent word: they would come by to wish us a happy Christmas, but two new friends at Sacred Heart had invited them to their home for the holiday. The father of the family was a wealthy banker with an estate on one of the lakes near Madison.

"They won't be here for Christmas dinner!" I exclaimed, waving the note under Francis's nose. "Can you imagine? Ida and Nita have decided to spend the day with friends! How could they do such a thing!"

"Because they want to, I guess," Francis said with a shrug. "Probably get a better meal there than they would here."

"That's hardly the point, is it?" I stormed. "Who cares what they'll eat! It feels to me like our family is breaking apart!"

"I don't know why you're so upset, Georgie. You always dramatize everything. They want to have dinner with their friends, so let them."

Ida and Nita came by, as they had agreed, and we all exchanged handmade cards. For Aunt Lola I had painted a small picture of a sleeping woman, and across the bottom Francis lettered "Beautiful Dreamer," the Stephen Foster song she loved. She was so pleased she burst into tears.

My sisters had also done little paintings, and I was sure I could see Sister Angelique's influence. I'd asked Ida about my favorite nun, but she wouldn't tell me anything. When I had a moment alone with Nita, I pried out of her the admission that the nun often praised my work. She made me promise not to let Ida know she'd told me. Ida never could stand being compared to me, and Sister Angelique's comments had sent her into fits of jealousy. Hearing what the nun had said did make me feel a little better.

My sisters stayed for less than an hour before they drove off in the carriage that had been hired to take them to "Trianon du Lac." I did my best not to show how upset I was that my sisters had chosen to be with their rich friends.

That Christmas dinner was surely the saddest I'd ever eaten. It had always been the ten of us, Mama and Papa, Auntie, and seven of us children, celebrating holidays and birthdays together. Now we were scattered everywhere, and it was just Francis and Aunt Lola and me with an undercooked turkey, each of us trying hard to be cheerful for the sake of the other two.

Francis and I had always been rivals, and we'd never really been close, but during a blizzard that paralyzed Madison he taught me to play poker. It became our entertainment that winter, and he almost always won. Winning cheered him up.

Classes that spring were uninspiring, but then I discovered music. As a child I'd taken violin lessons, and Mama had taught me to read music and made me practice scales and arpeggios, but I'd had no one to give me formal piano lessons.

One day when Aunt Lola was not at home, I opened the cover of the old spinet piano in the parlor and struck a few keys. The piano was badly out of tune, and two of the keys didn't play at all, but I found a book of piano exercises, like the one I'd had when I was six or seven, and I taught myself to play scales again. Arpeggios, too.

Day after day I practiced, though it was frustrating, with the piano in such terrible condition. Aunt Lola returned unexpectedly early one afternoon and heard me. She hired a piano tuner, and she wrote to Mama, suggesting that I take lessons. Mama agreed. Once a week I went to the dusty apartment of Miss Mildred Wentz, a friend of Aunt Lola's, and took a lesson. I kept practicing. I was improving.

A few houses down the street from Aunt Lola's lived a boy named Miklos, who was in my brother's class.

Sometimes he and Francis walked home from school together. They ignored me, and I returned the favor, until one day Francis stayed after school and I saw Miklos heading down our street with a violin case. He spoke to me, and we fell into step and walked the rest of the way together.

I mentioned that my father played the violin. "Mostly Irish folk music," I said.

"I sometimes play Hungarian folk music," he said. "The *czardas*, things like that." He explained that *Miklos* is the Hungarian form of *Nicholas*, and he asked if I played an instrument.

"I'm taking piano lessons."

"We must get together and play some time," he said. "You can teach me some Irish jigs, and I will teach you the czardas."

I had been at the high school for more than six months, and this was the first real conversation I'd had with another student outside of school. I was pleased—I'd never really had a male friend—but I didn't know what was supposed to happen next. Was I supposed to invite him to come to Aunt Lola's? Or was it up to him to suggest a time and place?

Then Miklos resumed walking home with Francis, and we resumed ignoring each other. I was disappointed—I thought it would have been nice to play music with him.

A letter arrived from Mama after Easter.

My dearest children, she had written in her small, neat hand, *I am happy to tell you that we have found* the perfect place to be your new home. Wheatlands, as it is called, sits on a hill surrounded by green lawns and huge shade trees. There is not nearly so much land as we had in Sun Prairie, but there is enough, and your father successfully negotiated a good price.

The stately old mansion has eighteen rooms, much larger than our house in Sun Prairie. Certainly enough for the O'Keeffe family! I am sure you will love the verandahs, the honeysuckle vines that perfume the air, and the roses that ramble everywhere.

What a pretty town Williamsburg is! The weather is delightfully warm. Papa has opened a store selling groceries as well as feed and grain and anticipates a brisk business.

It was not like Mama to write so glowingly, but I was glad that she seemed pleased with the house. But she went on to say that it was a bit like camping, since nearly all of our furniture had been sold with the house, but they would slowly acquire what they needed to make the mansion into a comfortable home.

We are settling in well in our new home, Mama ended, but of course we miss the four of you very much and look forward to having the O'Keeffe family together again.

"Well!" exclaimed Aunt Lola. "That sounds lovely, doesn't it?"

We agreed that, yes, it did.

Less than a month later I received a letter from Lena. We had both promised to write, but I'd never gotten around to it, and neither had she. Our lives were moving in different directions. I rushed up to my room with the letter and read it slowly—her handwriting was a mess and hard to read. Buddy was sick a lot, she wrote. Her oldest brother had married a girl from Milwaukee, and they were expecting a baby. Miss Belle's house in the village had caught fire, and only part of it could be saved.

At the end of the letter came the news I dreaded: She and William would be marrying in June. William was running the farm—*our farm*—and had hired all of her brothers to work for him. For the time being, she and William planned to live with her parents. She still had to help with Buddy, and the house—*our house*—had been rented out. "I still dream that one day I will be in your tower room," she wrote.

During the spring term I had made dozens of pencil sketches, but I'd lost interest in painting. I had a few of my old paintings in Madison, things I'd done in Sun Prairie that I planned to take to Virginia, but when I looked at them now, they seemed amateurish. I crumpled them up and threw them into the stove, along with Lena's letter, which I didn't mention to Francis.

Aunt Lola saw what I was doing and gasped. "Why on earth are you destroying them, Georgie? Such lovely pictures going up in flames!"

"It's only practice work," I said. "I don't want to keep them around to remind me of how poorly I've made them."

The term ended in June, and Aunt Lola and I attended Francis's graduation exercises. He had finished near the top of his class, with distinction in mathematics. Ida and Nita said goodbye to their friends at Sacred Heart. The four of us packed up, ready to leave Wisconsin and join the rest of the family in Virginia.

Aunt Lola cried and cried, wiped her eyes and sniffled, and then commenced weeping again. She said the last two years were the best she'd ever had, and I said we'd miss her, too.

That was true—but I was fifteen and eager to begin a new chapter in my life.

PART II

*"I'm going to live a life that's
different from yours."*

6

Williamsburg, Virginia—

Summer 1903

AFTER MANY HOURS ON THE TRAIN AND THREE changes at unfamiliar stations, my brother and sisters and I finally arrived in Williamsburg. The rest of the family turned out to meet us as we stepped off the train—Papa in high spirits, Mama smiling but reserved, Auntie dispensing hugs and kisses.

I hadn't seen the three youngest O'Keeffes since last fall, and it seemed they had each changed while still remaining the way I remembered them. Alexius, twelve, jumped up and down, nearly dizzy with excitement. Catherine, always shyer than the rest, tugged on my hand, wanting to tell me right away about her ninth birthday, while little Claudie was chattering a blue streak about the new kitty. The surroundings might be completely different, but it was my same dear family.

We loaded our valises and boxes onto a wagon with "O'KEEFFE & SONS FEED & GRAIN" painted on the sides—it had replaced the John Deere—and then climbed in for the trip to our new home. We must have made quite a sight as we drove past grand old mansions surrounded by untamed hedges and entangled in unruly vines. It seemed strangely quiet for midafternoon. No one was out and about to witness the passing of ten members of the O'Keeffe clan, as people surely would have been on a bright June day in Sun Prairie. Where was everyone?

It was very warm—much warmer than Wisconsin—and an army of tiny insects buzzed and flitted in the muggy air. Mama and Auntie were fanning themselves, and Papa was in his shirtsleeves.

"Sultry," Auntie said, swatting at a mosquito. "That's how they describe the weather here."

We came to the bottom of a steep, narrow lane. Tall pine trees lined both sides of the lane. Giant oaks threw shade on the broad lawn, and flowering bushes blazed with color. "This is Peacock Hill," Papa announced with a sweep of his arm. "One of our neighbors has peacocks. Beautiful birds!"

"But very noisy!" Mama added. "How can anything so beautiful make such a dreadful racket?"

Alexius demonstrated a peacock's squawk and, pleased with himself, did it again.

The draft horse, Danny Boy's replacement, plodded up the hill and halted in front of a huge white house with tall pillars and long verandahs and shutters on every window.

"There it is," Papa announced proudly. "Wheatlands! And nine acres of land, too!"

He flung open the front door with a huge brass knocker, and I stepped into the entrance hall. Our farmhouse in Sun Prairie was only a farmhouse, not nearly so grand or so grandly named, but it had been crammed with plush-covered divans and carved tables and Mama's beloved piano. Wheatlands was nearly empty. The rooms echoed hollowly.

I flew up the sweeping staircase to the second floor, and within minutes I had chosen my bedroom and claimed the room next to it for a studio.

"Why are you taking two rooms?" Nita demanded.

"Because I am an artist, and I must have a studio," I informed her loftily. I didn't say "going to be an artist," as I had when I was twelve. *I am an artist*, I said. I was still not sure exactly what that meant and hadn't done much painting lately, but I knew that it was important to keep saying it.

"You always get what you want," Ida said bitterly. She and Nita had become closer than ever since their year together at Sacred Heart.

That was true. I'd always had the tower room to myself, while my four sisters had to share rooms. They complained, but they didn't challenge me. They'd learned that it was useless: I always got what I wanted, and I took it for granted that I always would.

During our first few days in Williamsburg, Alexius and Catherine took us exploring. There really wasn't much to explore. What a quiet little town! "Only about five hundred people, counting the Negroes," Papa said, "and those black folks are mostly servants for the white folks."

Smaller than Sun Prairie! The main street, called Duke of Gloucester Street as though it belonged to English royalty, wasn't even paved, and it was ankle-deep in silky dust or, following an afternoon shower, sucking mud. A couple of shops, several churches, and an inn—that seemed to be the extent of it.

"There's a college," Alexius informed Francis. "You'll probably be going there. And a wrinkled old man who goes up and down the streets hollering out the price of oysters. They eat them raw here."

"Ugh!" said Ida and Nita, shuddering.

"And a lunatic asylum!" Catherine added brightly.

People moved slowly. In the afternoons the streets emptied, and the pace went from languid to motionless in those big old houses with the verandahs and pillars. Everybody rested and didn't begin to move around again until darkness fell and the temperature drifted downward a few degrees.

People spoke slowly too, dropping the g's and r's at the end of words. Their a's and o's stretched like taffy. Why would you say "doe" when the word is *door*? But when I spoke to people, I could tell that they thought *I* was the one who didn't speak correctly.

It didn't take long for me to realize that the O'Keeffes were outsiders. We were northerners, the side that won what I'd been taught in school was the Civil War but in Virginia was called the War Between the States, and the Union victory was still resented. We walked too fast and talked too fast. And we didn't have Negro house servants, except for Minnie, the cook Mama hired.

Papa often worked outdoors beside the Negro hired men, loading and unloading feed and grain, hauling groceries, and building things, his shirtsleeves soaked with sweat—just the way he'd always worked with our hired hands back in Sun Prairie. He was obviously not a "gentleman."

"Even the Negroes think there's something odd about Papa doing that," Francis told me after we'd been there a few weeks. "The older ones don't say anything, but Sammy, the fellow who makes the deliveries, said, 'White men here don't work with their hands, and they don't work next to coloreds.'"

"Does Papa understand that?"

"I don't think he cares. That's just how he is."

Other things we did, or didn't do, also must have made us seem strange to the people of Williamsburg. The streets were deserted on Sunday mornings because everybody was in church. Papa told us about the neighbor lady—the one with the peacocks—who'd stopped by the grocery one morning soon after he and Mama had arrived. "Mrs. Blanchard said she assumed that with an Irish name like O'Keeffe we'd be going to the Catholic church, and then she said, '*Of cohss, mos' ever'body heah is eithuh Bap-tist or E-pis-co-pa-li-an.*'" He mimicked her drawl perfectly.

Papa used to go to Mass at the little stone Catholic church in Sun Prairie on special holidays—I begged to go with him, because I thought it was pretty—and Mama sometimes drove into Madison to the "*E-pis-co-pa-li-an*" church where she and Papa were married, but as a rule we weren't a churchgoing family, and that didn't sit well with people in this town.

Mama fit into Williamsburg society better than the rest of us, because she carried herself like an aristocrat. In a way she *was* an aristocrat, thanks to her father, the Hungarian count who left and never came back. Soon after Mama and Papa moved to Virginia, she had been invited to a stylish afternoon tea at the home of our neighbor, Mrs. Blanchard. The weather had not yet turned unbearably hot, as it was when I arrived, and the black silk faille dress that Mama reserved for special occasions would have to do. With gloves and a hat, of course.

"Your mother was wearing her fine old Totto jewelry," Auntie reported proudly. "The gold and emerald brooch and earrings. That started a rumor that she is somehow related to Tsar Nicholas of Russia."

"But that's not true!" I said.

"Of course it's not true, and she denied it, but I don't think they quite believed her. If not Tsar Nicholas, then it must be one of the other Romanovs, they decided. And so now she's acceptable to the ladies of Williamsburg."

Maybe Mama was acceptable, but I surely was not.

I had been there for scarcely a month. We had just finished breakfast; everyone else had gone off to do their chores, and I was clearing the dining room table. Mama came in and saw that I was alone. "Georgie, I want to talk to you," she said.

I paused, my hands full of dirty dishes.

"Perhaps you should not go out by yourself every morning before the sun comes up," she said. "Young ladies here don't do that. The neighbor ladies have seen you out walking alone, and they've spoken to me about it."

"They have? What did they say?"

"Well, they think it's unusual behavior, and they wonder about it."

"Why is it unusual? I don't think it's unusual!" I insisted. "It's the best time of the day, while it's still cool. The sky is so lovely then. The birds are singing. And no one comes along to bother me."

It was true—no one had bothered me. If there were any girls my age in Williamsburg, they must have been well hidden behind those hedges. I hadn't thought much about it. The town itself was dull, but the countryside was lushly beautiful. I took my sketchbook whenever I went out on the morning walks that seemed to bother the neighbors. I was painting again, spending hours every day in the room I'd commandeered as my studio or painting in *plein air* whenever the fancy struck me. That must have *really* bothered people! There were times when I wished I had a friend like Lena. Ida and Nita were around, but they had each other. Mostly, anyway, I was content to be on my own.

"Georgie, please listen carefully to what I'm telling you." Mama followed me into the kitchen, took the dishes out of my hands, and set them on the table. "There's an old saying, *When in Rome, do as the Romans do.* The same could be said about Williamsburg. This is not Sun Prairie, and people here don't like to get their hands dirty. They inherit the property and hire Negroes to do the work. They don't regard your father as a gentleman, because he is the proprietor of a grocery. *They* wouldn't be doing such a thing." She paused, watching me pour hot water from a kettle on the stove into a tub and toss in the soap. Then she continued, "It might be helpful to your father's business if you would make an effort to speak and act more like the other young ladies here."

"The grocery needs help?" I dipped cold water from the barrel into the tub and began to scrub dried egg yolk off the plates.

"The feed and grain business, too. It's been slow getting started," she said. "Economic conditions weren't quite what we'd hoped for, and"—she hesitated, then went on—"and for some reason, people just don't come around to buy there. Some Negroes are his customers, and I suspect that has something to do with it. White people don't seem to want to patronize stores that cater to colored people. But it's more than that. We must make every effort to fit in. That's all I'm asking you to do."

I didn't understand that kind of thinking, nor could I see how my behaving differently would change anything. I stacked the clean dishes in a second tub to be rinsed. "What would you have me do?" I asked curiously.

"At the very least, wear shoes and stockings—going barefoot is so unladylike—and put on a nice dress. You might even consider letting me curl your hair."

"You want me to become somebody else!" I cried. "I don't want to curl my hair! It's far too hot for stockings, and I detest the silly clothes the girls wear—petticoats and lace and ribbons and tiny buttons on everything. I'd feel ridiculous, Mama."

"All right, Georgie," Mama said with a sigh. "I won't ask it of you again."

She turned her face away. I'd disappointed her, but I didn't see that whatever *I* did was going to help Papa's business.

At the end of summer Francis began classes at the College of William and Mary in Williamsburg, Ida and Nita were enrolled at a private day school, and Mama hired a tutor to come to Wheatlands to teach Catherine and Alexius and Claudie.

Without consulting me, Mama decided that I should attend a girls' boarding school that she'd heard offered excellent instruction in art. The headmistress herself was an artist and taught the classes. But there were no vacancies when Mama applied for my admission to the fall term.

"I'm sorry, Georgie," Mama said, when she finally got around to telling me her plans. "Your name is on the waiting list for next spring. I hope you won't mind very much staying home for a few months."

I didn't mind at all! I saw it as a chance to draw and paint to my heart's content.

But early in September Mama received a letter from the headmistress of the Chatham Episcopal Institute, informing her of a cancellation. Did Mrs. O'Keeffe wish to send her daughter to Chatham immediately? Classes had already begun, but it was not too late to enroll.

Three days later I was sent away. Again. This would be my third school in three years, and all I'd really wanted was to stay at home and paint and draw whatever I chose.

7

Chatham, Virginia—Fall 1903

EARLY ON A STIFLING MORNING IN SEPTEMBER, I left Williamsburg in a carriage to Norfolk, boarded a train from Norfolk to Lynchburg, and in Lynchburg caught a jitney that let me off by the courthouse in the center of Chatham. The sun had already set.

"That's your school, up yonder," the jitney driver said, pointing out a white clapboard mansion on a hilltop silhouetted against a lavender sky.

I climbed the winding path to the mansion, set down my suitcase by the front entrance, and rang the bell. When no one came after I'd rung a second time, I pushed open the door and stepped uncertainly into a reception room, dimly lit and silent.

Tired and hungry, I wandered down a hallway toward a brightly lit room. I found a dozen girls engrossed in their studies at long wooden tables.

"Hello," I said.

They looked up from their books and stared at the strange creature who had suddenly appeared in their midst. I was dressed in a light brown skirt and unfitted jacket with a row of tortoise shell buttons. I'd sewn every stitch of it myself over the summer. My hair was combed straight back from my forehead and plaited in a single thick braid that hung down my back, the end tied with a black grosgrain ribbon, the way I'd always worn it.

"Good evening," one of the girls ventured carefully, as if she thought I had just stumbled off the boat from a foreign country and didn't speak the local language. "May we help you?" She spoke in that thick-as-honey way they have of talking in the South.

"I'm Georgia O'Keeffe. I'm a new student." I wished they'd quit gawking at me.

A motherly-looking woman arrived in a flutter, caroling, "You must be Miss O'Keeffe! Welcome, welcome, welcome to Chatham! We're so happy you're here!" She turned to the girls at the table. "Miss O'Keeffe comes to us from Williamsburg. I know you'll make her feel at home."

"I'm actually from Wisconsin," I said. "Sun Prairie." My voice was clear and crisp as creek water.

A willowy girl with china blue eyes rose. "I'll show Miss O'Keeffe where she is to sleep, Miss Drummond."

Her blond hair fell in a cascade of curls caught up with a large satin bow. She looked like a pretty box of bonbons.

"My name is Susan Young," the girl murmured. "Miss Drummond is our housemother."

I followed Susan Young up steep, narrow stairs to an attic room with two long rows of cots, almost the same as at Sacred Heart. A potbellied stove squatted in the center of the room, and four washbasins were lined up at one end.

"It's hot and stuffy up here right now, but come winter, the place is an icebox if we don't keep the stove going all night. We're all expected to help carry firewood from the woodpile and stoke the fire, but at least we don't have to chop it. Billy's our custodian, and he'll take care of that," Susan assured me. "I'm afraid you won't find any luxuries here, and few comforts either. Mrs. Willis is hardening us for whatever lies ahead in our lives."

I could not imagine what might possibly lie ahead in Susan's life that she needed to be hardened for. "Mrs. Willis?" I asked.

"The headmistress. She's also the art teacher."

"I'm here for the art instruction."

Susan looked a little surprised. "Well, you surely won't be disappointed, Miss O'Keeffe."

"Please just call me Georgia."

"Of course—Georgia," she said, smiling. "And you must call me Susan." Her teeth were a row of perfect pearls.

She led me downstairs to a room next to the kitchen outfitted with a couple of laundry sinks and three large tin tubs. "This is where we take our weekly baths on Saturdays. Willie Mae and her helper do our bedsheets, but we must wash our own underthings."

Susan took a lantern down from a peg, and we made our way out to the yard behind the mansion to find the two outdoor privies before the tour ended back in the kitchen. We sat at the help's table, where the cook, a Negro woman Susan addressed as Elsie, served me a plate of green beans and ham and cornbread left from supper. The help at the Institute would all turn out to be Negroes, like all the servants in Williamsburg. There hadn't been a single colored person in Sun Prairie, and not many in Madison either.

I hadn't eaten since breakfast, and I was ravenous. Susan sipped tea while I ate. "There's a rule for everything, and if there isn't a rule, there's a tradition," she said. Lights out at ten o'clock, rise at six, breakfast at a quarter to seven. Grace before meals. Evening Prayer after supper, followed by supervised study. No walking out in the countryside or down to the village alone, or even in pairs—students always to be accompanied by a teacher when they leave the school grounds. School uniforms worn on Sundays, everyone marching down the hill in a column, seniors in the lead, for Morning Prayer at Emmanuel Episcopal. Weekly letters home.

Most of the rules were not much different from the ones we'd had at Sacred Heart in Madison. A few were new. Apparently no one censored letters for undesirable content or bad grammar—a good thing, in my opinion—but some of the rules, like not walking alone, seemed completely unreasonable. "What do they think will happen if one of us walks down to Main Street in Chatham to buy a new comb, or just to look around?" I asked.

"It simply isn't done. It could get you a question-able reputation, and that would reflect poorly on the Institute. I can tell you're not a Southerner," she said, as though that explained the silly rule. "You'll get used to our customs."

I don't think so, I thought.

Then she added, "You're here in time for the Scholars' Frolic. It's the first of our monthly dances."

"Dances? But this is a girls' school. Where do the boys come from?"

"There are no boys, but we still have dances. Half of us dress in our uniforms. You'll get yours soon. They're navy blue with red trim. The style is rather masculine. You might not object to it as much as the rest of us do. We wear them to church and on formal occasions."

I thought wistfully of the long black dress and veil I'd worn at Sacred Heart.

"The rest of us get to dress up in our party frocks for the dances," Susan went on. "Miss Cornwall, the music teacher, plays the piano, and we dance with each other. Then, at the next dance—that will be the Autumn Celebration in October —we'll switch places. Those of us who wore uniforms at the Scholars' Frolic will wear our dresses at the Autumn Celebration, and vice versa. The hardest thing when we're learning new dances is remembering how to lead. That's the boy's part."

Another ridiculous tradition! "I guess dancing the boy's part is harder," I allowed. "But what's the point?"

"The point is, we must learn to dance well, for when we eventually go out in society and dance with young men. That's what all of us girls dream about, as I'm sure you do, too, Georgia."

She was wrong about that. I'd never once dreamed of "going out in society" and dancing with young men.

I liked Mrs. Willis as soon as I met her. She was tall and always wore a green smock to class. One side of her face was paralyzed, and I wondered how that had happened.

On my first day in her art class, she came by my easel to observe. Mama must have told her I'd taken art lessons since I was ten years old, and she didn't have to watch for long to see that I already understood the basics: how to blend colors, which brush to use, how much detail to include and how much to leave out.

By the end of the week I had my own table in the art studio and permission to work there after supper when the other girls had supervised study in the dining hall. Either I worked alone in the studio, standing at my easel for hours at a stretch, totally absorbed in my painting, or I was poking around the studio, staring out the window, doing nothing at all. There was no in-between.

Mrs. Willis understood that. A strict headmistress who enforced all the rules, she turned out to be much more flexible as an art teacher and allowed me to work at my own pace, obeying my own rhythms.

I wore my tan skirt and jacket to church on my first Sunday—my uniform had not yet been issued. After we'd marched up the hill after the service, we sat on long benches at the plain wooden tables in the school dining room, bowed our heads, and murmured, "Bless this food and us to Thy loving service," which wasn't much different from what we said at Sacred Heart. Then Elsie set a steaming pot at one end of the table, and we took turns serving ourselves.

"What is it?" I asked, ladling a thick soup into my bowl.

"Brunswick stew," answered a plump, dark-haired girl named Lucille.

"Made with fresh squirrel," added Earnestine, who might have been pretty if her teeth hadn't been so crooked.

Squirrel? Back on our farm in Sun Prairie I'd tamed a couple of the bushy-tailed creatures to eat nuts out of my hand. I thought of their bright eyes while they waited for their treat, and I laid my spoon back in the bowl.

"Earnestine is teasing," said Susan. "In colonial times Brunswick stew was made with squirrel, but now it's chicken, and all the other things that good Virginia cooks add to the pot—tomatoes and lima beans, corn and okra."

I'd never heard of okra but decided not to betray any more ignorance.

"And a big ham bone," Lucille said.

"The same ham bone Elsie cooks with the collards."

Collards?

"It may be the oldest ham bone in the state of Virginia."

A plate of biscuits was handed around. The stew was quite tasty. I still didn't know what okra and collards were, but I had seconds.

The girls did not hide their opinion of my clothes. Lucille pronounced my tan suit "unfashionable." Earnestine and a few others, not including Susan, even formed a committee and told me in a sugary manner that they had some ideas for helping me to dress properly. As though those girls didn't look foolish in all their ruffles and laces and bows! "You should wear clothes that are properly fitted," advised chubby Lucille, "to show off your tiny waist."

Earnestine informed me that my braid was childish— "It makes you look ten years old."

Even Susan, who didn't like to be critical of anyone, laughed at my accent, even though *they* were the ones who spoke almost unintelligibly. Hardly anyone in Wisconsin would have understood a word they said!

The girls probably meant to be helpful, but I ignored their advice.

The politeness of these Southern girls made me want to shock them, or at least to rile them up. After we'd been subjected to an especially dull sermon by the rector of Emmanuel Episcopal and had given thanks for whatever Elsie was serving for Sunday dinner, I sighed dramatically and said, "She must get awfully tired of hearing the same thing week after week, year after year."

"Who? The rector's wife?" Earnestine asked. The chicken with dumplings was being passed around, and she took an extra helping.

"No," I said. "I'm talking about God. *She* must be bored to death by now, don't you think?"

Everyone stared at me, forks poised in midair.

"'*She*'?" Lucille asked timidly. "Georgia, did you refer to God as '*She*'?"

"Well, yes, I did. I mean, God is obviously a woman, don't you agree?"

I had come to that conclusion some time before, and when I was about thirteen, I'd had a fierce argument with Francis on the subject. I had expected Mama to agree with me, and I was surprised when she didn't. And if Mama didn't think God was a woman, I was sure none of these Southern belles would either. I was being provocative, and it worked. The girls were stunned.

"Oh, Georgia, you are most certainly wrong about that!" Lucille exclaimed.

"Not only completely wrong but probably blasphemous too," Earnestine said. "My daddy is a minister, and he would be shocked almost to death at what you're saying."

Susan hurried to be the peacemaker. "Aren't these just the fluffiest dumplings you've *evuh* tasted in your *liiife*?"

In spite of my habit of stirring up controversy, I got along with almost all the girls, except for one: Alice Peretta.

Alice was not pretty in the way the other girls were, but she carried herself like a queen. For some reason Alice had taken a dislike to me and treated me with utter disdain, mocking me, even calling me "Farmer O."

Susan tried to explain Alice's behavior. "It's just that she's stuck-up, and—well, I don't like to tell you this, but she says you walk like a farmer and you talk like a farmer and you dress like a farmer, but you think you're better than anyone else because you have your own table in the studio, and you say you're an 'artist' and get to do whatever you want." Susan imitated Alice, pronouncing *artist* with a curled lip, as though it had a bad taste. "The best thing is just to pay her no attention."

I had a different scheme in mind. I would change Alice's opinion and win her over, not because I liked her but to prove that I could. "I'll wager I can make her like me so much that she'll want to be my best friend," I declared boldly.

Susan shook her head. "No, you can't. Not Alice. She's a terrible snob. Her father owns a huge ranch in Texas and a bank and thoroughbred racehorses and I don't know what else."

"Just watch me!"

Most afternoons Alice practiced on the spinet piano in the dining hall. She played "Für Elise" over and over, but no one had the nerve to tell her how badly she played. One day I went down to the dining hall while she was practicing. I'd often done quick sketches of Auntie and my sisters, and I was good at it. I stood near the piano and sketched Alice's profile. Alice ignored me and kept on playing—worse than ever, repeating the same mistakes—but I knew that *she* knew I was there.

When I'd finished the drawing, I signed it *With admiration, Georgia O'Keeffe*, propped it on the music stand, and left without a single word.

After supper Alice showed up in the art studio. I was at my easel, working on a painting of a pewter pitcher with a curved handle. The reflection of light on the dark metal wasn't quite right, and I was trying to find some way to improve it.

Alice watched silently for a while. "Thank you for the drawing," she said stiffly.

"You're welcome." I kept working on the reflection and didn't even glance at her.

She tried again. "I don't understand why you gave me the drawing. Or why you bothered to draw it in the first place."

"It's merely a souvenir from an admirer," I said. I stepped back and studied the pewter pitcher. Maybe if I added a tiny daub of paint to the handle, that would do the trick.

"Well, it was very kind of you," Alice said. Her Southern manners required her to say something polite even if it wasn't sincere. Then her tone softened. "And it's a good likeness, too, Georgia."

Within a week or two, Alice had changed her tune and decided to be my friend. It was hard to say why—maybe she got over some of her snobbishness about Midwestern farm girls. I'd won my wager with Susan, and it turned out that once I got to know Alice, I really liked her—maybe because she had her own way of thinking, just as I did.

8

SCHOLARS' FROLIC: HOW DID THEY EVER COME UP with that name! Miss Drummond, the housemother, decided that for my first appearance at the monthly dance I would wear the regulation school uniform and be one of the "boys." The tailored navy blue skirt and jacket with red piping suited me much better than a party frock. I didn't even own a party frock! I would have had to borrow one.

The tables and benches in the dining hall had been shoved aside. Miss Cornwall took her place at the piano. "Gentlemen!" she called. "Choose your partners!"

Picking up my cue from the other "gentlemen," I stepped up to Lucille, who was decked out in a flouncy dress with a satin sash tied in a bow. I bowed stiffly from the waist. "May I have the honor of this dance, Miss

Trumbull?" I could hardly choke out the words without laughing.

Miss Cornwall launched into a waltz. I stood perfectly still, at attention, arms at my sides. "You're supposed to lead, Georgia," Lucille whispered.

"I don't know how," I whispered back.

"You've *nevah* danced *befoah*?" she asked.

"Not like this," I confessed. Papa had not taught us to waltz.

Miss Cornwall observed that there was a problem. Without missing a single note of "The Blue Danube," the music teacher directed "Miss Trumbull" to take "Mister O'Keeffe" aside and practice with me until I got the hang of it.

"Put your right hand on my waist," Lucille instructed. "Now I'll put *my* right hand in your left. Lead off on your left foot. One—two—three, and here we go."

I caught on fast, and soon we were waltzing. And when we moved on to the Virginia reel, forming two facing lines—"boys" on one side, girls on the other—I knew what I was supposed to do.

After an hour we paused for refreshments, in order to practice the art of balancing a cup of fruit punch and a plate of fancy little cakes and "finger sandwiches" that were literally no bigger than my finger, while carrying on a conversation between polite sips and nibbles.

A month later, knowing I'd have to borrow someone's "party frock" for the Autumn Celebration, I suddenly found myself indisposed, with a headache, tiredness, and stomach pains brought on by "the curse"—which had never bothered me before—and spent the evening in bed, listening to the *THUMP-thump-thump* of Miss Cornwall's attack on the Blue Danube.

But I could not use the same excuse to escape the Harvest Ball in November. It coincided with my sixteenth birthday, and Alice Peretta's, too, a week later. Elsie had decorated tiny little cakes with fancy icing as a special treat for us to practice eating daintily. Alice's rich family in Texas had sent her three new frocks, all of them ordered from Paris, and she offered to let me borrow one, because we were close to the same size and she had lots more.

I accepted and chose the plainest dress in her collection—pale blue with a minimum of ruffles. Lucille helped with the buttons. Earnestine insisted that I unbraid my hair, but when I protested, the girls agreed that I could tie it in back with a bow. "No black ribbon!" they insisted, and found a blue one that satisfied them. I had never felt more unlike myself.

After the Harvest Ball finally ended and we'd retired to our dormitory rooms and changed out of dresses and uniforms and into our nightclothes, I made a proposal: "Let's go down to the dining room, and if the tables haven't been put back, I'll teach you some dances that are much more fun, and you don't need a partner."

The girls stared at me as though I'd suggested robbing a bank. "In our nightclothes?" Susan asked.

"Of course! Why not? Who would know the difference?"

"But what if we're caught?" asked Earnestine. Being a minister's daughter—a lot of the girls at Chatham were—she was timid about breaking rules and worried about being found out.

"Is it a crime to go downstairs?" I asked.

"It's against the rules—leaving our room after lights-out."

But Susan stepped up boldly. "Oh, come on, girls! Georgie's had a splendid idea." I'd asked her and my other friends to call me Georgie, like my family did. "And besides, it's her birthday! We have to do something special to celebrate."

We tiptoed down the creaking wooden staircase, suppressing giggles. A lamp had been left burning in the empty kitchen, and it provided just enough light to the dining hall that we could see without running into anything. We were in luck: the tables and benches hadn't been pushed back in place. I demonstrated a few simple Irish jig steps and provided the accompaniment by whistling. Francis had taught me how.

Alice declared that because her birthday was the following week and this was partly her celebration too, she would raid the pantry and see if there were any of those little cakes left over. There were, and we made short work of them.

Our dancing lesson/birthday party was in full swing when a bright light suddenly flared in the dining hall. Billy, making his rounds with a lantern, gaped at us, a dozen girls in nightgowns dancing a jig.

"It's a class, Billy," I called out. "We're rehearsing."

Billy held up the lantern and squinted in my direction. "You have permission, do you, Miss O'Keeffe?"

"Of course!"

"Uh-*huh*," Billy said and went away, shaking his head.

The girls stood in shocked silence. "That's an untruth, Georgie," Earnestine said quietly.

"No, it's not, Earnestine. I haven't seen any rule against dancing in the dining hall in a nightgown. And I'm the one who gave permission."

The girls laughed nervously, but that was the end of the dancing, and we trooped back upstairs.

It wasn't the end of the adventure, though. Someone—maybe it was Billy, maybe it was one of the girls who hadn't joined in the dancing, Bea Morrison or Annabelle Jeffries—reported me to Miss Drummond for "being out of bed after the lights-out bell had sounded."

"I am disappointed in you, Miss O'Keeffe," the housemother said. "Such behavior is unbecoming to a Chatham girl. I must assign you the usual punishment of writing five hundred times, 'I shall obey all the rules of the Chatham Episcopal Institute.'"

The other girls, including Alice, had to write it only a hundred times. "Why are you getting off easy and I'm not?" I demanded.

"Because you're the ringleader, Georgie! You always are! Everybody knows that!"

My punishment consumed an entire Sunday afternoon while the rest of the girls went out for a walk. It was a waste of time that failed to cure me of my determination to do things my own way. But I also thought it was funny that my classmates recognized me as the ring-leader. I was not rebellious, exactly, but the rules felt like a dog collar attached to a leash, and I looked for ways to wriggle out of it.

Early in December the young ladies of the Institute gave a holiday recital. The townspeople of Chatham filled the benches in the dining hall, plus the chairs Billy brought in. I played "Anitra's Dance" from Grieg's *Peer Gynt Suite*, a piece I'd been working on since the beginning of the term, with Miss Cornwall's encouragement. I couldn't afford to take lessons from her, but she lent me exercise books and sheet music, and sometimes when I was practicing she stopped by and gave me advice.

Everyone said I gave a fine performance, and for a while I wondered if I might not be a better pianist than artist. "You do have talent, Georgia," Miss Cornwall said. "But discipline is the key. You must put in long hours of practice every day if you truly wish to become a fine musician."

But that was not how I worked; I had to be inspired. I either painted for hours at a time, or I didn't paint at all, sometimes for days. It was the same with music. There was something else: when I finished playing "Anitra's Dance," it was done, and nothing remained of my performance. But when I finished a painting, it continued to exist—unless I decided to burn it. I realized that I was temperamentally better suited to being an artist than a musician.

At Christmas, almost all the Chatham girls went home to be with their families. I did not. It was a day's journey, and it cost too much. I didn't mind. If I stayed at Chatham, I would have plenty of time to paint and not be bothered by anyone until the other girls came back in January.

Mrs. Willis and a few of the teachers also stayed at the school over the Christmas and New Year holidays, and they did their best to make it less lonely for those of us who remained—along with me, two first-year girls whose parents were missionaries in China and my friend Alice Peretta. Laredo, Texas, on the Mexican border, was too far even for Alice, who could afford to travel wherever she wanted. We went together to the midnight service on Christmas Eve at Emmanuel Church, with lots of flickering candles and anthems by the choir and carol-singing by the congregation. I did like that part.

Mrs. Willis invited us to her home for Christmas dinner. Her pretty little house had once been the caretaker's cottage, and the walls were hung with interesting paintings, mostly landscapes. Some were signed "E. Claridge" and others "E. C. Willis." I asked who E. Claridge was, and Mrs. Willis explained that she was Elizabeth Claridge before she'd become Mrs. Harold Willis. I knew right then that I would sign my name and *only* my name on my artwork. Even if I someday decided to have a husband, I would not use his name. I would always be Georgia O'Keeffe.

We feasted on baked ham and candied yams, served by Mrs. Willis's maid, Cora. Cora was dressed in a black uniform with a starched white apron and cuffs and a collar, an outfit that—except for the ruffles on the apron—I thought was every bit as handsome as the robes worn by the nuns at Sacred Heart. After we'd had our Christmas pudding, Alice volunteered to play the piano so we could all gather around and sing carols. Her playing had not improved much, but I liked to sing and the wrong notes didn't matter.

On New Year's Day the four of us who'd stayed over the holidays ate dinner in the school dining room. Elsie fixed rice with black-eyed peas and some ham left over from Mrs. Willis's Christmas dinner, to eat for luck in the New Year, she said. She'd warned us that chicken would not be served.

"Why is that, Elsie?" I asked.

"'Cause a chicken scratches backward and a pig roots forward," Elsie explained. "Don't you folks up North know that?"

When I was a student at Sacred Heart, I'd paid attention to my regular classes, and I'd done enough to get decent grades in Madison. But during that first term at Chatham, I did as little as possible. I thought most of the subjects were a waste of time. I refused to practice my French lesson three times a day, as was required. I was a loathsome speller—I didn't even know how to spell "loathsome"—and I hated the drills.

The only class I truly enjoyed was Mrs. Willis's art class, but around the beginning of the second term I stopped painting. Nothing I'd been working on interested me. Restless and bored, I distracted myself by annoying the other students. They complained to Mrs. Willis. "Georgie pulled my hair," grumbled Annabelle Jeffries, the smartest girl in all the other classes but without even a shred of artistic talent. "She hides our brushes," whined Bea Morrison, who whined about everything.

"Leave her be," Mrs. Willis advised them. "When Georgia is inspired, she does more in a few hours than all the rest of you combined can accomplish in a week." I loved her for saying that—not only for telling the girls to quit complaining, but for understanding that I had my own way of working or not working.

By the time wildflowers like bleeding heart and bloodroot and lungwort were bursting into a frenzy of color in that part of Virginia, and the air was so heavy with their scent that I was almost drunk with it, inspiration had returned. Inspiration wasn't something I could turn on and off like a faucet. It was more like an underground spring that disappeared for a time and then came bubbling up to the surface again. I started painting more intensely than ever.

The girls in my classes sometimes resented me for my special privileges, and it was plain that even my good friends—Susan and Lucille and Earnestine and Alice—thought I was a bit odd. Their conversation was usually about clothes and parties and often turned to boys they knew, or hoped they'd meet someday, subjects that didn't interest me. When *The Mortarboard*, the yearbook, came out at the end of the term, this rhyme appeared with my photograph:

A girl who would be different, in habit, style and dress,
A girl who doesn't give a cent for men—and boys still less.

But my classmates also marveled at the quick sketches I seemed to toss off so effortlessly. Even Annabelle, who was used to being the best at everything, agreed that I was talented, and Bea admitted grudgingly that my work was superior.

"You're going to be a famous artist someday," Susan said. "I believe that with all my heart."

I believed it, too. But how was I going to become a famous artist? And a *great* one?

9

Williamsburg, Virginia—
Summer 1904

AFTER NINE MONTHS AT CHATHAM, I MADE THE trip back to Williamsburg and my family. For the first few days we stayed up talking until late. Francis had completed a year at the College of William and Mary and seemed little changed, just as quiet and reserved as he'd been when we stayed with Aunt Lola in Madison. Alexius at twelve was still a good-humored boy with a bright smile and a sunny disposition. Fifteen-year-old Ida and Nita, two years younger, lamented that the private day school they attended was a humdrum place with lots of snobbish girls. "They let us know that we're not quite up to their standards," Ida said, sighing.

Catherine and Claudie were being tutored at home. "I like it," Catherine told me, and Claudie, now five, agreed. "I get to do whatever I want," she said.

I envied those two their freedom, and I looked forward to three months of doing whatever I wanted, too.

To escape the suffocating heat of the town, Papa rented a ramshackle house on the York River a few miles from Wheatlands. We piled our featherbeds and some cooking pots and utensils into the O'Keeffe & Sons Feed & Grain wagon, assembled a table out of planks and sawhorses, turned empty crates into stools, and set up housekeeping in the rented house. Papa showed us how to pry oysters open and suck them, raw and briny, from their shells. Francis and Alexius found an old rowboat, rigged up a sail, and figured out how to maneuver it. For long, solitary hours I waded barefoot along the water's edge, and as the sun dropped lower I scrambled up the riverbank and filled pages of my sketchbook with pencil drawings—the river, the old rowboat among the reeds, a single oyster shell.

In July Susan Young accepted my invitation to come out from her home in Roanoke for a visit. The poor girl did not do well at sleeping on a featherbed on the floor and "roughing it" with the O'Keeffe family, but she was a good sport—except when we all ran down to the river in the early morning, wearing only our underclothes, for a swim before breakfast. This was simply too much for Lady Susan, as Francis called her. Completely dressed in her embroidered cotton lawn dress and gartered stockings, she watched us from the shelter of a shade tree. She might have wanted to join us when we jumped into the water, or baited hooks to catch fish to fry over a campfire for breakfast, but she could not bring herself to do it.

"She lacks only a parasol," Francis said after Susan left. I could tell that he'd been attracted by her delicate beauty, and that she was attracted by the lack of polish and pretense that set my brother apart from most Southern boys, but each took care not to let the other know.

We moved back to town at the end of summer, and I spent part of every day in my studio painting still lifes: flowers and leaves stuck carelessly in jars, a bowl of purple grapes and oranges. Most often I worked with watercolors, pinning a sheet of paper to my easel, dampening it with a wet brush, and letting the bold strokes of paint blossom and blend into one another in unexpected ways.

I did pencil sketches of Francis and Alexius and Auntie—Auntie was the one who never seemed to change. I coaxed Claudie to come and sit while I drew her picture. She sighed and agreed to put on her best dress and shoes, and I tied a bow in her hair. I sketched quickly when Claudie posed for me, because she was a restless child who hated to be still for long. A bowl of fruit was so much easier.

My mother didn't bother framing my pictures anymore. "There are too many of them," she said with a little laugh.

Too soon the summer ended, and with it the freedom to do whatever I wanted. I was resigned to returning to Chatham for one more year. I was nearly seventeen and sick to death of being escorted by chaperones on our weekly visits to the town, as though we were still children, constantly in danger of some undefined threat, with no idea how to take care of ourselves. As a child I'd roamed the farm on my own, and no one thought anything of it. But at Chatham, even an afternoon walk off school property was forbidden unless a teacher went with us. I wanted to wander alone, poke into dark corners, discover whatever I could. But that was not allowed.

I chafed under these restrictions. Why couldn't I just take my sketchbook and pencils and go where I pleased? Set up my easel and paint in *plein air*, if that's what I felt like doing? It was what artists did, and I felt that as an artist I deserved that independence.

So I looked for ways to ignore the rules without getting caught. Pulling off harmless escapades, like swiping onions from the garden and eating them raw, didn't win me any artistic freedom, but it did make me feel I had some control over my own life.

The girls still talked about how we had once danced the Irish jig in the dining hall after lights-out, as though that had been a wild adventure. They wanted to learn to be naughty and counted on me to show them how.

Thanks to Francis, I knew how to play poker, and I offered to give them lessons. We played for "chores," like carrying an extra load of wood up to the stove in the dormitory, or making up someone's bed for a week, or smuggling out an extra dessert at supper. They were thrilled to be doing something we knew would be disapproved of by nearly everybody.

One night when Elsie was off, Willie Mae, who did our laundry and sometimes filled in for her in the kitchen, fixed leaden biscuits and lumpy sausage gravy for a supper that nobody liked. Lucille pushed away her plate and said, "Our cook back home makes the most wonderful roast chicken you've ever tasted," and Alice said, "Oh, my goodness, Lucille, just *thinkin'* about our Consuelo's chicken makes my mouth water!"

After Susan and Earnestine raved about *their* cooks, I said, "Let's get ourselves a chicken and cook it!"

The girls rolled their eyes. "Just where do you think we're going to get ourselves a chicken, Georgie?"

"We'll kidnap one from the henhouse."

After a good deal of scoffing and laughter, Lucille and Alice and I sneaked out to the henhouse, Lucille and Alice stood watch, and I grabbed the first chicken I saw— it was too surprised and sleepy to object. Since I was the only girl with experience in life on a farm, I wrung its neck. Annabelle and Earnestine drew short straws and had to clean and pluck it, gagging as they did, and Alice buried the incriminating remains in the garden. I was amazed that she knew how to handle a shovel. Surely her family had a whole team of gardeners!

"Daddy's crazy idea," Alice said. "He says he wants me to be 'capable.' Of what, I don't know. Digging, I guess."

We cooked our stolen chicken in the woodstove in our attic dormitory. It was burnt on the outside, half raw inside, and tough all the way through, but we ate it out of plain stubbornness and felt immensely proud of ourselves, because *we'd gotten away with it!*

When I wasn't figuring out ways to break school rules, I painted. I'd become more adept at watercolor, and I'd gained better control of the shapes and colors in the wet-on-wet technique, painting on dampened paper. My best works early that year were of a bunch of lilacs and another of ears of red and yellow corn—I won a prize for that one. And I did an oil painting of our red barn back in Sun Prairie, simple, geometric, and bold. It reminded me of my childhood and how much my life had changed.

Six of us were graduating seniors, and we often talked dreamily about the future and what we hoped our lives would be like in five years. All of them seemed to be thinking of the same thing: marriage and a family. Those girls had been sent to Chatham by their parents for an education that would make them desirable marriage material and would attract husbands who were guaranteed to support their wives properly.

I asked Susan exactly what "marriage material" meant.

"It's not just how to balance a punch cup or dance well, Georgie," she explained. "It's more than that, like how to carry on an intelligent conversation—"

"Not *too* intelligent, though," Alice interrupted. "Boys don't like girls who are smarter than they are."

"Annabelle will have to be careful, because she gets the highest grades in everything," Bea teased.

"I'm smart enough not to let on that I know more than they do," Annabelle replied airily.

All of this seemed pointless to me. I had no interest in boys, or in the men they would someday be, much less in finding a husband.

"Georgie, tell us what *you* think!" said Susan. "What is your life going to be like five years from now?"

"I don't want what the rest of you want. I'm going to have a life that's different from yours," I told my friends. "My art is the most important thing, and I'm willing to give up everything else for the life of an artist."

"You mean you're never going to marry?" Lucille asked in disbelief.

"Maybe one day I will, but not for years and years. How would I have time to paint if I had a husband and a houseful of children?"

"You could hire servants to look after them," Earnestine suggested. "Of course you'd have to marry a man of means."

"Even if I was somehow able to marry a man with money, someone has to supervise the servants and run the household. And all of that would keep me from painting."

I'd been chosen art editor of our class yearbook. I decorated the pages with my ink drawings, but I was not responsible for the two lines that appeared beneath my photograph:

O is for O'Keeffe, an artist divine.
Her paintings are perfect and drawings are fine.

My classmates clearly saw me as an artist, and I saw myself that way. But I had no idea how I'd reach my goal of dedicating my life to my art. All the artists I'd ever heard of were men. Of course Mrs. Willis was an artist, but she was headmistress of a school and taught art classes besides. When did she have time to make art? I wondered.

Nearer to graduation, Mrs. Willis invited me for tea. A table in the garden had been laid with a linen cloth and china teacups. Mrs. Willis added cream and stirred it with a silver teaspoon. I wondered what we'd talk about. I admired her roses, and she told me their names and said they'd been planted by Mr. Willis before he died. Then she changed the subject.

"Georgia, I'd like to discuss your future plans. That's the main reason I've invited you here today."

"I want to be an artist, Mrs. Willis."

She nodded. "Yes, and I believe you have the talent to succeed. But you need more training than I can give you. When I was young, I enrolled at the Art Students League in New York to learn to paint, and then I studied at Syracuse University in New York State to earn my teaching credentials. Perhaps you might consider following a similar path."

Mrs. Willis was observing me expectantly, waiting for me to say something. But I did not know what to say.

At home the previous summer, after we'd returned to Wheatlands from the rented house on the banks of the York River, I felt a thick cloud of uneasiness hanging over my family like a swarm of mosquitoes. Although no one talked about it, it was plain that business had not picked up for Papa's grocery store, and he wasn't selling much feed and grain. I realized then that my parents could barely afford to send me to boarding school and to make sure that my brothers and sisters got an education too. In her most recent letter Mama had mentioned that Papa was looking for a new line of work, and I guessed that money must be getting tighter.

Art school seemed impossible. Where would the money come from? I could not say any of this to Mrs. Willis.

"That's a very good suggestion," I said at last.

The maid brought a plate of cookies to the garden and a fresh pot of tea. Mrs. Willis refilled our cups. "I invited you here for a second reason—not just to talk about your future. You have done well enough with most of your required subjects, French and mythology and geometry. But you have another challenge, Georgia. Your spelling is atrocious."

My china cup rattled in the saucer as I waited to hear what I knew was coming.

"Miss Stevens has sent me a message," Mrs. Willis said gravely. "She tells me that you've failed your spelling test again. I cannot let you graduate in June unless you pass that test."

Not graduate? I'd been dreading this. "No matter how much I drill, I can't make sense of it! Why are words not spelled the way they sound?" I asked. My voice was trembling. "Miss Stevens says that English is derived from many different sources, and spellings don't always make sense. She's told me that I must write the words over and over until I've memorized them. And I've done that, but it doesn't seem to help." I blinked back tears. What if I couldn't graduate? Mama would be so disappointed!

"I understand. Nevertheless, you must pass the test. I shall instruct Miss Stevens to schedule another test for you. In the meantime, one of your friends might help you with spelling drills. Annabelle, perhaps?"

"Thank you, Mrs. Willis." My hand was still shaking when I picked up the teacup again. "I'll ask Annabelle."

"Good. You have an extraordinary talent, Georgia, and I would be remiss as an educator if I didn't do everything in my power to help you find your way. I shall write to your parents about the possibility of further study, if you have no objection."

I had no objection, but what good would it do if there was no money?

And, as Mrs. Willis had pointed out, it was possible that I wouldn't even get my diploma. In order to pass that test, I was required to spell seventy-five out of a hundred words correctly.

Abstemious bellicose evanescent fiduciary incontrovertible . . . Why did I need to know how to spell such words when I didn't know their meanings or how to pronounce them and would never use them? I stared at my speller and tried to make the peculiar arrangements of letters stay fixed in my mind.

Annabelle tried to help. She dictated words from the list, but I always left out a letter—the *i* in *abstemious*, the *s* or the *c* in *evanescent*. I got frustrated, and then Annabelle did too, and said she couldn't do it anymore. I was on my own.

Miss Stevens, a tiny, birdlike woman with thick glasses, harped endlessly on what she called my "over-indulgence in the use of dashes" and my "deplorable disregard for correct spelling." The first time she gave me the test, I got exactly half of the words wrong.

"But I got half of them right!" I reminded her, and she reminded me that I had best get serious quickly or I would not receive my diploma.

The second time I took the test, I did a little better, but the third was worse. Then Bea began drilling me and I actually improved, because she was not as intimidating as brilliant Annabelle. I had trouble sleeping, and of course I didn't paint at all—I was thinking of how Mama and Papa would feel if I failed to graduate and had wasted the money they'd spent on my education.

I failed the fifth try, although I came close—seventy-two right. Then, a miracle! On the sixth attempt to pass the awful test, I spelled seventy-six words correctly! I was so relieved that I burst into tears. I was never one to weep easily, but then, I'd never before feared failure. I would graduate!

We were required to wear white dresses for the ceremony. Alice offered to lend me one of hers—she had several to choose from—and I picked the only one without lace. From then on, I vowed, I would dress like a nun and wear only black and plain white. Mrs. Willis made a speech, and our teachers said complimentary things about each of us. Miss Cornwall pounded out "Pomp and Circumstance" on the piano as the graduating seniors, our backs straight as broomsticks, walked to the front of the dining hall to receive our diplomas. My name was inscribed on parchment in Gothic letters—*Georgia Totto O'Keeffe*—the only time I'd used my middle name. I wished that at least someone in my family had been there, but Mama had already let me know that it wasn't "practical." Meaning, I knew, that they could not afford to make the trip.

After the ceremony the six graduates observed the tradition of planting a tree, and that evening Billy, dressed in his Sunday suit with a flower stuck in the buttonhole, piled wood for a bonfire. I'd been chosen to light it. I picked what I thought were my five best paintings and gave one as a gift to each of my classmates. The rest of the paintings I rolled up to use as a torch to light the fire. It was what I'd done with a lot of my pictures before I left Aunt Lola's— burned up second- and third-rate student work that I did *not* want to be associated with in the future.

Susan leapt up and tried to stop me. "Oh, Georgie, surely you don't want to do that! They're all so lovely!"

"Of course I'm sure," I told her. "I'm always sure about what to do."

That wasn't *entirely* true, but I said it so convincingly that I believed it myself.

10

Williamsburg, Virginia—
Summer 1905

THREE WEEKS AFTER GRADUATING FROM THE Chatham Episcopal Institute I was in the kitchen at Wheatlands, making pies. A half dozen pie tins were lined up on the table. Mama sprinkled flour on the table and flattened a ball of dough with a rolling pin, a few deft strokes one way, then the other, into a perfect circle. My job was preparing the fillings: lemon sponge, egg custard, strawberry rhubarb. The heat in the kitchen climbed. I wore a kerchief wrapped around my forehead to keep perspiration from dripping into the batter.

Several loaves of bread cooled on wire racks. When Ida and Nita had finished frosting two spice cakes and a sponge cake, Mama sent them to deliver the bread to Papa's grocery—Alexius was tending the store that summer—and bring back a sack of sugar and two dozen eggs. She sighed. "I wish we had our own chickens. They were such good layers, the ones we had on the farm!"

Ladies who'd invited Mama to tea when we first arrived in Williamsburg would send their colored maids later this afternoon to pick up the cakes and pies they'd ordered for their teas and dinners and birthday parties. Mama's pies and cakes were in demand, even if her presence was not. It had been many months since she'd been invited to a tea.

Claudie and Catherine had gone out to the barn to feed and groom Penelope. Those two were practically inseparable from Auntie's horse—especially Catherine, who loved to ride and could coax the elderly horse into a brisk trot. Auntie herself was off shopping for darning needles and thread. All of our stockings were full of holes. "Like Swiss cheese," she said.

Mama and I were alone in the kitchen. "Your father and I have been talking," she began.

I broke another egg into a bowl and waited to hear whatever she was going to tell me.

"We've exchanged some nice letters with Mrs. Willis," Mama went on. "Such a kind lady! She speaks highly of you."

I concentrated on beating the eggs. "Mrs. Willis did say she was going to write to you."

"She believes you have a great deal of talent, and she thinks you could earn a living as an art teacher. She wants us to consider sending you to the Art Institute of Chicago. There's a program there for training art teachers, and she suggests that you enroll in it."

I added buttermilk to the eggs. "Mrs. Willis said that?"

"She did. I agree with her that you're very talented. But I have to tell you, your father is not pleased by the idea. It's not just the cost. He's heard that men pose almost naked in some of the classes, and you'd be drawing pictures of them. He wanted to know if this is true. Mrs. Willis explained that the models in the life classes wear very little clothing, but there are separate classes for male and female students." Mama gathered up scraps of pastry dough, formed them into a ball, and rolled out the last piecrust. "You'd get used to seeing such things, I guess."

I measured sugar and flour and folded them into the eggs and buttermilk, almost as nervous as I was taking those spelling tests. "And Papa says it's all right?"

"He worried that you wouldn't be properly supervised, but I reminded him that my sister and brother live in Chicago. You can stay with them, you'd be chaperoned, and it would save money. Once he was persuaded that your morals were in no danger, he agreed with Mrs. Willis and me that it's a good idea. You must have a way to earn a living on your own."

I'd been holding my breath, and I let it out slowly. "So it's settled then? I can go to Chicago?"

"Yes, if you want to. She'll write you a letter of

recommendation, and that will be enough for you to be admitted. Will you pass me the batter for the lemon pies?"

My hands were shaking when I handed her the bowl. "But—the cost," I stammered. "How . . . ?"

"We'll get along somehow. Your father is optimistic about starting a new business soon."

She smiled brightly, and I did something I hardly ever did: I threw my arms around her and pressed my cheek to hers. "Thank you, Mama," I said.

We went back to making pies, and I could not stop smiling and thinking, *I am going to Chicago! I'm going to art school! I'm going to become an artist!*

The hot, suffocating days of summer crawled by, but this year there was no money to rent the house by the river. I felt a little guilty that whatever money might have been used for rent was going to pay for me to go to Chicago. Also, though, we were busy baking.

When I was not perspiring in the kitchen, I escaped upstairs to my studio and painted. During the long twilight evenings I stitched two long black skirts, one black jacket, and three plain white shirtwaists. Auntie had taught me how to make French seams so there were no raw edges. My clothes were so neatly sewn that I could have worn them inside out.

Aunt Ollie, Mama's oldest sister, wrote that she and their brother, my uncle Charley, were pleased I was coming, and I would have the spare room in their apartment, only a few blocks from the Art Institute. I wouldn't even have to take a streetcar.

I'd been leaving home to go to school since I was twelve. I was now seventeen and should have been used to it, but as September approached, my uneasiness grew. I had never been to a big city. Madison had seemed big at first, but it wasn't, really, and I couldn't imagine what Chicago was going to be like. And the Art Institute! I lay awake at night wondering, *What if I'm not good enough?* I wrote to Susan Young and Alice Peretta and told them what I'd be doing. They both wrote back with congratulations, and Alice added, "You'll be a shining star, just as you always are."

But still I fretted.

At the end of September my father drove me to the depot in the O'Keeffe & Sons Feed & Grain wagon. Mama, Auntie, my sisters, and Alexius came along. Francis had already left for Boston to study architecture.

"Remember to write," Papa said as we waited for the northbound train.

"Let us know if you need anything," Mama added.

I saw again how tired they both looked, how gray Papa's hair had grown while I was at Chatham, but they never talked about what was worrying them. I'd asked Alexius, who worked at the store when he wasn't in class at the private academy he attended, if he knew what was going on. Alexius looked away. "Business stinks. That's all I can tell you, Georgie."

The train arrived, and I climbed aboard with my two small suitcases. Everyone waved and smiled as the train pulled out, except Alexius, who ran alongside, shouting, "Goodbye, Georgie! Goodbye, goodbye!"

I waved back, trying to ignore the sick feeling that lay like a heavy stone in the pit of my stomach. Would I be a shining star, as Alice predicted, or a failure? And what was going to happen to my family if Papa's business failed?

PART III

"A new part of my life began to unfold."

11

Chicago—Fall 1905

CHICAGO WAS BIGGER, NOISIER, AND MORE FRIGHT-
ening than I expected. There were elevated trains and
electric streetcars, and the streets were crowded
with horse-drawn carriages and even a few horseless
carriages—I'd seen only one before, rumbling down Duke
of Gloucester Street and stirring up clouds of dust. Tall
buildings, skyscrapers, crowded together and lit up at
night with electric lights.

"You're in the big city now," Uncle Charley said
proudly. "More than two million people live and work
here. There's nothing like it anywhere!"

Two million people, all going somewhere in a hurry,
but life with Aunt Ollie and Uncle Charley was quiet and
ordinary. No one had time to fuss. Miss Alletta Totto—
she'd always been Ollie to us—worked as a stenographer.

Every morning she left for her office wearing a black hat with a large feather and carrying a black umbrella, rain or shine.

Aunt Ollie had never married, but I would not describe her as an old maid, like Aunt Lola. She was strong-willed and independent, and she assumed that I was, too. She gave me whatever I needed, except affection. I admired my aunt and I wanted to be like her, but I didn't see much of her, and I couldn't really talk to her when she *was* around. Uncle Charley managed a business that had something to do with finance. A confirmed bachelor with a huge mustache, he didn't have much in common with a seventeen-year-old girl. The three of us ate Sunday dinner together, but the conversation was brisk and impersonal, usually about politics and business. They discussed the Teamsters strike (it ended before I came, but twenty-one people had died!), and they argued about who should be the next mayor of Chicago. Aunt Ollie was voting for the Democrat, Uncle Charley supported the Republican, and I didn't care the least bit about either.

Alone in the tidy kitchen after Aunt Ollie and Uncle Charley left for work, I had a breakfast of bread and tea and tucked a boiled egg, sometimes two, into my bag for my noon meal. Then, dressed in my black skirt and jacket and white shirtwaist, a black ribbon tied at the end of my braid, I set out on the half-hour walk to the Art Institute, an enormous building near the shore of Lake Michigan with a pair of bronze lions guarding the broad marble steps. On the first day of classes I had to force myself to climb those steps, past those lions.

Hundreds of students had registered. The first-year students, more than forty of us, were gathered in a huge gallery with dark green walls. As our first assignment we were to make a drawing of a larger-than-life-sized plaster bust of a curly-haired Greek god displayed on a table in the center of the gallery. I thought I was beyond drawing plaster casts and was ready for something new, something more challenging.

I remembered Sister Angelique's criticism of my drawing of a baby's hand: *Why have you made it so small and black? It looks like a lump of coal.* Since then, I'd learned to make my sketches larger and filled with light. If drawing the bust was the assignment, I would do it, and do it well. I worked quickly, and the face of the Greek god emerged on the paper.

The instructor made his rounds, offering a comment here, a suggestion there. He stopped by the easel of the student next to me, tapped a finger on the dark, dense rendering, and remarked to the young man, "A lighter touch would improve this." Then he moved on to mine. "Well done, miss!" My neighbor glared at me, ripped the drawing from his easel, and crumpled it into a ball that he flung to the floor.

It wasn't always like that. Many of the other students were very talented, and as the days went by, I could see that their work was richer, more complex, *better* than mine. My paintings and drawings had been praised since I was a child. I was recognized as the best, the most talented, in Sister Angelique's class and then in Mrs. Willis's. But now I quickly discovered that most of the students were more accomplished than I, and I was no longer the star. I had felt confident of my talent at Chatham—so confident that I worked when I was inspired and didn't work at all when I wasn't; Mrs. Willis had allowed that. Now I began to doubt myself. I would have to work very hard to catch up.

Then it got worse.

I was assigned to an advanced life drawing class. The students were all female, as Mrs. Willis had promised, but most of them were older and, I thought, more experienced. A male model wrapped in a blue robe strolled into the studio, took his place on a small raised platform, and casually dropped the robe. His privates were barely concealed by a flimsy loincloth. He was almost completely naked! My face grew hot, and I was sure that my blush must be obvious to everyone.

If the other girls in the class felt any embarrassment, they didn't show it. Maybe they were more sophisticated than I was, more worldly. Or maybe they were bothered, too, but I was too flustered to notice. *I won't be able to do this*, I thought. *It's just too much. Maybe it means I'm not cut out to be an artist after all.* I wished I could talk to Aunt Ollie about this, but I didn't know how to bring up the subject. Anyway, I had a pretty good notion of what my no-nonsense aunt would say: *You're beginning to sound like one of those delicate Southern belles! Totto women are made of sterner stuff. Learn what is required and get on with it.*

I took the advice I thought she'd give me and forced myself to keep going. After four or five classes, I stopped being embarrassed by the model's near-nakedness, and I could concentrate on my drawing.

My work improved steadily, and when it was judged at the end of the first month I found that I'd been ranked fourth out of the forty-four and promoted to the intermediate level.

I signed up for an anatomy class taught by a Dutchman named John Vanderpoel. He used a wooden pointer to call our attention to certain parts of the model's anatomy, drawing with black and white crayon on big sheets of tan paper while he talked. "Notice the clavicle, here, and how it curves to meet the scapula, there."

Mr. Vanderpoel was quite short and had a hunchback, and he stood on a stool while he lectured. Some of the students made fun of his appearance, and that bothered me, because I'd become fond of him. I had gotten over my self-consciousness in the life drawing classes, and I looked forward to Mr. Vanderpoel's weekly lectures.

"I recognize what a struggle it was for you in the beginning, Miss O'Keeffe," Mr. Vanderpoel said in his heavy Dutch accent, tapping my drawing, "but you are getting better, much better."

Art Institute classes were very competitive. Each month the teachers pinned our most recent drawings up on the wall and ranked them. It was important to show improvement. A good ranking won you the chance to set up your easel near the front, where you'd have the best view of the model. But if you were ranked fifteenth, say, you found yourself toward the back of the hall. You certainly did not want to be among those who ranked lowest, because eventually those students were asked to leave.

My confidence grew. Each month I advanced. In December the instructors ranked me fifth in the class of twenty-nine women, and in February they placed me first. I was thrilled, of course, but being first didn't win me any friends among students who were ranked lower. Because the classes were so competitive, and we always had to be proving ourselves better than the next person, I had made only one friend, Madeleine Connor.

"I'm going to call you Patsy," she said, "because with a last name like O'Keeffe you should have a first name that's more Irish than Georgia. And you must call me Mattie, not Madeleine."

From then on in Chicago, I was Patsy.

We often ate our noon meals together—my boiled egg, her sardine sandwich—and sometimes we went to see the new exhibits at the Institute, shows of work by contemporary French artists and another by Americans.

"Have you noticed how few women artists are represented?" Mattie asked.

I hadn't, until she mentioned it. "I wonder if that's because there are so few women artists, or if it's because the men who select the paintings don't like women's art?"

"It's odd, isn't it?" she said. "There are about twice as many women as there are men in our classes. But it's the men who end up having their work exhibited in museums."

I'm going to change that, I thought. *Someday my work is going to hang in a museum.*

In midwinter Mama wrote to me that my sister Catherine had come down with malaria, and although she was feeling better, she wasn't able to keep up with her schoolwork.

Catherine is tired all the time, Mama wrote, *but not too sick. Nobody recovers in a hot, damp climate, one gets well in bitter cold, and for that reason I am sending her to you. She is bored and does not know what to do with herself, especially since we will not allow her to ride Penelope until she is better. The change will be good for her and possibly good company for you also.*

Catherine traveled alone all the way to Chicago with a note pinned to her coat and arrived looking as limp as a sack of laundry. Uncle Charley set up a cot in my room for her, and Papa sent extra money to pay for her food. My sister and I were left to fend for ourselves.

"How did you catch malaria?" I asked Catherine.

"Lots of mosquitoes back home," she said. "They bite you, something bad gets into your blood, and you get sick."

Catherine was eight years younger than I was but a sober-minded little person, and we understood each other. She had developed an interest in art and was beginning to show a real talent for drawing. I found a book of chromos and helped her figure out how to sketch a horse that was supposed to be the beloved Penelope.

We braved the blustery Chicago weather, but we'd both grown up in Wisconsin winters and weren't bothered by the plunging temperatures. Mama was right; the cold weather perked her right up. Catherine had come without a warm winter coat, but a friend of Aunt Ollie's passed along a bright red coat her daughter had outgrown, along with a stylish hat. I persuaded my sister to pose for me in that coat and hat, sprawled on a green baize settee in the parlor. I enjoyed working with the bold reds and emerald greens—I was falling in love with color! I didn't work fast enough to suit Miss Catherine, but I did succeed in capturing her impatient expression.

Meanwhile, Catherine had fastened her affections on Aunt Ollie's cantankerous old parrot, Lucifer, who had generally regarded me with bored silence. My sister stopped drawing horses and borrowed my colored pencils to draw the parrot, which preened and posed for her. He must have been starved for attention.

By spring she was almost completely recovered, and I registered her to attend the nearby public school for the rest of the year. It would give her something to do, and she would be with girls her own age.

"How was school today?" I asked after the first week.

Catherine gave me a look with one eyebrow raised. "School is school," she said with a shrug, and I knew just what she meant. "How was yours?"

"About the same," I admitted. "Dull."

I'd read that exciting things were happening in the Paris art world. Mattie and I had gone to see the exhibit of work by French artists whose names we'd heard, but our teachers hadn't even mentioned the exhibit or suggested that we see it. They insisted that most contemporary European painters weren't accomplishing anything worth much, and that we should study the Old Masters and learn from them. I saw that the other students in my classes seemed to be stuck more or less where they were when we started, and I recognized that I was getting better. But what, exactly, did that mean?

"Sometimes I wonder if I'm learning as much as I should at the Institute," I told Catherine.

"You're probably smarter than everybody, Georgie," my sister declared with an airy wave of her hand. "Maybe you should go someplace else."

Maybe she was right. None of the teachers—not even Mr. Vanderpoel—favored any of the latest trends, like the French Impressionists. Only art produced at least a half century earlier was valued. Mattie and I often discussed our feeling that perhaps we didn't belong here, but we could not come up with a plan. I kept on doing what I was doing and hoped it would somehow work out. Mattie did, too.

After a few more weeks, Catherine announced that she was ready to go home. She missed our family and her friends—she'd been much more successful at making friends in Williamsburg than I was. I put her on the train with Lucifer, that raucous parrot, a gift from Aunt Ollie. Why Aunt Ollie thought that was an appropriate gift, I had no idea, but Catherine was delighted, and they made the long trip down to Virginia together.

June came; Mattie would be going to her family in Boston, and I was ready to leave, too. My plan was to paint and draw, paint and draw, for three months in Virginia, until it was time to return to Chicago for my second year. Mattie suggested that we find a cheap place and room together in the fall, but I knew I could not afford to leave Aunt Ollie and Uncle Charley's home, no matter how cheap another place might be.

As the train headed south and the miles rolled by, I felt weighed down by a leaden weariness that had settled in my bones. The clamor of a huge city was exhausting. But that was only part of it. Mr. Vanderpoel had ranked me first in the class and given me several honorable mentions but no awards. The constant pressure—not only to do well, but to do better than everyone else—had worn me out.

Lulled by the monotonous *click-clack* of iron wheels on iron rails, I slept. It was as though I hadn't slept in months. Even after I reached Williamsburg, all I wanted to do was sleep.

12

Williamsburg, Virginia—
Summer 1906

IT STARTED WITH A HEADACHE. I HAD NO APPETITE.
Then came the fever.

"You've worn yourself out, Georgie," Mama said.
"Take some time and just rest."

But resting didn't help. The headache got worse.
The fever climbed higher each day. When the stomach
cramps began, Mama knew there was more to it than
simple weariness, and she sent Claudie to the clinic to
ask the doctor to come by and examine me.

White-haired and courtly, Dr. Hunter sat by my bed-
side and asked me questions that I struggled to answer.
He went downstairs to talk to Mama, and I drifted off
again into feverish sleep. Later, when I woke up, my

mother was sitting quietly beside me with a basket of mending.

"The doctor has diagnosed typhoid fever—there are many cases of it around here just now. It comes from dirty water or contaminated food, and it can be very dangerous. He says there's nothing to be done but let the ailment run its course."

"Yes," I said, too weak to ask how long letting it run its course was going to take.

I remember almost nothing about the days that followed. I slept and slept. I was too weak to get out of bed. My fever raged, and I endured dreadful dreams that tormented me both awake and sleeping. "She's delirious," I heard Mama whisper when Papa came. I didn't know if he stayed for minutes or hours. They coaxed me to take sips of water, tried to tempt me to taste a little of this or that. I turned my head away.

The doctor visited often to listen to my chest.

"How long have I been ill?" I mustered enough strength to ask Mama after he'd gone.

"Three weeks."

"How much longer will it go on?"

"We don't know."

Am I going to die? I was afraid to ask her that.

When I first got sick, my fever was low in the mornings, rising higher and higher as the hours passed, but now it stayed high all the time. I felt like I was burning up. Red spots appeared on my stomach.

My sisters were not allowed into my room and peered at me from the doorway with big, worried eyes.

My hair began to fall out. "I think it would be better if I cut off your braid," Mama said, and I was too weak, too exhausted, to argue. She helped me to roll onto my side, and I heard the scissors and felt the tug. Tears rolled down my cheek and onto the pillow. She laid the braid on the table by the bed, like a dead thing, and then one day she took it away. Even the short hair that was left came out, fistfuls at a time. Soon I would be bald and ugly as a baby bird. Auntie sat close by, crocheting a lace cap to cover my naked head.

Then one day the fever didn't climb quite so high, and the next day it was lower, and the day after that, lower still. The bedroom, stifling in summer, felt a little cooler. When I was able to sit up for a few minutes, Mama urged me to try to stand. My legs were too weak to hold me. My arms were thin as matchsticks. I refused to look in the mirror.

There was no question of going back to Chicago that fall. Francis left for Boston in September. I felt even worse when Ida and Nita were sent to Chatham. I couldn't hide how much I hated being left behind. They sent cheerful letters about how Mrs. Willis had welcomed them at my old school. They discovered Susan Young, who had visited us the summer we rented the house on the York River. Susan had returned for an extra year and taken up painting on porcelain, and they'd all become close friends. I envied my sisters so much I wept.

The most I could do was shuffle from my bed to a hammock on the verandah. At last there was a bit of breeze. A whole summer was lost, gone forever.

Only the three youngest O'Keeffes—Alexius, Catherine, and Claudie—were still at home. Alexius was enrolled at the academy at William and Mary, and the girls had set up a classroom in our vast attic and studied up there with a hired tutor. As I grew stronger, I took over some of their lessons, and the tutor came to Wheatlands just three days a week, then two, and then not at all. I was glad to be able to save my parents some money, because it was obvious by then that they were in dire need of it. They never spoke of it, but it must have been a terrible strain to continue to provide a good education for six of their children.

Papa's businesses were barely surviving. He'd never been able to overcome the fact that we were outsiders. For the past year Mama had been baking pies and cakes and bread to make ends meet. Now she decided to open our home to table boarders, students from the College of William and Mary who came to Wheatlands for their meals.

"I'm cooking for seven anyway," she said with a shrug. "May as well prepare meals for a dozen or so and bring in a few dollars."

How humiliated she must have felt! And how weary with all the extra work! She was up long before sunrise, cooking breakfast, sending half a dozen young men off with box lunches, and welcoming them back at suppertime for another big meal. Between meals, she baked. I did what I could.

The baking and the tutoring didn't leave me much time or energy, but I offered to help Miss Murphy, who ran a private kindergarten nearby, and took the children for afternoon walks. I tried to teach them how to see, pointing out flowers and clouds, as Miss Fellers with her yellow stockings and the violets on her hat had once taught me. I didn't earn any money, but I did enjoy watching those eager young faces light up at each new discovery—or not. Some of the children were more interested in creating mischief than in observing nature. There were days when I wondered if I'd do well as a teacher, if I had to deal with resistant young students.

Fall elided into winter, a weak imitation of the brutal winters we'd endured in Wisconsin and Chicago, and there were fewer walks with the children. I started painting again, and tried very hard not to think about the world I was missing, the life I didn't have.

Then spring came, and I felt completely well again, but I'd made no friends. At nineteen I had almost nothing in common with other girls my age in Williamsburg, Southern belles interested in clothes and boys and parties even more intensely than the girls at Chatham had been.

In April I made the acquaintance of Jetta Thorpe, whose mother regularly ordered Mama's cakes to serve at the luncheons she gave every Thursday. When I delivered a cake to their house, Jetta invited me to stay and visit. We sat on a swing on the Thorpes' verandah, surrounded by lilacs and dogwood, and the maid served us glasses of sweet tea.

"You're so different from the rest of us," Jetta said, after we'd talked awhile. "You cut your hair short when everybody else's is long, and your clothes are so . . . so *unusual*. I guess that's the way artists dress up north—is that true?"

"No, it's just the way *I* dress. And I'll probably braid my hair when it gets longer." My hair was growing back, a mass of short curls, and I knew how odd I must look to her.

Then Jetta surprised me and said she was having a dance, and would I like to come? I surprised myself and accepted.

I had never been invited to a party in Williamsburg, and I didn't own a proper party frock. I'd worn a plain skirt and shirtwaist to dances at Chatham on the off months when I wasn't required to be one of the "boys," or borrowed one of Alice's dresses for special occasions. I found an old dress that Nita hadn't taken to Chatham with her, much too big for me now that I'd gotten so thin, and Auntie helped me take in the seams and darts until it fit.

The Thorpes' house was decorated with vases of peonies and candles in silver candelabra. Mama had worn herself out baking dozens of little tarts, and Auntie and I finished Mrs. Thorpe's order for platters of tiny sandwiches cut into triangles and diamonds. Catherine proudly made three trips to deliver everything while I dressed for the party. Mama lent me a pair of fancy shoes someone had passed on to her—they hurt so much, I don't know how she could bear them—and let me wear her emerald earrings.

Two hours later, uniformed maids passed the platters of sandwiches and served strawberry punch from a crystal bowl. Hired musicians played waltzes, and perspiring young men in formal dress steered me around the polished dance floor. Sumner Something-or-Other zealously described his interest in fox hunting in Albemarle County. Philip What's-His-Name lectured me passionately on the novels of Zola. My duty was simply to nod and smile and not notice when they stepped on my aching feet or when they couldn't talk and keep time. It was all exactly the way we'd practiced at Chatham. And just about as dull.

O'Keeffe & Sons Feed & Grain officially closed its doors early in the summer. Francis came home from Boston, and he and Papa launched a new business: making hollow building blocks out of concrete they'd bought cheaply and piles of clamshells that were everywhere for the taking. The Williamsburg newspaper announced the opening of O'Keeffe & Sons Building Materials. Lots of curious visitors showed up, but hardly any paying customers.

Next, Papa made the painful decision to sell the rambling Wheatlands house, except for a small piece of land along the road, and move the family into a much smaller house. I helped Mama pack up our belongings. There wasn't much. After four years, the house was still mostly unfurnished. It had always had an empty feeling. Papa hadn't had enough cash to afford the divans and chairs or the piano that Mama wanted.

The summer dragged by. I befriended some of the children in our new neighborhood and persuaded a few to pose for me. The mother of a little girl named Letty asked me to give the child painting lessons, but I grew frustrated with Letty's lack of talent and her unwillingness to do anything but waste a sheet of paper with uninspired scribbles and muddy colors. Lessons ended after the third session—another reminder that I wasn't suited to teaching young children.

I tried to figure out what to do. My course of study at the Art Institute was supposed to cover two years, the first year for general study and the second to earn a teaching certificate. Papa had been hard-pressed to pay for that first year; a second year was impossible. I wondered if I could find a school that would hire me for a teaching position without a second year of training. I had to do something to earn money, and I didn't know where to start.

"It won't hurt to ask one of your teachers at the Art Institute to write a recommendation for you," Mama said.

I followed her advice and wrote to Mr. Vanderpoel. It took me three tries to write a letter I thought was good enough to send—without misspellings.

His reply came neatly typed on Art Institute stationery: *Miss O'Keeffe is a young lady of attractive personality, and I feel that she will be very successful as a teacher of drawing.*

I was elated! To help me figure out the next step, I wrote to Mrs. Willis.

I trust that you have recovered from your dreadful illness and are again at your easel as productively as ever, she responded. *I understand your urgency in wishing to obtain a teaching position, but you are correct in assuming that you must obtain the proper credentials. I wish to suggest that you consider enrolling at the Art Students League in New York City. It is known to be the most advanced art school in the country. I studied there myself. Although you will not earn a teaching certificate, you will receive excellent training and can perhaps then go elsewhere to obtain the certification. Please let me know if I can assist you in any way.*

I showed the letter to Mama. Looking completely exhausted, she sank onto a chair to read it.

"We have a little left from selling Wheatlands. Perhaps we can manage somehow," she said, sighing. "But only for a year, Georgie. No more than that."

A year! I'll have that—a year! I wouldn't have the credentials I needed for teaching art, but I would be *doing* art, and that was what mattered most.

13

New York—1907

NEW YORK WAS MORE CROWDED THAN CHICAGO—
was more of everything—and the Art Students League
was a handsome building right in the middle of it, on
West Fifty-Seventh Street between Broadway and
Seventh Avenue. Across the street was Carnegie Hall,
where great symphony orchestras played. But there
was no Aunt Ollie, no Uncle Charley, to give me practical advice or a place to live. From the minute I stepped
off the train in this completely strange and bewildering
new city, I wondered how I would ever survive here. I
was on my own.

While I was registering for classes, I made the acquaintance of a girl as poor as I was, Florence Cooney, and we
decided to rent a place together. Flo found a cheap room
in a rundown old brownstone only two blocks away. It

was small, but I was sure we could make do. We bought a hotplate and kept a few things cool on the fire escape. I set a pot of bright red geraniums out there, too.

The League had no required courses; I could take whatever I wanted and pay for it monthly. The first class I signed up for was taught by Mr. Luis Mora, who had studied in Europe and particularly admired the paintings of Velázquez and other Spanish old masters. I learned from him to apply a base of brilliant white paint to the canvas before I began. Layers of color eventually covered the base, but I found ways to let some of the white show, as though white itself was a color, something I'd discovered when I was a high school student in Madison and learned how to use the white of the paper in a watercolor. Every morning I attended a life drawing class. Nearly nude bodies were no longer an embarrassment, although drawing them well was still a challenge. I was not fond of sour-faced Kenyon Cox, who taught the anatomy class and never had a kind word to say about anyone's work.

My favorite was William Merritt Chase. With his perfumed beard and brushy whiskers, he made a dramatic entrance to his afternoon still life class, nattily dressed in a pin-striped suit, silk necktie and jeweled stickpin, top hat, and silver-headed walking stick, a black cape swirling behind him. His pince-nez dangled on a black ribbon. He had a reputation in Europe as well as here as a painter of portraits and still lifes, but he was also a respected teacher. At the start of each class he charged one of us with rearranging bottles and bowls of fruit on a length of cloth draped on a table. We were expected to complete a new painting every day, right over the painting we'd done in the previous session, until the layers of paint were too thick to add any more.

Mr. Chase moved from one student to the next, encouraging and suggesting. "Don't waste time making little sketches and fussing with details. Be bold!" he commanded. "Seek the bigger picture and do it quickly. Don't be afraid to fail! Simply paint and paint and paint! This is how the French Impressionists used to work. Now let's see what you can do."

It was a new beginning, and a new part of my life started to unfold. I was becoming bolder in my painting—and making friends, lots of them. I told them that everyone called me Patsy, which wasn't really true, because it was just Mattie, who'd given me the nickname in Chicago. Every boy I met wanted to run his fingers through my short curls. Someone was always showing up and saying, "We're going out dancing, Patsy, and you must come!" They hired street musicians to come into the League building and play, and we'd shove the easels out of the way and dance. I'd never had so much fun!

During my first weeks in New York I went dancing whenever I could, but I soon discovered that if I danced all night I couldn't paint for the next three days.

I began to ask myself, "If I do *this*, will I be able to do *that*?" I bought a notebook and printed YES at the top of one page and NO on the other. Every time I had to choose between being popular and being a serious artist, I asked myself which page I would put it on. That was how I learned to say no. I might never again have a chance to become the artist I believed I was destined to be. I had to seize it.

But it wasn't always easy to follow through after I'd made that choice. Other students wanted me to model for them. I could earn a dollar for a four-hour pose, and I needed the money badly. Eugene Speicher, an older student everybody admired, often asked me to pose, and I always refused because that meant time away from my classes. Gene was not used to hearing no.

One morning as I was rushing up the stairs to my life class, he loomed above me. He was very tall and muscular. When I moved to the left to evade him, he moved left, and when I stepped right, so did he.

"I won't let you pass until you say you'll pose for me, Patsy," he said.

"I'm on my way to class!"

"I know you are, but it really doesn't matter if you go to class or not," Gene said, laughing, "because someday I'll be a great painter, and you'll be teaching art in a girls' school somewhere."

That infuriated me. How dare he! I shoved past him and stormed on up the stairs and down the hall to my life class. The model was about to take his place on the raised platform. I recognized him from earlier sessions—his body lacked any sort of definition, and he was unable to hold a pose for any length of time. What a bore! I made a quick and perhaps foolish decision: I turned around and walked out.

Gene offered a smug little smile when I showed up at his studio in the basement. "Changed your mind, did you, Patsy?"

"Yes. But just this once."

He lifted a half-finished painting from the easel and reached for a new canvas. It was already prepared, as though he knew I'd give in. "All right, then. Sit there, your hands in your lap. And move your head just a bit to the left. Yes—perfect."

He worked quickly. We stopped once for tea and fruit and cheese and then continued through the afternoon. He would not let me look at the canvas until he was finished, and when I did, I was surprised. He had captured something about me that I didn't know I had—a quiet self-assuredness.

"I'll give you this one, Patsy, and you may keep it, but only if you give me your word that you'll pose for me again."

I promised. I liked the portrait very much, and I decided that I liked Gene after all.

Early in January I returned to Gene's studio. While I was sitting for this second portrait, several students burst in. "We're going to see some drawings by that French sculptor, Rodin," one explained. "The photographer Alfred Stieglitz is showing them at his gallery. Mr. Henri says they're trash and nonsense, that Rodin must have drawn them with his eyes shut. But he told us to go see what it's all about. You must come with us!"

Gene and I agreed to join the group. Robert Henri was one of our most influential teachers; everyone did as he said. It was a snowy, blustery day, but we were in a gay mood as we hurried down Fifth Avenue to Thirty-First Street and the gallery known as 291. An ancient elevator creaked and groaned up to the fifth floor of an old mansion, and we spilled out into a small room with drawings hung on all four walls.

A middle-aged man with wild, uncombed hair seemed startled by this bunch of boisterous intruders. "I'm Stieglitz," he said. He gestured grandly around the room. "And *this* is Auguste Rodin."

The drawings were no more than careless lines in ink or pencil, a few with a watercolor wash. Many were of nudes, and it was as if the sculptor had never had a lesson in human anatomy. In some drawings the intimate parts of the naked bodies were obscured by an arm or a thigh, but others revealed *everything*, and I was too shocked to say a word. These scribbles made no sense to me.

Gene and the others were loudly outspoken in their disapproval.

"This is not art!" one cried. "It is depravity of the worst kind!"

"Completely offensive, even to the most liberal of us!" shouted another.

"Please explain, sir, why you've chosen to display this travesty of art!"

"Rodin is first and foremost a sculptor," Mr. Stieglitz replied calmly. "I suggest that you take note of how he uses just a few strokes of the pen to convey the idea, the *essence* of the subject." He was trying—successfully, I thought—not to let the young art students bully him.

But our League boys were having none of it. They engaged Mr. Stieglitz in such a violent discussion that he was shouting, his whole body quaking. I'd been standing quietly in a corner. Had I come alone, I might have examined the drawings more closely, but with all the noise and shouting I was too embarrassed to show any interest at all in the drawings. I simply wanted to get out of there.

At the last moment, as the others crowded into the elevator cage, Gene seemed to remember me. "Come along, Patsy!" he boomed, seizing my arm. "No need to expose you further to this filthy stuff."

The gate closed, and as the cage began its clattering descent, I saw Mr. Stieglitz standing with his fists on his hips, glaring fiercely at us.

"So now you've seen the famous Alfred Stieglitz, Patsy," Gene said. "He may be a fine photographer, but he's certainly no judge of art. What a joke, that Rodin!"

14

New York—Winter 1908

GIVING UP DANCING WHENEVER I FELT LIKE IT DID not mean I'd given up a social life.

One of the students in my still life class was George Dannenberg, who'd come to New York from San Francisco. George was twenty-five—five years older than I was—and ruggedly handsome. He attended classes on a scholarship, and he was so poor that, when class was over, I sometimes saw him eating the apples or grapes or whatever edible items that had been so carefully arranged on the table.

I called him the Man from the Far West.

When George invited me to a costume party on Valentine's Day, I dressed as Peter Pan in boys' clothing I'd borrowed from a friend of Flo's. Flo had a knack for getting acquainted with lots of people quickly. And she was a free spirit: she convinced me that it was all right to wear trousers in public.

Two weeks later, George escorted me to a Leap Year dance. I was supposed to wear masculine attire. He lent me his only suit—trousers, threadbare coat, white shirt and bowtie—and showed up himself in a long gown with a moth-eaten fur wrap thrown over his shoulders. I have no idea where he found that ensemble, but oh, did we have fun! All evening we reversed roles, and I pretended that I was a boy, even when we danced. Those monthly dances at Chatham prepared me for that—I was the only girl who knew how to lead.

George belonged to the Society of American Fakirs, about two dozen League students who had founded a group dedicated to painting parodies of works of our teachers and other established artists, like Sister Angelique's favorite, Winslow Homer, and the portraitist John Singer Sargent. George had lampooned Sargent's portrait of a wealthy society couple, transforming them into dressmaker's dummies. The Fakirs renamed the paintings and the painters with puns. They even mocked our favorite teacher, Mr. Chase, who seemed amused by it. George talked me into joining the group.

Every spring the National Academy of Design held a show at its Venetian-style building on Fifth Avenue, with the New York upper crust assembling to drink champagne and pay top dollar for works of the best-known artists, like Homer and Sargent, as well as some of our teachers, such as Mr. Chase, whom we liked, and Kenyon Cox, the anatomy teacher, whom we didn't.

The Fakirs staged a mockery of the Academy's gala, pouring cheap wine into old glasses and jars and dressing fit to kill in whatever tattered finery we could find. We put on our own show of paintings at the League that parodied the work of those famous artists and went to great lengths to produce a catalogue filled with satiric cartoons and articles headed with the Fakirs' motto, "Never let art interfere with pleasure." The idea was to sell our "fakes" to raise scholarship money. My parody of Winslow Homer's two farm boys in a pasture sold for five dollars. Sister Angelique would have been horrified—and maybe secretly pleased.

For a year I had worked hard to absorb whatever Mr. Chase had to teach in his still life class, and at the end of the term my painting of a dead rabbit lying next to a copper pot was chosen to receive the Chase Award. The prize was a hundred dollars and a scholarship to spend the summer at an art colony on Lake George. A rustic lodge set among towering pines in the Adirondacks at the southern end of the long, narrow lake had been turned into a retreat where artists of all kinds, including writers and musicians, could get away from the city for a few weeks to pursue their projects. The retreat was called Amitola.

I was thrilled to win such a prestigious prize, grateful to receive the prize money, and excited to be spending the summer at Amitola. But it was wrenching for me to leave New York, not knowing when I'd come back. When I wasn't in class at the League, I was painting, and when I wasn't painting, I was visiting galleries and exhibitions. New York was where I was forming my opinions about art.

All of my friends were making art, talking about art, arguing about art. The arguments sometimes got quite fierce, among the students as well as among the artists who were our teachers. Mr. Henri, who'd urged his students to see the Rodin show, was very controversial: his realistic paintings were considered ugly by Mr. Chase. Mr. Henri detested the National Academy of Design, saying it was much too conservative and too powerful. And we had all heard the story about Mr. Chase arguing with Mr. Stieglitz about the Rodins and banging down his silk hat so hard that he smashed it flat.

Instead of going south to Williamsburg in June, I took the train north to Lake George. Amitola had spectacular views of the lake; at night the lodge was lit by lanterns. The evening meal served in the timbered dining room was communal, and conversation was encouraged among the artists. Often there was music. Breakfast could be solitary or not, but I'd never liked to talk in the mornings, and kept to myself. The kitchen help packed lunches that we took with us to eat whenever and wherever we wished.

I was surrounded by beauty—a field of daisies, a sailboat with a red sail on the dark lake, a line of blue mountains in the distance—but none of it inspired me. I started a few paintings and then lost interest, preferring to go on long walks alone and then return to my room, make a few sketches, and let it go. I'd been like that as a student at Chatham, but soon after I enrolled at the Art Institute in Chicago, I had recognized that I could not afford to be so lackadaisical, and I worked steadily to catch up to the others. Now I fell back into my old pattern—working hard when I was inspired, not doing much of anything when I wasn't.

Twenty other students from the League had been invited for the summer. Among them were Eugene Speicher and George Dannenberg. Gene had won the fifty-dollar Kelley Prize for his portrait of me. Gene and George were competitors at the League, and now they were competitors for my attention. Gene was both *per*-sistent and *in*sistent, but I was *re*sistant. George was an extraordinarily disciplined worker. His creative energy always seemed to be focused. He'd work like a demon until all hours, but he felt happiest tramping through the woods. I often went with him. We were spending more and more time together.

Near the end of July we were all invited to display our work, competing for a prize that would be awarded by a jury of local art collectors. Gene entered his portrait of me. One of the judges was a rich businessman named Stieglitz, who turned out to be the father of wild-haired Alfred Stieglitz at the 291 gallery. The younger Stieglitz helped his father pick the winning painting: Gene's portrait. By then I had been in New York long enough to become familiar with Stieglitz's reputation as a photographer. It was ironic that he'd awarded Gene the prize, given that Gene had deplored 291's showing of the Rodins.

Late one afternoon George knocked on my door. "I have an idea," he said. "There's a grocery store in the village on the other side of the lake, where all those big mansions are. Let's row across and find that store. I bet they have fruit and cheese and a decent loaf of bread. Maybe even a bottle of wine! We'll buy something and have a delightful little picnic on the shore and then row back with the rest."

It was an appealing idea. "What about a boat?"

He grinned. "I've arranged to borrow one. Your ship awaits you, mademoiselle."

We collected our sketchbooks and pencils, because we were, George pointed out, dedicated artists and not a couple of bohemians drifting idly through summer days without serious purpose.

The rowboat was tied up at a wooden dock. I was about to climb in when I heard a familiar "Halloooo!" It was Gene Speicher. "Off for a little excursion, I gather?" Gene asked.

"Pretty obvious, isn't it?" George muttered under his breath, and began untying the rope.

"We're going across the lake to get some things for a picnic," I explained, adding impetuously, "Want to come along?"

George's head jerked up, and he was scowling. I'd said it out of politeness, thinking that Gene would just as politely refuse.

But Gene was oblivious—maybe intentionally. "A capital idea!" he said. "It's a magnificent day for an outing!" He took my hand to help me down into the rowboat. I didn't need his assistance, but there it was.

George pushed the boat away from the dock and set the oars in the oarlocks. Gene tipped his cap down over his eyes and settled in comfortably to soak up the afternoon sun. "I'll row coming back," he said.

George rowed sullenly all the way across the lake. There was no conversation. I concentrated on the sound of the creaking oars and the gentle splash of water and tried to ignore the growing irritation of the two rivals. I liked both men, George far more than Gene, and I should never have suggested that Gene come along. But it had happened, and there was nothing to do now but put up with it until we'd bought the groceries and rowed back. George would surely think of some diplomatic way to ditch Gene, and that would be the end of it.

When we reached the western shore, George tied up the boat, and the three of us set off in search of the grocery store. It was not as easy to find as we expected, and we wandered aimlessly until we encountered an elderly fellow on a bench, puffing on a pipe and watching a mallard and her ducklings. He pointed his pipe in the direction we should go.

The grocery catered to well-heeled summer people, who must have sent their cooks or housekeepers when they ran out of Russian caviar or preserved pheasant or pâté de foie gras. Gene explained, in a tone that plainly irritated George, that pâté de foie gras was French for goose liver paste. We eventually filled a basket with delicacies that neither George nor I could afford. Flush with his fifty-dollar prize money for my portrait, Gene paid for it all.

"It's the least I can do," he said. "If it hadn't been for you, Patsy, I wouldn't have won that prize." Then he couldn't help bragging: "The League has promised to publish it in next year's catalogue as a example of excellent student work, and they've hinted that they may hang it as part of their permanent collection."

George grimaced. "You can treat Patsy. I'll reimburse you for my part. Let's go."

When we got back to the dock, the rowboat was not there.

"The rope must have come undone," George said, "and the boat drifted off. Surely it can't have gone very far."

We walked up and down the shoreline, searching for some sign of the missing boat, until we met the elderly pipe-smoker again. "Two young fellers climbed in a boat like the one you're talking about and rowed off with it."

"When was that?" Gene asked.

"'Bout half an hour ago, I'd guess. Headed up toward Diamond Point." He waved his pipe in that direction.

We looked at one another.

"Stolen," George said. "Obviously, it's been stolen."

"It appears that we have a nice long stroll ahead of us," Gene said.

We set off glumly. It would be about an hour's walk, George estimated. We had left late in the afternoon and spent quite a lot of time selecting groceries, and now it was getting on toward evening. We stopped long enough to eat some of the bread and cheese and pâté, which none of us enjoyed, and then began to make our way around the southern end of the lake. Soon we found ourselves slogging ankle-deep through marshland created by underground springs that fed the lake. We were wet, mosquito-bitten, and thoroughly miserable when we came upon a large pond. A stand of cattails reflected on the black water. Invisible insects pricked the shimmering surface. Beyond the pond, the woods, dark except for flashes of white birch, appeared mysterious, unfathomable. It looked the way I felt—wet and gloomy and mysterious. I stopped to take in the scene.

"Do you need to rest, Patsy?" Gene asked solicitously, reaching for my hand in the deepening twilight.

I yanked my hand away. "No. I just want a moment to look," I said, adding, "and to feel."

A sliver of moon was rising when we finally emerged from the marsh and stumbled up the outdoor stairs and onto the wooden porch at Amitola. Lamplight glowed. Voices were hushed. We said good night and went to our rooms. I was still hungry, but Gene had taken the rest of our delicacies with him. I was too tired to care. I kicked off my wet shoes and lay down, still in my clothes. In seconds I was asleep.

I woke up before sunrise the next morning. Without bothering to change my clothes, I stuck my feet into my damp shoes, grabbed my watercolors and paper, and found my way back to the marshland and the place where the cattails had been reflected in the still water. Morning mist rose from the marsh. The cattails stood silhouetted against a sky the color of pearl. The light had changed, but the mystery I had experienced the night before was still there—without the gloom. It came to me, suddenly and overwhelmingly, that the way I felt dictated how I saw that scene. I worked fast to capture the feeling in deep greens and black.

I knew that it was the best work I had done since I'd arrived at the lake. Later, I showed it to George. He studied it for a long time. I didn't have to explain a thing.

"Will you give it to me, Patsy? Then I'll have a part of you."

I nodded *yes*.

George took a long step toward me, buried his fingers in my curls, and kissed me. I returned his kiss. It was the first time. I had been waiting for this kiss, and I knew that it would not be our last.

From then on we were together as much as we wished, paddling a canoe on the lake—the "stolen boat," taken as a prank, had been recovered, but we decided to borrow a canoe the next time so that Gene wouldn't invite himself along. We spent hours tramping through the woods, sometimes talking, sometimes not saying a word. We were so closely attuned that there was no need for conversation. I wondered if this is what it was like to be in love. George was the first man for whom I'd had strong feelings, and it touched me deeply. Gene had finally figured out that something serious had developed between George and me, and he didn't interfere.

One night darkness came on faster than we'd expected, and we lost our way. We fell asleep on a bed of pine needles and crept back to Amitola at dawn without being detected. It was the loveliest night I'd ever spent.

At the end of summer we prepared to go our separate ways, George home to California and I back to Virginia. Our parting was sad—I even wept a little—and our futures uncertain, but we promised to write. That was the only thing either of us *could* promise.

15

Williamsburg, Virginia—Fall 1908

DURING THE YEAR THAT I HAD BEEN AWAY, MY father had changed into someone I hardly recognized. The fun-loving Irishman who had once played the fiddle and danced with his children, the forward-looking businessman who was the first to install a telephone in his Sun Prairie house, had now become withdrawn and silent. After the grocery and the feed and grain business folded, he had launched O'Keeffe & Sons Building Materials. But people in Williamsburg wanted only traditional houses of brick and sometimes clapboard, and they were not interested in buying the concrete-and-clamshell blocks. He still owned the nine-acre strip of land next to the gracious old mansion we'd once lived in, and he decided to use the inventory of unsold blocks to build a new house on it.

He'd made a few rough sketches of what he wanted. Francis, newly graduated with a degree in architecture, helped with the construction. Fourteen-year-old Alexius pitched in as well.

"What do you think?" I asked Francis. "Did you advise him on the design?"

Francis rubbed his eyes. "It's what he wants. He didn't ask for my advice, and when I made some suggestions, like the placement of the doors and windows, and eliminating the awkward gables, he didn't want to hear anything I said."

"Maybe Mama can get him to listen."

"She says it's his project and he'll do what he wants."

"That two-story concrete porch on the front—"

"I know. It's clumsy; there's no other word to describe it. And the design of the roof is all wrong—it will let rainwater leak down inside the concrete blocks, so the house will likely always be damp. I can't imagine anyone wanting to live there." Francis looked at me with a wry grin. "Except those oddball O'Keeffes."

The oddball O'Keeffes moved into the house, and we tried to make the best of our situation. Almost all of the money Papa had made on the sale of the property in Sun Prairie was gone, and he had not yet hit upon a way to earn more. A partnership set up to sell land came to nothing. An arrangement to ship peanuts and watermelons from a pier rented on the York River went nowhere.

"You know I'd send you back up to New York if I could," he told me. "But right now, I can't do it. Pretty soon, though, things will work out."

But things did not work out. There was nothing left to send any of us back to school, except Alexius. Although Mama badly wanted Ida and Nita to have another year at Chatham, she explained that it was more important for Alexius to finish at the academy. I was almost twenty-one, and I couldn't expect my family to keep on paying for my education. I would have to figure out some way to earn enough money to support myself.

But how? Doing what? I had gone to New York with the idea of eventually going on to earn a teaching certificate, but I needed another year of training to achieve that. What school would hire me without it?

Mama, I knew, would be pleased if I'd make a good match and get married. She'd hinted at it. Jetta Thorpe, the only girl I knew in Williamsburg, was making wedding plans. It was what most girls did. Susan Young sent me an announcement of her engagement, and most of the other girls in my class at Chatham were probably either married or planning to be. I'd insisted then that I would not marry, because I would have no time to paint if I had a husband and a family, even if I married a rich man and had servants.

George Dannenberg would soon be on his way to Paris to study and paint. I wished I could go with him, but that was impossible. I had time now, but I could not paint. I stopped drawing. I had no energy. I had no idea what to do.

As if on cue, along came a new pastor at Bruton Parish Episcopal Church.

The Reverend Tucker Lawrence was tall and blue-eyed with a winning smile. All the girls at Bruton must have been setting their caps for him, their mothers wracking their brains for a way to snare him. For some reason I, of all the possible candidates available, was the one the pastor chose to call upon. Mama encouraged this, going so far as to invite him for an evening meal, without even consulting me. I wanted nothing to do with any of it.

In those lean days, we were living mostly on vegetables from Auntie's garden accompanied by plenty of rice and cornbread, but for this important occasion Mama sacrificed a chicken and made it stretch to feed all of us. There were also deviled eggs and sliced tomatoes and a lovely peach cobbler.

Conversation was strained. "I understand that you've come here from Michigan," said the pastor.

"Wisconsin," Papa said. "My parents came over from the Old Country in 1848 and settled in Sun Prairie. Bought land from the government for a dollar an acre. My brothers and I were all born there. My wife is descended from Hungarian nobility."

Alexius kicked me under the table. I expected him to burst out laughing.

"And your people, Pastor Lawrence?" Mama asked pleasantly. She'd learned in the five years she'd lived in the South that talking about ancestral roots was the best way to start a conversation with a new acquaintance.

"My grandfather served with Robert E. Lee in the Mexican-American War and again in the War Between the States. My father was a drummer boy during that conflict."

Mama tried again. "And your mother's family?"

"Mother is a Beauregard from New Orleans," he said, pronouncing it *Nawlins*. "Her father, General Beauregard, was a great friend of General Lee."

The conversation lumbered along, all of us being excruciatingly polite, and excruciatingly dull. My classmates from Chatham would have been mad for him.

A week later, without waiting for an invitation, Pastor Lawrence stopped by when I was not at home and left a bouquet of flowers and a note inviting me to go canoeing on the York River.

I was foolish enough to agree to the boating expedition. As if I hadn't learned my lesson crossing Lake George in a rowboat! But it was a bright September day, and I was happy for an excuse to get away from the gloom of the concrete house—until I discovered that Pastor Lawrence hadn't the least idea how to handle a canoe. I had mastered that skill at Amitola with George, and it must have been hard for Pastor Lawrence to accept that I was the one who grabbed a paddle and turned the canoe around before we could be swept out to sea.

Mama surely knew that the project was hopeless—I could not settle for a man I didn't love. It was the Man from the Far West, George Dannenberg, who occupied my thoughts as our letters crisscrossed the entire country.

I began to believe that art was not a practical path for me to follow, and I tried to quit thinking of myself as an artist.

For the sake of my family, and for my own sake as well, I had to make my way in the world. Without a teaching certificate, I would have to seek some other kind of work.

In November, after three months at home and two days before my twenty-first birthday, I boarded a train for Chicago—not to return to the Art Institute, but to hunt for a job. When I left, my mother looked even wearier and Papa gloomier than when I'd returned from Lake George in August, but Aunt Ollie and Uncle Charley were exactly the same as the last time I'd seen them, immersed in their own affairs but willing to have me stay in their apartment. This time I was not their only boarder: Aunt Lola had moved there from Madison, and I had to share the spare room with her and her off-key singing.

I found work almost right away, drawing lace and embroidery illustrations for fashion advertisements in newspapers. The supervisor would distribute renderings of women wearing plain, unadorned coats and dresses, and I would add highly detailed fancywork to sleeves, collars, necklines, and hems. I was fast—I'd learned that from doing a painting a day in Mr. Chase's class—and since it was piecework, I earned more than slower girls, but the company paid such a low rate that I ended up with very little. It was tedious and boring, foolish and meaningless. I dreaded going to work in the morning, and I had no energy left for painting, even if I'd wanted to.

Chicago no longer appealed to me. It was dirty, noisy, cold, and gloomy most of the year, with none of the tremendous excitement and constant stimulation I'd found in New York. And I thought I'd go mad if I had to listen to Aunt Lola warbling "Beautiful Dreamer" one more time.

I stuck it out for two years—two years of doing work I hated, in a place I didn't want to be, with people I could barely tolerate. Two years of my life, gone. Two years in which I did not make one painting or one drawing of my own. I felt numb.

Then I came down with measles. I was sick for weeks. Measles weakens the eyes, and even after I'd recovered, I could not see well enough to draw fine lace and dainty embroidery. I told my employers I was leaving, thanked my distracted aunts and uncle, and boarded the next train out of Chicago for Virginia.

Pastor Lawrence had been charmed by another young lady, and that was a good thing—one of the few good things about going home. Papa had become even more morose; no matter how hard he worked, the results were dismal. His plans to open a creamery had come to nothing. Even more worrisome was Mama's health. She had looked pale and tired when I left for Chicago. Now she rarely had the strength to get out of bed. She coughed and coughed.

"Consumption," Papa explained dully. "It carried off my father and my three older brothers, and I feared it would come for me as well. I brought my dear Ida here so as to avoid all that, and now it has come for her!" His voice cracked, and he turned away.

"Why did no one tell me this?" I asked.

"We didn't want to worry you. There's nothing you can do."

I hurried to the clinic to find Dr. Hunter. He ushered me into his office, pointed to a seat, and sat down on the opposite side of a cluttered desk. "I've come about my mother," I said. "My father thinks she's consumptive."

The doctor sighed. "I'm afraid your father is correct, Miss O'Keeffe. Your mother is exhibiting the early symptoms of tuberculosis. It is a terrible disease, as your family knows from tragic experience. There is no cure. Progress of the illness is inexorable and ultimately fatal. The dampness here will only worsen her condition. I have recommended to Mr. O'Keeffe that your mother be removed to a higher, dryer climate."

And so that's what we did. Mama, my four sisters, Auntie, and her horse, moved to Charlottesville. They chose Charlottesville not only because it was in the mountains but because Ida and Nita had attended a summer class at the University of Virginia and found the town more to their liking than Williamsburg had ever been. All our lives we had been used to having almost limitless space inside and out, and the house Mama rented in Charlottesville had neither. But it was close to the university, and Mama decided, weak as she was, to take in table boarders to help cover expenses. Her illness had to be kept secret, or she would have had no customers.

Papa and my two brothers stayed behind in Williamsburg, and I stayed too, to keep house for them while my father searched doggedly for work and tried to sell the house. I learned to bake biscuits and to make soup from most anything that was handy and cheap—we ate a lot of almond soup that winter. We took turns traveling up to Charlottesville to visit the other half of our family.

The one thing that kept me going during those dispiriting months were my letters from George Dannenberg. George was in California, trying to earn extra money and preparing to leave for Paris, where he planned to stay for as long as he could. His letters were affectionate, showing concern for my eyesight, encouraging me to continue painting. He hinted that he wanted me to be with him.

I long to have you as the little black-haired girl I knew at the lake. You stunned me into a daze that I can't shake off. I read his letters over and over, building castles in the air based on what he wrote: *I want very much to see you before I sail. I wish I could take you with me. It is not so very impossible, so don't laugh.*

I didn't laugh. I dreamed. When a week went by with no letter, I entertained the fantasy that he might be making his way across the country to see me. At any time I might hear a knock on the door and open it and find him standing there. Another week passed, and another, with no word from him. At last a letter arrived, postmarked Paris. *Paris!* He had gone there without coming to see me first, without even telling me that he was on his way to France.

So it had been impossible, after all. I could hardly bear to open it, or to read his bold script on the flimsy blue paper.

The night before I sailed from New York, I sat all night on a bench in the Battery, trying to decide if I should come to see you or not. But in the morning I sailed without seeing you—crazy, or maybe stupid, because if there is anything in the world I want, it is Patsy.

If he had come for me, I would have married him. But he didn't. I was disappointed and hurt. This was the first man I had cared for, and he had done this. He may have wanted me, but he didn't want me enough.

Nevertheless, we continued to exchange letters. *I should like to have you here*, he wrote.

What did that mean, I wondered, and then decided that it meant nothing.

Later I wrote to him that I had given up painting. It had nothing to do with him, I said—I simply had come to understand that I didn't know what to do that was any different from what I had been doing. I'd been repeating myself, and I could see no way forward.

It's all or nothing for me. If I can't give myself to it completely, I cannot do it at all.

He replied, *The fact that you have abandoned painting does not mean that you have given up art. You are and always will be an artist.*

PART IV

*"Art is the way you see things,
the choices you make."*

16

Chatham, Virginia—Spring 1911

I WAS TWENTY-THREE AND FEELING UNMOORED AND adrift. What could I do? I still was not painting, but if I couldn't paint, perhaps I could teach children to paint. I applied to the Williamsburg public schools for a position. They refused to hire me without a certificate.

Then, a small miracle: Mrs. Willis wrote that she planned to take a temporary leave from the Institute for six weeks in the spring. Would I be willing to teach the art classes in her place?

Of course I would!

How happy I was to be back at my old school, happier still to find that Susan Young was living nearby with an aunt and teaching a class in painting china. It was almost as though no time had passed since we first became friends. Susan had returned to Chatham after our graduation, while Ida and Nita were there, and she'd met Walter Wilson, a teacher at a nearby boys' school. (Had there been a boys' school when we were taking turns as "boys" at our dances? I couldn't remember.) Susan and Walter were to be married in June.

I enjoyed teaching more than I ever thought possible. I hadn't forgotten what it was like to be very young and subject to all sorts of silly rules. Those rules no longer applied to Susan or to me: we walked into town together at least twice a week, and I went off alone into the beautiful countryside whenever I felt like it. Both were harmless activities that were absolutely forbidden for students. I had been given a small private room in the dormitory and routinely turned a blind eye to girls who thought they were terribly daring to sneak down to the kitchen at night to raid Elsie's icebox. They seemed bolder than we were as sixteen-year-olds.

Susan happened by one evening when I was stitching a shirtwaist with pintucks down the front and a bit of lace trimming on the sleeves. She admired it enthusiastically, amazed at how I'd finished the seams on the inside. While I sewed, she described plans for her wedding, which would be a grand affair at her home in Roanoke. Details of the church ceremony and a reception at the Youngs' private club were often the subject of our conversations. I could not afford to attend the wedding or give her a proper wedding gift, but when I finished the shirtwaist, I wrapped it carefully and presented it to her.

"For your trousseau," I told her.

"Oh, my dear Georgie, how very kind of you! How I wish you'd come to the wedding!"

I hoped she'd understand that I couldn't, without my having to explain.

By the time I left Chatham at the end of the term, I recognized that I was a good teacher—even an excellent one. The students respected me, and I knew they had learned from me. Maybe teaching was how I could earn a living and make a life for myself. I had no work of my own to show for those six weeks in Chatham, but I felt as though I was waking up from a bad dream. I could see a way forward. I still didn't have a teaching certificate, but I did have experience, and I resolved to use that to get to where I wanted to be.

Papa finally sold the house he'd built in Williamsburg, and he and Alexius and I joined the rest of our family in Charlottesville. I was not sorry to leave.

With the bit of money he had left after he'd paid off his debts, he opened a creamery, an idea he'd first had in Williamsburg. "If there's one thing I know, it's cows," he said. He bought milk from dairy farmers and then sold the milk, cream, butter—even ice cream—to private customers. But the O'Keeffe Creamery struggled from the beginning.

Ours was the poorest house on an otherwise fashionable street of gracious homes belonging to Charlottesville's aristocratic old families, including the president of the university. If we had never been accepted in Williamsburg, the social structure of Charlottesville was even more rigid, and the O'Keeffes even more rigidly excluded. Auntie still had her old carriage horse, Penelope, but we no longer owned a carriage. No one in Charlottesville was impressed with Mama's Totto jewelry. They would have been appalled if they knew she took in boarders.

The University of Virginia had changed its "gentlemen only" policy and for the first time began admitting women, but only to the summer sessions. The courses were aimed at girls from around the state who wished to become public school teachers. Ida and Nita had taken a drawing class the previous summer, and they'd signed up for another. Both of them had always shown a great deal of artistic talent, and I was pleased that they were continuing to study.

Nita could not say enough about her instructor, a New Yorker named Alon Bement. "You must come with us, Georgie," Nita insisted. "One class with this man and you'll want to start painting again."

"He's almost too peculiar," Ida warned me. "He's vain, he puts on airs. And he's short and round, and dresses in outrageous outfits, and he speaks in such a funny, squeaky voice. Nobody likes him. You probably won't either."

Ida's description was enough to make me want to turn right around and go back home, but Nita wouldn't hear of it. "Never mind what Ida says," Nita insisted. "He's a brilliant teacher, and he has some unusual ideas. I learned that just from the first class."

Nita was twenty, three years younger than I was, but she had a good head on her shoulders. I'd learned to pay attention to what she said, and not shrug her off as I often did with Ida. I agreed to go with them to the art building on the campus, listen to what Mr. Bement had to say, and make up my own mind.

I attended Mr. Bement's class the next day. Although Ida had described him to a T, Nita was right: his ideas and theories about art started me thinking about painting in an entirely different way. He'd learned these ideas from an artist named Arthur Wesley Dow. My teachers at both the Art Institute in Chicago and the Art Students League in New York had taught us to learn how to paint by imitating the work of the old masters. Arthur Wesley Dow challenged that idea. He believed that copying was the wrong way to approach painting. What interested Dow—and Mr. Bement—was filling a space, any space, in a beautiful way. Art should be grounded in personal experience and harmonious design, Dow said. *Interpretation is more important than representation.* I would always remember that.

Mr. Bement agreed with Dow's theories. "Art is the way you see things, and the choices you make," he said. "Even about something so simple as buying a cup and saucer."

At the end of the class that day I was ready to enroll. It was a six-week course, and I had already missed the first few sessions, but Mr. Bement allowed me to join his Drawing IV class, the most advanced. One of Mr. Bement's early assignments was to start with a blank page and draw a line, dividing the space into rectangles. "By doing so, you have made an artistic choice."

Mr. Bement's ideas were exciting. He did not insist that I look at the world in a particular way or do something a certain way. He left me to find for myself the ways of looking and doing. With no effort and no struggle, my imagination came alive again.

I began a series of watercolor paintings of the beautiful university campus designed by Thomas Jefferson. I left out the fussy details that William Merritt Chase favored, concentrating instead on the geometric shapes and simplifying classical elements of the handsome Rotunda and the Law Building. I painted trees and shrubs as outlines; then I returned to the same tree or shrub and painted it from a different perspective. These paintings were not like anything I had ever done.

When the course ended, Mr. Bement called me to his office. "I'm giving you the highest grade in the class," he said. "Ninety-five. And I should like very much to have you as one of my teaching assistants next summer."

I accepted immediately. "But I need to work in the meantime," I told him bluntly. "I can't bear to go back to Chicago and take some meaningless job drawing embroidery and lace, but if that's what I have to do, or something like it, then I suppose I must."

"Oh, my dear, dear girl!" Mr. Bement said in his fluttery little voice. "I shall do my best to find you a regular teaching position for the winter. But you will need to have more experience to be hired."

How do you get teaching experience when you have no teaching experience to begin with? I saw no way around the problem until a telegram arrived from Alice

Peretta. The wealthy girl from Laredo, Texas, whom I had made my friend when we were students at Chatham, was teaching in Amarillo. We'd kept in touch in the seven years since we graduated. We didn't correspond for weeks and then we'd pick up again exactly where we'd left off. Alice knew I needed to find work, and she wired this message:

DRAWING SUPERVISOR POSITION AVAILABLE HERE STOP WIRE IF INTERESTED

I reread the telegram with growing excitement. A teaching job in Texas! What an adventure! I loved the idea of the Wild West that I'd read about as a child, and this was just the kind of thing I knew I'd like to do.

I rushed to show the letter to Mr. Bement and to ask his advice.

"Glorious news!" he trilled. "I shall write you an utterly irresistible letter of recommendation."

"But I don't have certification," I reminded him.

"Oh, dear, dear, dear!" Mr. Bement dithered. "Well, you need have no concern. None whatsoever! Banish all worry! We shall see what can be done!"

I wired back to Alice immediately:

VERY INTERESTED STOP LETTER FOLLOWS

The next day Mr. Bement called me to his office and showed me the letter he had written on university stationery. He described my work and my qualifications, noting that I had studied in New York and Chicago "with such masters as Luis Mora and William Merritt Chase." He also stated that I had trained at Pratt Institute in Brooklyn, where I had achieved the highest degree known to my profession.

"But I've never attended Pratt Institute!"

"Really? No matter. No one cares. I have no doubts—none whatsoever—about your qualifications. You have the makings of a splendid teacher." He started to wave me out of his office and then changed his mind. "Let me have the letter, Miss O'Keeffe, and I'll make sure that it is mailed."

I hesitated. The line about Pratt was an outright lie, and I was reluctant to have it included. But if Mr. Bement saw no harm in making the false statement, then I decided to let it pass. I left the letter for him to mail.

Through most of July I existed in a kind of limbo, not knowing if I would be hired or not. At last the letter arrived offering me the position. I had been accepted! The pay was adequate, a little better than I'd earned in Chicago, and I'd be doing something I'd enjoy, maybe even love.

School would begin in Amarillo at the beginning of October, but I was instructed to be there for a meeting with the teachers and administrators on the last day of August.

Papa declared that he was proud, and Mama said she was pleased, although I could see that she was weak and needed help. Selfishly, I could hardly wait to escape the gloom that hung over the house where my studio had been reduced to a dingy space in the basement. In Amarillo I would teach, I would paint, I would have the different kind of life I'd yearned for. Yet I felt torn. I was needed at home.

Nita saw my hesitancy. "You must go, Georgie. It's a glorious opportunity for you, and you mustn't worry about Mama. I'm here, and Ida and Auntie too, so Mama will be well cared for. You know this is what she has always wanted for you. I love to paint and draw, and I believe Ida and I have some artistic ability, but you're the artist, not us. I'm thinking of studying to become a nurse, and Ida has talked about it, too."

I hoped Nita was right about Mama, and I made her promise she'd let me know if the situation became dire.

Letters flew back and forth from Amarillo. Alice was enthusiastically planning how we would share the cabin she was renting. *It's a plain little place, barely above a hovel, but you won't be spied upon by the other teachers, and I guarantee that you won't be lonely at all,* she wrote in the last letter I received before I left. *There's even a piano in the parlor—I call it a parlor, just to be funny—and we can entertain our beaux with musical evenings.*

I remembered her incessant playing of "Für Elise," and laughed. Maybe she had improved, but it wasn't likely.

She also reminded me to bring warm clothes, because Amarillo was in the middle of the Texas Panhandle, and the winters could be much colder than I imagined, and very windy. *More like Chicago, I'm afraid,* she said.

I finished packing and saying my goodbyes. I was almost twenty-five, and finally my life as a teacher and an artist was about to begin.

17

Amarillo, Texas—1912

AFTER SEVERAL BLISTERING-HOT DAYS CROSSING the endless flatness of the Midwest, the train pulled into the depot in Amarillo. I looked for Alice, who had promised to meet me. When there was no sign of her, I hired a carriage to take me to the address she'd given me in her last letter, a rustic cabin on a ranch at the edge of town. A woman in a shapeless calico dress, her face lined by harsh sun and worry, came out of the main house.

"You must be Miss O'Keeffe," she said, and I said I was. "I'm Mrs. Randall, and I am mighty sorry to have to tell you that Miss Peretta came down with a fever about a week ago, and the good Lord took her just three days past."

I gaped at the woman. "She's dead?" I asked. "Alice is dead?"

"Yes, ma'am," the woman said. "Doc Gibson tried everything he could, but nothing seemed to help, poor thing. Her folks come by yesterday and took her away to their home in Laredo to bury her. They was pretty broke up about it."

I stood there, dazed, unable to take in what I'd just been told. Alice, dead? How could that be? My knees were weak as water, and I had to lean against the dusty carriage to keep from falling down. I was too shocked for tears. I couldn't think clearly, and I had no idea what to do next.

"I can rent the cabin to you at a fair price," Mrs. Randall said. "It's close to town—just a good walk to the high school."

Mrs. Randall opened the door, and I stepped into the cabin I'd expected to share with Alice. It was as bare as a cell. Her parents must have taken everything of Alice's with them. Even the piano she'd talked about.

"Such a nice girl. She spoke highly of you. Had a picture she said you painted, hanging on the wall, right there. Guess her folks took it." She hesitated, and we both tried to collect ourselves. "Miss Peretta surely liked living out here. I think you would too."

"No. No, thank you, Mrs. Randall." I shook my head. I didn't have the money even if I'd wanted it.

The driver was waiting to be paid. I'd forgotten about him. "You want your suitcases, ma'am?" he asked.

"No, please just take me to a hotel in town," I said. "Any place will do."

I thanked Mrs. Randall and climbed numbly back into the carriage. I tried to pay attention as the driver drove back toward town, going on and on about the wonders of Amarillo—the new Grand Opera House that seated two thousand music lovers, the trolley that ran up and down Polk Street, the new high school that wasn't quite finished. I had noticed a handsome new hotel, Harvey House, at the depot when I got off the train, but I feared a room there would be more than I could afford.

After some discussion he deposited me at the Magnolia Hotel, a rundown-looking place with two lilac bushes drooping by the front porch. "Not the fanciest place in town," he said, "but as good as any to start off."

The manager showed me to a room on the third floor—small, with a narrow bed, a straight-backed chair, a washstand, and a couple of hooks for my clothes. I paid him for two weeks in advance, and after he'd gone I unpacked a few things, washed my face, and went downstairs to the combination saloon and dining room. Although I wasn't in the least hungry, I ordered the nightly special: beefsteak, beans, cornbread, and coffee. A card game was under way at a nearby table, and a few rough-looking men leaned on the bar, knocking back shots of liquor and chatting up a couple of rough-looking women. I left half my meal uneaten, climbed upstairs, and crawled into bed. Outside my window the wind whistled and groaned. I had never felt so lonely in my life.

The next day I walked up Polk, down Taylor, up Fillmore, and so on. All the streets running north and south in that part of town were named for U.S. presidents, and the cross streets were numbered. It would be easy to find my way around the dusty town. But there was none of the genteel charm of Williamsburg, none of the elegant Jeffersonian architecture of Charlottesville or the well-tended cottages I'd admired at Lake George— just banged-together lumber, whatever was practical to create shelter without much regard for style. For some reason that attitude appealed to me.

I thought of Alice. Her friendship had meant a great deal. I was grateful that she'd brought me here, because somehow I felt immediately that I had made the right choice to come. But I missed her sorely, and I struggled to come to terms with her absence.

The people who'd hired me must have realized from the first meeting that I had no experience teaching in high school, and I could not think how I was going to put to use anything I had learned in my classes at the university. I was the youngest of the teachers. The other teachers had years of experience—I was out of my depth, and they knew it. I still dressed in tailored skirts and jackets and shirtwaists I'd made. And because I loved to walk wherever I pleased, I wore flat-heeled men's shoes that were much more practical than the dainty footgear most women teetered around in. I'd gotten used to my hair, still too short to braid. It was obvious from the start that I stood out in Texas just as much as I'd stood out in Virginia.

The female teachers lived with families, two or three to a household. I wanted to be on my own, independent. They didn't come right out and say so, but they did let me know that the Magnolia was not a respectable place for a young lady and would tarnish my reputation. I ignored their hints that I should look for "more suitable" lodgings.

For a few more weeks, until the high school was completed, I would not have a room for my classes. In the meantime I was to use a one-room cabin that must have been a schoolhouse at one time. It reminded me of Town Hall School in Sun Prairie. The location was inconvenient, but it was not a bad thing to be away from the other teachers for a while.

The teachers brought their noon meals from home and ate together in one of their classrooms, and I was expected to join them. I asked Max, the bartender-cook at the Magnolia, to boil a couple of eggs for me to take for my dinner. Max was a tough-talking man with a soft side, and he not only boiled the eggs but sent along a square of cornbread or a slice of pie and whatever else he had on hand. Not much grew in this dry, sun-bleached, wind-parched prairie, but Max was friendly with a cook over at Harvey House. Fresh fruit and vegetables were brought in by the Harvey's arrangement with the Santa Fe Railroad, and Max made sure I got a dose of lettuce or green beans whenever a shipment of such luxuries arrived.

"Cowpokes don't give a dang about any kinda beans except pintos," he said.

I'd been in Amarillo for about two weeks, eating supper alone in the Magnolia among a crowd of local ranchers and cowboys in town for a rip-roaring Saturday night, when we heard gunshots outside. Everybody rushed to the door, and I followed them. A body lay sprawled in the middle of the street, and a bearded man with a smoking six-shooter stood over it.

"What's going on?" Max called.

"Not a dang thing," snarled the gun-toter. "Thought he could steal my cattle *and* my wife, and I just showed him otherwise." He got on his horse and rode off, and we all went back inside.

I wondered aloud if the sheriff wouldn't soon arrest the killer. One of the patrons at the bar explained that it wasn't the shooter's first time. "Beal Sneed's already shot his father-in-law dead for insulting him. But he'll get off, you'll see."

And he did. The trial lasted half a day, the jury acquitted Mr. Sneed after ten minutes of deliberation, and his defense attorney celebrated by buying a round of drinks for everybody at the Magnolia.

There I was, a naïve schoolteacher who'd grown up in the Midwest and been an outsider in the South, now living in the Wild West. I could look out my window and see herds of cattle miles away, a thousand or more head at a time, making their slow, steady way across the prairie in a cloud of dust that never entirely disappeared. Moving no more than fifteen miles a day—the cattle would lose too much weight if they did any more—they took as long as two months to make the journey from ranch to railhead, where they'd be loaded onto cattle cars and taken to slaughter. At night the cowboys' campfires flickered in the inky blackness beneath a starry sky.

I found that I was crazy about all that wonderful emptiness. I walked for miles under the hot sun and through wind that sandpapered my skin, soaking up the vastness of the sky and the plains as blank as a newly primed canvas. I wasn't painting, not even sketching much, but I was content. I was absorbing my new world.

My students were mostly fifteen and sixteen, some a little younger, some older, children of ranch hands and nearly all of them poor. We liked each other immediately. I had no trouble with discipline: I listened to them, and they listened to me. Two of my pupils, Horace and Cornelia, were enthusiastic about everything I tried to teach them. They accompanied me on long walks on the prairie beyond the city limits, and we sat on the grass with sketchpads and pencils and drew. I drew and they drew, and we talked about the ways an object could be drawn. Sometimes they brought along little brothers and sisters, and we all had a grand time, talking and drawing and *seeing*.

That first year in Texas I turned twenty-five, and it was not my students but the older people and those closer to my own age who were judgmental, who thought I didn't fit in the way I was expected to. I wondered how Alice had stood it, but she was a Texan, so perhaps it had been easier for her.

I tried to impress upon the boys and girls in my classes that art was not just a picture hanging in a museum. Most of them had never been to a museum and had no notion of what I was talking about. I showed them pictures—chromos were still around—but that was not the same. "Art is the way you see things, the choices you make in your everyday life, in the way you live," I told them. *Filling a space in a beautiful way,* as Mr. Bement had quoted our much-admired Arthur Wesley Dow saying.

At first I had none of the supplies I believed were necessary to teach students about art. But after we'd been given drawing paper and pencils, I taught them how to divide space. "Draw a square on your sheet of paper," I instructed. A variety of rectangular shapes appeared, some neatly squared at the corners, others freer, looser. "Now put a door in it," I said.

They looked up from their papers and stared at me. "A door, Miss O'Keeffe?" Cornelia asked, frowning at her perfectly drawn square. She was the type who liked things well formed. "Where should it go?"

"Wherever you want it to go," I said.

Horace, predictably, set his door off to one side and then decided to add a window. He didn't ask my permission; he just did it.

But it did not take long for me to get into a struggle with the principal of Amarillo High School. The woman I replaced had required her students to copy from a Prang drawing book, the very same chromos that Mrs. Sarah Mann had used to inspire me back in Sun Prairie. I strongly opposed this method. I thought the book didn't do a thing to encourage free expression. Many of my students couldn't afford the Prang books, and so I didn't order them.

"You don't need a book to learn to draw," I told my class. "You take whatever you have at hand and *look* at it."

What we had at hand was the dappled pony named Barney that Horace often rode to school. I suggested that Horace bring Barney into our classroom, and we'd use him as a subject. With much laughter, Horace and his friends coaxed the placid little pony onto a platform. We had a lively discussion of how to draw him and then tried out our theories. When the bell signaled the end of class, no one wanted to leave.

Word about the pony got back to the school board. I received a stern letter from the superintendent, informing me that this was against school policy. What was the school policy, I wondered—no horses in the classroom? I ignored the letter, and for a while I heard nothing more. That winter the Texas legislature met and debated the issue, and they backed the superintendent's requirement that teachers must use textbooks approved by the board of education. I could have told them that the board of education knew nothing about art or how to teach it—but I didn't. I just kept on ignoring them and doing things the way I thought they should be done. My students brought in whatever they wanted to draw—a china teacup, a battered straw hat, a one-eyed doll—and we drew them. No more ponies, though.

I should have known the battle wasn't over. The superintendent called me into his office and ordered me to buy the drawing books. "It's the law, Miss O'Keeffe," he informed me, as if I were weak-minded.

"The law is based on ignorance, and it's wrong," I insisted.

I simply "forgot" to order the Prang books for the rest of the school year, and my memory never did improve.

Every now and then I'd received a letter with a French postmark. George Dannenberg, my Man from the Far West, continued to write to me, although we had not seen each other in more than three years—not since we were together at Lake George. In February he reported that he was enjoying the celebration of Mardi Gras in Paris, with music and dancing in the streets, and from there he would travel to the Riviera. I doubt that anyone in Amarillo had the slightest idea what Mardi Gras was—and I wrote back about the desolation that I found exotic in its own way. In his next letter he said that he planned to return to America early in the summer, and he would come to Virginia to see me.

I saved his letters. I thought of George often and wanted very much to see him again, but we had chosen such different lives that I doubted we could ever again share a common one, as we had at Lake George.

I had fallen in love with the wild, free openness of the Texas Panhandle, so different from the Midwest, where I felt I could reach out and touch the horizon, and certainly from the suffocating closeness of the East. That vastness was influencing even my small watercolors. But I'd become weary of Amarillo. I was thought odd for my dress, for my insistence on living at the Magnolia Hotel, for my unorthodox teaching methods—I was in a standoff with the school superintendent.

The small-mindedness of the town was the complete opposite of the exhilaration I'd found in the land, and I was desperate to leave it when in June I boarded the eastbound train headed back to Virginia.

18

Charlottesville, Virginia—
Summer 1913

THE O'KEEFFES WERE AS CLOSE-KNIT AS EVER, and the chilliness of our Charlottesville neighbors reinforced our clannishness. These families had been Virginians practically since the Creation, and we would always be newcomers of dubious background and questionable status. I'd been a misfit in Williamsburg, a misfit in Amarillo, and of course a misfit in Charlottesville, too. It didn't bother me.

I began my summer position as Mr. Bement's teaching assistant at the university, assigned to two classes for high school teachers.

I began painting again. Our house had no garden or grassy lawn to speak of, only a few hollyhocks blooming bravely in the mean little yard, but they were inspiration enough. I painted them over and over, always seeing something new in them, something I hadn't seen before, or trying another combination of colors, or altering the perspective. It was a habit I'd developed the summer before, when I painted trees and shrubs on the university campus and then painted the same tree or shrub a different way.

Francis was working in New York and Alexius had begun studying engineering at the University of Wisconsin, but my four sisters were still at home, Ida and Nita teaching, Catherine finishing high school; Claudie, the baby of the family, was just fourteen. My sisters and I kept to ourselves, mainly by choice but also because no one else chose to include us. Sometimes we picked up ice cream cones from Papa's creamery to enjoy on our walks out into the rolling green hills, so different from those wide-open spaces in Texas! We avoided discussing Mama's condition—she was obviously getting worse—or Papa's business, obviously getting worse, too. I worried about our parents, and I'm sure my sisters did as well, but we were a family who rarely talked about unpleasant subjects, preferring to pretend they didn't exist.

For a time I thought I had made a new friend, Miss Anna Barringer, who also taught art classes at the university. Her father, a prominent member of the faculty at the medical school, had a marvelous greenhouse where he raised orchids, and she invited me to set up my easel there. It was thrilling, because I'd had no idea so many varieties of orchid existed, so many shapes, sizes, and colors—dozens of them, each exotically beautiful in its own way.

But Miss Barringer turned out not to be serious about art, or even her own painting. She was more concerned with the social life of her small, exclusive circle.

"Oh, Miss O'Keeffe!" she rhapsodized. "My friend So-and-So is being courted by the handsomest fellow, and she is so hoping that So-and-So will ask her to marry him. She's been dropping hints about the kind of engagement ring she'd like, and we've been secretly planning the wedding sometime next—"

On and on prattled Miss Barringer, but I had stopped listening. I was concentrating on the colors of a particular orchid, a pale green with dark red spots, imagining how I might capture that particular blood red, and her endless chatter about who was courting whom and whose family had just purchased a new carriage horse or automobile didn't interest me. That we really had nothing in common except our watercolors and brushes must have been as plain to her as it was to me, and soon we didn't bother to try to paint together.

The student in my class who showed the most promise was my own sister, Nita. She had always been talented, and I felt that she drew on a far larger reserve of natural ability than I did. I gave her a high grade, of course, because she worked hard enough to earn it, but Nita lacked boldness, daring—*nerve*. She painted beautifully, but she took no risks. I knew she would never become an artist. Talent was not enough; it is never enough. She recognized it, too.

"Georgie, you're the artist, we all know that. We've known it all along. I couldn't choose the path you've chosen, any more than you'd choose mine."

The path Nita chose when the class ended was to go into nurses' training at a hospital in New York City.

I heard from George Dannenberg several times that summer. His letters were always warm, always dangling possibilities of something more. He'd promised to visit me in Virginia, but the months went by, summer was coming to an end, and George did not appear. There was a time that the broken promise would have mattered a great deal to me, but no longer.

In September I made the long train ride back across the country to Amarillo. I was welcomed at the Magnolia Hotel like an old friend by the manager, who believed that I brought a certain amount of civility to the rowdy clientele, and by Max, the cook. "How can you eat so little, Miss O'Keeffe, and stay alive?" he marveled. "You'll turn into a skeleton!" It was true—I was leaner than ever, and my hair had grown out straight and was now long enough to wear pulled back in a bun.

Day after day the cowboys stomped into the Magnolia, coated with dust, sunburned and bleary-eyed. Max had spent years as a cook for the cowboys driving cattle from ranches all around Texas, and he knew from experience that when a new crew arrived in town, he'd better have plenty of beef on hand to feed them. More than once I observed a tableful of cowboys plow through their platters of thick steaks, order another round, and then go for a third! After the serious drinking began, they were a boisterous bunch, and I was glad my room on the third floor was in back, away from the ruckus and racket.

I loved the landscape; I even loved the whip and whine of the relentless wind. I loved my young students, their enthusiasm undimmed, open to the wonder and joy of creating art, starting with just the merest suggestion from me. If I put the egg I'd brought for my midday meal on the table and said, "Let's talk about this egg," we'd have a discussion of the elegant shape, and then they'd draw it, or make it part of a larger arrangement, and we'd talk about what made the composition better, or not.

I got along with the townspeople, even those who weren't afraid to tell me they thought I dressed oddly and had peculiar ideas, but I did not get along with the Texas state legislature, the bullheaded board of education, and the implacable superintendent.

When I went home to Charlottesville at the end of the spring term, I was unsure what I would do next. Mama was frailer than ever. Auntie tried to keep on taking in table boarders, as Mama had, but word had gotten around that Mama was consumptive and no one wanted to eat food from our kitchen. Papa had finally decided to give up the creamery venture. He found work as a construction inspector for the government, but he was required to travel and was away a great deal. I had once been close to my father, but he had changed so much—and I suppose I had, too—that we had little to say to each other when he did come home.

The previous summer, fussy Mr. Bement had tried to convince me to go back to New York. "Miss O'Keeffe, I urge you, beg and implore you! Please, please, enroll at Columbia Teachers College and earn your teaching certificate."

"I would love to do that, Mr. Bement, but I have no money," I told him then. "And I do love Texas and the West. I believe it's where I need to be, to explore the kinds of painting I want to do."

But after I had again encountered the obstinacy of the educational system in Texas—the superintendent's office ordered the books, but they sat unopened in the box—I came home in the spring discouraged and worn out. And I'd done hardly any painting.

Now Mr. Bement resumed his crusade to convince me to go to New York. He must have spoken to Nita, who must then have spoken to Mama. My mother spent most of her days in her bedroom and left it only in a wheelchair. She was so weak that talking was hard for her, but one morning when I carried in her tea and toast before I left for class, she asked me to stay for a minute or two.

I sat down on the bed beside her and took her hand. I could feel the bones in each finger. "Please, Georgie," she whispered, "I'm going to ask you a favor." I nodded. "Will you promise me that you'll take care of Claudie when I'm gone?"

I started to protest that she was a long way from dying—although that was not the truth—but she shushed me.

"She's very young, only fifteen, and she'll need someone. Auntie is getting old, and Papa is gone. Will you do it? Make sure Claudie's all right?"

"Yes, Mama, I will. I promise," I said, although my own life was so uncertain that I had no idea how I would keep my word.

Mama mustered a weary little smile. "Something else. I decided to ask Ollie if she'd lend you the money you need to go to New York." She laid her finger on my lips before I could protest. "I've already written to her. I'm sure she'll agree. I want you to do that—for me."

I was wiping away tears when I hurried off to teach my class. A week later I had a letter from Aunt Ollie, offering me the loan. "At no interest and with no repayment," she wrote. "Since that year you spent with Charley and me when you were at the Art Institute, I've felt that I'm partly responsible for you becoming an artist." The check she enclosed wasn't huge, but I knew I could make it last.

At the end of the summer of 1914 I sent my resignation to the superintendent of the Amarillo schools. I loved my students, but I despised the small-mindedness of the officials, who pretended to want an education for their students and then resisted any attempt I made to provide exactly that.

And then I left for New York for the second time. It would be the third year of my education as an artist, and I was ready.

PART V

"I felt that I must stop using color until I couldn't get along without it."

19

New York—Fall 1914

I STEPPED OFF THE TRAIN IN NEW YORK AND KNEW
that this was exactly where I wanted and *needed* to be.

Newspaper headlines screamed the start of a war
in Europe, one country after another declaring war on
the others—Germany, Russia, France, England. But the
war seemed far away and of no concern to me. The city
was humming with new ideas about art, and that was the
conversation in which I was swept up.

Artists and art students were still talking about an
exhibition that had taken place the year before, the
Armory Show, with work mostly from Europe. I would
have given anything to see it, especially the most controversial work, *Nude Descending a Staircase*, painted by
a Frenchman, Marcel Duchamp, in ochers and browns.
The image was splintered, so that it looked as though it

was in motion. A critic described it as "an explosion in a shingle factory." A lot of people, many of them American artists, were furious about Matisse's *Blue Nude*, because she really was done in blue, and not in natural skin color.

I was a little shocked that Robert Henri, who had despised Rodin's drawings, had also entered a nude in the show—not splintered or blue, but looking so very real that it was as if she was about to step right out of the canvas. Kenyon Cox, the instructor who never had a good word to say about anybody, proclaimed that it all looked like the work of savages. And some were demanding that the exhibition be shut down because it was a menace to public morality.

I'd missed the show, but I hadn't missed my chance to hear about it. It was so controversial, so radically different from everything we'd been taught, it was still being hotly discussed for many months afterward.

I was different, too: I had changed since my first arrival in New York seven years before, nervous and unsure of myself, believing that the men in my classes knew so much more than I did, so easily intimidated by the likes of Gene Speicher. *Someday I'll be a great painter*, he'd said, *and you'll be teaching art in a girls' school somewhere*. I'd painted and painted, and I knew my work was good and getting better all the time, but I wasn't yet sure what my ideas were. I was experimenting, still finding my way.

I enrolled at Columbia Teachers College, where I met Anita Pollitzer in a drawing class. Anita was just twenty, seven years younger than I, and bursting with energy and enthusiasm. She was sometimes disorganized, apt to misplace things or lose them entirely, but that was part of her charm. We got to know each other well. Her spontaneity and the variety of her interests attracted me, and I wondered if Anita could afford to indulge her whims because she had no money worries—her father was a cotton broker in South Carolina, and her family was quite well off. My situation was so different—I had to be very careful of my expenditures. I could stretch Aunt Ollie's "loan" for a year in New York, but after that there would be no more.

I did not want a roommate; I'd become much too accustomed to living alone in Texas, and I found a room for four dollars a week. I looked up Dorothy True, a friend from my year at the Art Students League—she was one of the Fakirs—and she soon became part of a tight little trio with Anita and me. Anita and I had been calling each other "Miss Pollitzer" and "Miss O'Keeffe," as was customary in those days, but when she heard Dorothy call me Patsy, my Chicago nickname, Anita began calling me Patsy as well.

The three of us signed up for a drawing class with Charles Martin, who was my age; he'd studied at the Teachers College and also with Arthur Wesley Dow, Mr. Bement's mentor. This was his first year of teaching. Since we were advanced students, he allowed us to have a private corner in his studio and to arrange our own still lifes. We could draw whatever we wanted, while on the other side of the curtain Mr. Martin's regular students were drawing those abominable plaster casts of heads of Greek gods with perfect ringlets of hair. Oh, we were so proud of our advanced status and the freedom it gave us!

In a printing class I experimented with monotypes, painting directly on a glass plate and then transferring the image by pressing a sheet of paper on the inked surface. I made monotype portraits of redheaded Dorothy and dark-haired, brown-eyed Anita, and both girls pronounced them brilliant. Anita called the one I did of her a masterpiece.

I took a color class with Arthur Wesley Dow, who had a show of his paintings of the Grand Canyon. His bold use of color was breathtaking. Mr. Dow was a nice man, and everybody in the class fell all over themselves flattering him, but I could not bring myself to be so worshipful.

I saw Mr. Bement often—he taught there during the fall and spring terms—but I didn't take his courses. I liked some of his ideas, but I wasn't going to let him tell me *what* to paint, much less *how* to paint. I wanted to move forward on my own.

All I thought about was art and painting and drawing. There wasn't room in my head, or in my life, for anything else. This was a problem, though, because I had enrolled at Teachers College to earn a degree in fine arts education, and although I was immersed in the "fine arts" part of the degree, I was not interested in the "education" part. I'd already taught at Amarillo High School and the University of Virginia, so I simply ignored "Principles of

Teaching." The instructor liked me and gave me a grade of C. I barely passed the English course; my abominable spelling had not improved one bit since my days at Chatham.

Anita and Dorothy and I made the rounds of the galleries and art shows, to see what was happening in the art world and to compare what we saw with what we were trying to do. The fall show of the American Watercolor Society seemed dull as dishwater.

"It would be no problem at all to paint something as good as any of these," I snorted.

A few days later I painted a girl in black next to some red flowers, and that winter, when the Society asked for submissions for the spring show, I entered my painting. It was accepted, as I'd known it would be. When the show came down, I reclaimed my picture, ripped it to shreds, and dropped them in the trash bin.

Anita and Dorothy stared at me, appalled. "Why on earth did you do that?"

"Because that picture was as boring as everything else hanging in the show. Ten years ago when I graduated from boarding school, I destroyed most of my student work. I didn't want to be associated with such mediocre work in the future, and I still feel that way. Now let's go have tea somewhere."

When Alfred Stieglitz opened a show of new work from Europe at his gallery, 291, the three of us naturally went to see it. There were abstract drawings by a Spaniard, Pablo Picasso, and Georges Braque, a Frenchman, so similar that I could hardly tell which was which. Mr. Stieglitz also exhibited sculpture by a Romanian artist, Brancusi. One piece, titled *Sleeping Muse*, was a large marble egg lying on its side with only the suggestion of a face with closed eyes. There was almost nothing to it, yet it was so elegant and so simple that I could not stop looking at it. I really didn't know what to make of this radical new style.

It was not just European artists who were breaking all the rules—the Americans were too. I wanted to learn more. I'd seen a reproduction of a pastel called *Leaf Forms* by an American, Arthur Dove, and I was excited by its bold, abstract forms and vibrant colors. In the spring a new show opened at 291: four dozen watercolors and oils by John Marin, mostly seascapes and landscapes, but I was just crazy about his watercolor of the Woolworth Building, so full of energy it looked as though it was flying!

The work Mr. Stieglitz exhibited was intriguing, but I was put off by Mr. Stieglitz himself. When I had traipsed down to his gallery with my League friends, I hadn't liked Rodin's scribbles, and I hadn't liked Mr. Stieglitz much either—so pugnacious and argumentative. And he hadn't changed! Whenever Dorothy and Anita and I went to 291, Anita always got into intense conversations with him—she was the kind of girl who got into intense conversations with everybody—while I went off by myself to look at the paintings and ignored whatever the two of them were going on about.

"Mr. Stieglitz truly appreciates the work of women artists," Anita said to Dorothy and me one day as we left the gallery. "He's shown Marion Beckett and Katharine Rhoades when no one else paid attention to them because they're not men!"

"They may be women, but I'm not sure they're really artists," I said. "I didn't think much of their work. They paint the way somebody told them to, not the way they really want to."

Anita was surprised by my reaction, but Dorothy wasn't. "I think Mr. Stieglitz's interest in Beckett and Rhoades is more romantic than aesthetic," she said dryly.

"Oh, you two!" Anita said, laughing. "Let's go get something to eat. I'm starving!" She must have noticed my hesitation, because she added, "My treat!"

My New York year was finished, and I returned to Charlottesville. I had new confidence in myself and my work, but I didn't yet have a teaching certificate. I could not bear to go back to Amarillo and engage in constant warfare over teaching materials and heaven knew what else. I could, I thought, return to New York and look for work. I loved New York, and I loved the excitement of the art world. But if I could find a job that paid enough to live on, I would not have time to paint—and painting was the most important thing. Not to paint was not to be alive. I would have to find another way to support myself.

Back in Virginia that summer, I taught again as Mr. Bement's assistant. There were eighteen students in my class, and I decided to introduce them to the idea that art doesn't try to present an accurate picture of reality, in the way that a photograph does, but uses colors and shapes and forms to convey the *idea* of reality.

Most of them had never seen anything like abstract art, and as I expected, most rejected it. I wanted to change that.

"Pick up some colors that appeal to you, and show what you're feeling on paper," I told them. "Don't *think*, just *do*. It doesn't matter what—just *do*."

They looked at me as if I were half mad, but one girl boldly snatched up red, orange, and green crayons and began making big wavy shapes on the paper.

"That's it!" I cried, and showed the paper to the class. "That's exactly what I'm talking about."

The others looked at her as though *she* were half mad. A few made some feeble attempts, but I was fairly certain that only one student in that room would ever suggest such an exercise to her high school class. The others were Prang people, working by the book of chromos, and they weren't about to change.

My friendship with Anita Pollitzer continued to deepen even after I'd left New York. Her letters always lifted my spirits. I found time to paint, and the colors in my paintings were bright, glowing, full of life—the opposite of how I felt, which at that point was drab, dull, lifeless, with my mother ill, my father seldom at home, my brothers gone, my sisters involved in their own lives. I rolled up my old watercolors and drawings in cardboard tubes and mailed them to Anita, mostly because I felt that keeping old work around took up too much breathing space. At the same time, I always felt that sending out my work, even to my closest friend, was a huge risk. As much as I craved a response, I felt exposed, as if I were walking around completely naked.

Then I met Arthur Macmahon.

Arthur had come to Charlottesville to teach summer courses in political science. Three years younger than I, he had graduated at the head of his class, won prizes in oratory, earned a master's degree, and was already a professor at Columbia. Besides being brilliant, he was also an avid outdoorsman—and desperately good-looking! Someone at the university had organized walking excursions into the mountains nearly every weekend, and that was where we met.

Arthur gave me many new things to think about. He described his liberal political theories—he was interested in feminism and the women's suffrage movement, which demanded that women have the right to vote—and recommended books that he thought I should read on the subject. Mostly he talked and I listened, but he also let me rattle on and on about new ideas in art and why I'd stopped paying much attention to Mr. Bement's suggestions.

By the time the summer courses finished in August, Arthur and I had become great friends. He stayed on for four extra days, and we tramped through the woods, completely at ease with each other. One hot day when we stopped beside a stream to eat the picnic we'd brought along, I boldly peeled off my stockings and put my bare feet into the cold water. I wondered if he might be put off by my daring, but he could not have been too shocked, because he took off *his* shoes and socks and put *his* bare feet in the water, too. It seemed funny when fish swam up and nibbled at our toes, but with Arthur everything was amusing and delightful. Things never got slushy between us, and we had a beautiful time. When Arthur left for New York, we promised to write, but that was the only promise that had been made.

I still had not made up my mind about what to do next. At the end of the summer a letter arrived offering me a position as the art teacher at a small college in South Carolina that trained girls to be music teachers. There would be plenty of free time for my own work—I was to teach only four days a week—but I wasn't sure if Columbia College was the right place for me. The college was small and the town was small—remote, isolated, far from a big city.

I could see Mama growing weaker and weaker, and I wavered. She sensed my hesitation and lectured me firmly. "You have a career ahead of you as an artist, and your father and I sacrificed so that you'd have the training you need. You are twenty-seven years old, and you will be letting us down if you don't go where your talent takes you. I have all the help I need here. Go, Georgie."

But there was another reason I delayed making a decision. I hoped that Arthur would ask me to come to New York. When time passed and I didn't hear from him,

I decided to write to him. It would be bold of me to write first—I knew it was not proper for a woman to take the initiative—but *not* to write seemed like playing a game, and I refused to do that. I wanted to write to him, and so I did.

Arthur's reply was warm, but there was no invitation to come to New York. That was a disappointment, but it pushed me to make up my mind. Four days before classes were to begin, I sent a wire accepting the position in South Carolina. I would earn enough to support myself, and I would have time to paint. My mind would be freer there than in New York or Texas, and it would be good just to work alone for a year.

That's what I told Anita Pollitzer, and what I told myself.

20

Columbia, South Carolina—
Fall 1915

DURING MY FIRST WEEKS IN SOUTH CAROLINA I explored my new surroundings. The architecture of Columbia, the state capital, was handsome, and the campus of Columbia College was a short trolley ride from the center of town and surrounded by pretty countryside. I was in an optimistic mood: I would be able to do so much for my students, and the change would be stimulating for my own work.

But disillusionment set in quickly. The town was even duller and more backward than Williamsburg and Amarillo, and the pace ranged from sluggish to half dead. It may have been livelier in good times, but these were not good times. This was cotton country, and the demand for cotton had almost vanished because of the war raging in Europe. This was the first evidence I'd seen of the effects on people here of the fighting on the other side of the Atlantic. My students were the daughters of cotton growers, girls whose families could no longer afford the tuition. Enrollment had plummeted to one hundred fifty. Half the teachers had resigned—there wasn't enough money to pay them.

I'd been hired, I realized, because they wouldn't have to pay an uncertified teacher much—a tiny salary, a sunless room in a dormitory that had seen better days, and three tasteless meals a day in the gloomy dining hall. But far worse than the financial poverty of the college was the intellectual poverty of faculty and students. There was no interest in art or literature or ideas or much of anything. Mediocrity lay like a thick layer of dust over everything. It would take a huge amount of effort for me not to wither away entirely.

The young ladies, who supposedly wanted to be music teachers but more likely wanted to be brides, showed no curiosity about what I was trying to teach them. I attempted in the first weeks to introduce them to ideas of abstract art. I showed them lithographs of what Matisse and Picasso were doing. "Interpretation is more important than representation," I said, quoting Arthur Wesley Dow. I showed them photographs of Brancusi's egg-shaped sculpture of the sleeping head and Duchamp's *Nude Descending a Staircase* and John Marin's watercolor of the Woolworth Building that I found so exciting. The girls stared at the pictures in utter boredom.

"That's supposed to be art?" asked one young lady, curling her lip. "It doesn't look like much of anything." The others nodded.

I thought of my summer school student in Charlottesville who had snatched up red, orange, and green crayons and gone joyfully wild when I'd instructed the class to do something crazy with nothing in mind but a feeling. There was no one like her in my classes.

I didn't mention any of this in my letters to Arthur, who was teaching at Columbia University, but poor Anita—also in New York, at the Art Students League—caught the full force of my disappointment and misery. *I feel all sick inside, as if I could dry up and blow away,* I wrote, feeling very sorry for myself.

Anita urged me on, warning me not to slacken. *Just grit your teeth and bear it. Ordinariness might actually be good for you for a change, Patsy!*

Tramping in the piney woods allowed me to escape from my listless students and find myself again. In November, when the wild chrysanthemums were in bloom, I came back from a walk with my arms filled with flowers, and arranged bunches in my dormitory room and the classroom and my little studio next to it. When my students admired the flowers, I was suddenly moved to announce, "Tomorrow we shall go for a walk. I want you to see how important it is to pay attention to the world around you."

The next day was sunny and warm, and I led the girls along the banks of the Broad River. The wood ducks were migrating from the north. As we walked deeper into the woods, we stopped to listen to the breeze singing high up in the tall pines. I learned that a few of the students were more interested in local history than they were in art. Melanie told me that General Sherman had marched through the town in 1865. The school, called Columbia Female College then, had to close. Fanny, a talented violinist, chimed in that the college was saved from being torched when the professor of music stood in the doorway where Union troops could see him.

The walk did not transform the girls into art lovers, but when I showed that I was interested in their stories, they became more willing to hear what I had to say about art.

Being alone agreed with me. I painted every day, even when I didn't feel like painting, and the foul humor I'd been in drained away. I'd imagine abstract shapes that were like nothing I'd seen, nothing I'd been taught, and then I'd paint what I imagined, the same picture over and over, trying it first one way, then another. I was developing a new language, a new form of expression that had never existed before. Those abstract forms came to me in bursts, almost like music, surging in a bold crescendo and then subsiding in a sensual melody, and that music was what I painted. For days on end I taught, painted, slept—and woke up with more imaginings.

Letters arrived every few days from Anita, and almost every letter had something exciting to report—usually another visit to 291, with raves about Mr. Stieglitz and how important it was for her to "breathe his air." Although I could not imagine wanting to breathe Mr. Stieglitz's air, I did subscribe to the magazine, named *291*, that he'd begun to publish. Anita had shown me copies of his older magazine, *Camera Work*, that had originally been devoted entirely to photographs but had gradually changed to include drawings as well. The new magazine had just four or six oversized pages, with drawings by Picasso, the French artist Braque, and other modernists, and poems and essays about art. There were no photographs, except for one in the October issue. Mr. Stieglitz had inserted a large reproduction of his photograph *The Steerage*, showing passengers on the lower decks of a steamer.

The more I heard from Anita about the exhibitions at Mr. Stieglitz's gallery, the more I began to wish that I could somehow get his opinion on the direction my work was taking. If I ever painted something that satisfied me even a little, I would find a way to show it to him and ask if he thought it was any good. But I knew I was a long way from making art that would satisfy me enough for that.

At about this time I experienced one of those random moments when I stopped thinking altogether and simply started *feeling*. I had always loved color, but now I felt that I must stop using color until I could not get along without it. I put away my watercolors and began to work only in charcoal. I spread large sheets of the cheap sketch paper used by students on the floor and crawled around on my hands and knees, drawing and drawing the shapes that came straight from my imagination. I had no teacher to please, no one else's ideas of what made good art, no one to satisfy but myself, and it was exhilarating.

I worked until my hand ached so much that I couldn't do any more. And I promised myself that I would continue until I knew—*felt*—that I had said everything I could possibly say in black and white, even if that took months. Only then would I use color again.

I had no close friends among the faculty and only one or two who were casual friends. There was no one at the college with whom I could share my ideas about art, and I found myself relying more and more on my correspondence with Arthur. He was constantly on my mind. His beautifully written letters sustained me. Arthur was not much interested in art, certainly not passionate about it in the way that I was. In fact, he was rather cool to it. He didn't see things the way I did, although we *thought* about things in much the same way. His approach to life was intellectual, and mine was purely emotional, yet the attraction between us was powerful.

My growing feelings for Arthur may have had something to do with my decision to work only in black and white. What I felt for him was an explosion in every primary color, every secondary color, and every shade and hue in between. I worried that the intense emotion might eat me up and swallow me whole. But did he experience that same intensity of feeling? Sometimes I believed he did; other times, not.

I was falling in love with him, I wasn't sure I wanted to, and yet it was happening and I did nothing to stop it. That filled me with happiness, and it frightened me, too.

A few days before Thanksgiving he wrote that he had been invited to give lectures in Virginia and North Carolina the week after Thanksgiving, and he wanted to spend a few days with me in Columbia. There had been no hints that he was even considering making a trip south, and so nothing could have been a bigger surprise—like a thunderbolt out of a cloudless sky.

Be calm, I cautioned myself. But then I wrote to him immediately, throwing caution to the winds, telling him, *I'm the gladdest person in the world!* Then, my pen practically scribbling off the page, I wrote to Anita, *I am so glad about something that I'm almost afraid I'm going to die.*

Three nights in a row I stayed up late, stitching a new shirtwaist, adding bits of lace. Sewing helped to keep me calm. It was a wonder that I slept at all.

Arthur arrived Friday morning, having spent the night on the train after a Thanksgiving Day visit with his parents in New Jersey. I stood waiting at the depot with a ridiculous grin on my face as the train pulled in. I wanted so badly to kiss him, but we greeted each other with a comradely handshake, and I escorted him to a boarding house near the college.

"You must be exhausted," I said. "Probably you'd like some time to rest."

Arthur laughed. "Do you think I'm going to waste one minute resting when I can be with you?"

Exactly what I wanted to hear.

We had four whole days together, walking and talking. We took photographs of each other in the woods outside the city and ate picnic lunches by the river. And we made plans. He would come back in the spring, his mother and brother would come with him, and we would rent a rustic mountain cabin that I'd heard about. It was wonderful to have something to look forward to!

The time came to say goodbye, and Arthur boarded the train for New York. And yes, we kissed for the first time. I made the first move, put my hands on his face and drew it to mine. Later I wrote to him, apologizing for being so forward. He wrote back, reassuring me that I had not behaved badly, that it was perfectly fine, he was so glad I had done it.

We continued to exchange the tenderest messages—there was nothing I couldn't say to him—and I knew that my deepening feelings for him were the source from which so many of my drawings were coming. I sent one, all rounded shapes and swirls, to him with a note: *I said something to you with charcoal.*

All the students and nearly all the teachers had gone home at Christmas, and the campus was nearly deserted. Arthur and I had talked of meeting at Christmas—I would go home to Charlottesville, and he would come there to visit—but in the end I knew that I could not afford the expense of the travel. I made up my mind to enjoy the solitude, embrace it—it would give me time to work, with nothing else to think about. Nothing else but Arthur, of course, and I thought of him a great deal. I wrote to him boldly, *I want to touch your face and kiss you, not on your lips but your forehead.*

One night I was sitting on the floor in front of my closet with a stick of charcoal and my rough sheets of paper, and my head began to throb. I had such a ferocious headache that I couldn't do another drawing. And then I thought, *I might as well do something with this headache,* and I drew it.

I had done dozens of charcoal drawings, and a few days later I chose several of them, spare but sensuous shapes, and mailed them to Anita in New York. I hadn't really planned to do that, but I found I wanted her reaction. I had always told her I didn't want her to show my work to anyone else, but, without consulting me, she took the drawings to 291 and showed them to Mr. Stieglitz.

It was New Year's Day, Anita wrote to me later, and he was alone in the gallery:

I unrolled them, two earlier ones and the ones you just sent. The room was quiet, with one small light, and his hair was mussed—you know how he looked, you've seen him. It was a long while before he said anything. And he kept looking at them, squinting at them, analyzing. After he stared at them for a long time, Stieglitz said, "Finally, a woman on paper." Then he added, "Tell this girl they're the purest, finest, sincerest things that have entered 291 in a long while. They're genuinely fine things, and I wouldn't mind showing them one bit."

I read Anita's letter, and reread it, over and over. My whole world suddenly shifted.

Nobody at Columbia understood my drawings or what I was trying to do. One of the professors whom I considered a friend had looked at one and exclaimed, "Why, it's as mad as a March hare."

But Mr. Stieglitz didn't think they were mad, and impetuously I wrote to him. It took all my nerve to ask why he liked the charcoals and what they said to him. *I make them just to express myself—things I want to say— haven't the words for.*

I was nervous when I sealed and stamped that letter, jittery when I stuck it in the mailbox, on edge wondering if he'd bother to reply. When an answer came, Mr. Stieglitz seemed to have succumbed to the same kind of wordlessness that I'd felt when I made the drawings. *If you and I were to meet and talk about life, possibly then I might make you feel what your drawings gave me.* He made no promises about showing them, though. He ended his letter, *The future is hazy—but the present is very positive and very delightful.*

That answer was even more than I had hoped for—it left me struggling for breath. When I'd calmed down, I wrote to Anita, *I just like the inside of him.*

21

New York—Spring 1916

I WAS IN A DILEMMA. AFTER ANITA'S LETTER ABOUT the drawings, another letter arrived, this one offering me a position in the fall as head of the art department at West Texas Normal School in Canyon, about twenty miles south of Amarillo—beyond the reach of the wretched superintendent of the Amarillo schools but still in that wonderful empty Panhandle. I was delighted.

But there were problems. I could not accept the offer unless I left South Carolina and went back to Teachers College to complete one more course for my teaching certificate. Just one more course! But I would need a place to stay plus two hundred dollars to cover expenses in New York, money that I did not have.

What a temptation! Arthur was in New York, and I wanted to see him. I'd written to him, saying that I wanted to kiss him. I knew that I loved him, and in a letter I had even told him so. I was the bold one! Sometimes I believed he loved me; more often I doubted. In some letters he would come very close, but in others he seemed to pull away. If I went to New York, I would be with him—and we would talk, and I would see and hear and feel just how close or how far away he was, and then I would *know*.

Anita solved one of the problems when she offered me a place to stay with her uncle and aunt. Then she solved another by offering to lend me two hundred dollars.

Still I could not make up my mind, leaning first one way, then the other. The second term was beginning at Columbia College, and I had to make a decision.

My dilemma would soon be resolved. Within days after students returned from the Christmas holidays, several of the parents complained to the president of the college about the outlandish things they had heard their daughters were being taught in art class. It took a few weeks for the complaints to percolate through the system, but in mid-February, while I was still considering the offer from Texas and debating whether or not to go to New York, the college president, the Reverend Mr. Gladstone, called me into his office.

"Miss O'Keeffe," he began in a fatherly tone, "the mothers and fathers of our young ladies expect their daughters to learn to paint pictures of flowers and landscapes and perhaps to make drawings of people and buildings. Not the sort of scribbles in charcoal and splashes of random color that look like nothing at all or are in some cases possibly indecent. The Methodist ministers on the board of regents have made objections as well, suggesting that some of this so-called 'art' you're teaching is a travesty of God's marvelous creation."

My face was burning, and I'm afraid I lost my temper when Mr. Gladstone delivered an ultimatum: I must agree to teach traditional methods of painting and drawing or tender my resignation. It was a near-repeat of my experience in Amarillo with the superintendent and his insistence that I use a textbook I abhorred.

I didn't waste a minute thinking it over. "I cannot teach what I do not believe. I resign, effectively immediately."

The usually placid Mr. Gladstone reared back in his chair and stared across the desk at me. "Please do not make a hasty decision that you may come to regret, Miss O'Keeffe."

"It is not hasty, and I assure you, I shall not regret it. I'll begin immediately to collect my belongings, and I'll be on the northbound train Monday morning."

"You're leaving us without an art teacher!"

"It should be easy enough for you to find someone who will teach the mindless kind of art you prefer to have taught here."

Mr. Gladstone's face turned red. "You understand, Miss O'Keeffe, that if you break your contract I shall be unable to furnish you with a positive recommendation for any future position."

"I think you would be unable to do that in any case. Good day, sir."

230

Those were my final words to the Reverend Mr. Gladstone. I marched out of his office and back to my room, wrote a letter of acceptance to West Texas Normal College, and started packing. It didn't take long, for I had very few things to take with me.

I was going to New York.

How wonderful to escape from South Carolina, beautiful and somnolent as it was, and to jump into the taut nerve and kick of the city! I arrived in New York at the beginning of March—I'd already missed the first weeks of Arthur Dow's "Methods of Teaching" course—and settled quickly into a big, bright room on the top floor of Dr. Pollitzer's elegant brownstone on East Sixtieth Street. I arranged to eat all my meals in the cafeteria at Teachers College and went out of my way never to bother the family. The only one I got to know was Anita's nineteen-year-old cousin, Aline, who by coincidence was enrolled in a political science class at the university with Professor Arthur Macmahon. I took care not to let Aline know about my relationship with her professor.

I'd written to Arthur as soon as I knew I was coming to New York, and of course he was the first person I wanted to see when I arrived. From then on we saw each other often, although, for me, it never seemed to be often enough. He took me to lunch with his mother, an interesting woman deeply involved in the suffrage movement, and the three of us had a lively discussion about what the effects on society would be if women could vote. I liked Mrs. Macmahon, and I was sure she liked me. Arthur and I met in Central Park for long walks that usually ended at a coffee shop on Columbus Avenue. Sometimes he accompanied me to galleries, but Arthur's interest in art had never been nearly as intense as mine—how could it be? And I did not care much about political issues that absorbed Arthur. He supported the reelection campaign of President Woodrow Wilson, who was running on an "America First" platform to keep the country out of the war raging across Europe.

I had not seen any of my family since I left Virginia for South Carolina in September, but I corresponded regularly with Ida, who was teaching art at the high school. I worried about Mama, of course, as her health steadily worsened, but she always insisted to all of her children that our duty was to go on with our lives, and we had all obeyed her. At the end of April Ida wrote to me with upsetting family news—not about Mama, but our sister Nita. Nita had left nursing school and begun taking courses at the university, where she had fallen in love with a nineteen-year-old student and eloped with him. Nita was twenty-five.

His name is Robert Young, Ida wrote, *he is from somewhere in Texas, they met in class and they have been seeing each other secretly for several months. Now they've moved to New Jersey, and Nita says he's working for a chemical company.*

I could hardly believe that Nita had done something so foolish. Whatever could she have been thinking? I wrote back, asking what Mama had to say about it, but my letter had not yet reached Charlottesville when I had a second letter from Ida:

Our dearest Mama is gone. The landlady, Mrs. Philips, came to collect the rent. I explained there was no money to pay her right then. Papa promised to send it. Mrs. P demanded to see Mama and refused to leave until she did. Claudie and I went in to Mama and helped her get out of bed and walk to the front door where the awful Mrs. P was waiting. Mama didn't make it. She coughed up blood, collapsed, and died.

No matter how prepared I thought I was for this news, I was not. I felt as though I was drowning in grief.

Our family was in many ways no longer a family. My father traveled constantly and was completely absent, Francis was an architect in Cuba and was rarely in touch, Alexius was working in Chicago, Catherine had become a nurse and was back in Wisconsin. And now Nita, married and gone! The only ones still living in the rented house were Ida, Claudie, who was still in high school, and dear old Auntie.

The letter had been delivered in the morning, and I decided to leave for Charlottesville that night. I needed to be there. Maybe it was where I should have been at Christmas, or at other times, in spite of Mama's insistence that what she wanted was for me to go on with my life.

Before I left New York, I went to the sculpture studio and began to work the clay, softening it in my hands, looking for an outlet for my feelings of loss and regret. Slowly the shapeless mound of clay began to take on form. The elongated figure of a woman emerged, her head bowed in sorrow. I left the sculpture on a shelf with a note, asking that it be cast in plaster.

That night I took the sleeper to Charlottesville, and although I'd barely slept, I wrote to Arthur the next morning to tell him what had happened. I confessed how afraid I was of what the coming days would be like, and how I dreaded them. I laid my heart bare to him as I never had before: *I wish you would love me very much for the next few days.*

Arthur responded with a proper note of condolence, but not much else—not the love I had asked for, *begged* for.

After Mama's funeral—only a handful of people attended; my father was not among them—I dragged myself back to New York to finish out my required course. Feelings of overwhelming sadness were followed by a long period of emptiness. I continued to meet Arthur for walks in Central Park and coffee at little restaurants, but he might as well not have been there at all, leaving me bleak and alone.

Toward the end of May I had just begun my noon meal in the cafeteria when a student I didn't know approached my table and asked, "Are you Virginia O'Keeffe?" I told her that I was not. "Well," she said, "a new show opened at 291 gallery with drawings by someone named Virginia O'Keeffe, and I thought perhaps it was you."

I was sure that "Virginia O'Keeffe" was me! I'd made it a habit to go to 291 whenever I heard that a new exhibit had opened, but I hadn't heard from Mr. Stieglitz since he'd written to me about the drawings Anita had shown him. I had no idea that he was planning to hang my work, and he had done it without my permission. I leapt up from the table, leaving my meal unfinished. It was quite a long journey from the college at Morningside Heights all the way down to Thirty-First Street, but I was still angry when I reached 291, ready to give Mr. Stieglitz a piece of my mind.

Edward, the elevator operator, recognized me from my former visits. "Mr. Stieglitz is not in today," he informed me in his lilting West Indian accent. "He has jury duty, but I'll take you up anyway. I'm sure he wouldn't mind."

I stepped into the silent room. My drawings hung on the muted green walls. They were beautifully mounted, and filtered light from a skylight lit them perfectly. How elegant those charcoals looked in this setting!

I left, furious at his boldness, his effrontery, yet deeply pleased, too—a curious mixture. The next day I went back, still angry but calmer. Mr. Stieglitz was there. His disheveled hair was longer than I remembered and streaked with gray, his eyebrows even bushier—he was much older than I, but still quite handsome. This was the first time I had actually spoken with him.

"Who gave you permission to hang these drawings?" I demanded.

"No one," he said, unperturbed, as if he didn't need anyone's permission.

"You have to take them down."

"You are mistaken about that," he said calmly.

"Well, I made those drawings," I informed him. "I am Georgia O'Keeffe."

"You have no more right to withhold those pictures than to withdraw a child from the world," said Mr. Stieglitz.

Did he think *he* had the right to make such a pronouncement? "You apparently take me for a fool, Mr. Stieglitz!" I snapped.

"Not a fool, Miss O'Keeffe," he said. "Not at all. But I think you don't understand intellectually what you've done here."

I caught my breath and allowed him to lead me into the back room that served as his office, dingy except for what hung on the walls: a pastel by Arthur Dove and a small blue crayon drawing by John Marin, whose watercolor of the Woolworth Building I so admired. Mr. Stieglitz wanted to talk about my drawings. When I balked at answering his questions, he tried a different approach and invited me to lunch. "It would be so much more pleasant to discuss your work at a quiet restaurant over a nice meal," he said.

We went to a little French café, and after he'd ordered a quiche and salad and wine, he calmly defeated all of my arguments. I found him difficult to resist. I left my drawings at 291.

At the end of May I finished my course at Teachers College and left New York for Charlottesville. The house seemed terribly empty now without Mama. Mr. Bement had once again asked me to teach summer courses at the University of Virginia. I accepted, but I could barely muster the strength to do it. Every morning after teaching my early class I climbed back into bed and stayed there until I had to get up again to teach the next class.

I could not get Mr. Stieglitz out of my mind; he had left a powerful impression. He photographed the nine charcoals he'd hung at 291 and sent them to me—and I was crazy about them, even though I sometimes thought I hated those drawings. And I learned that he'd decided to keep them on display a month longer than he had planned, into July.

I asked him why. "Because, Miss O'Keeffe, your pictures have provoked so much discussion and speculation and argument about what the pictures *mean* that I have no choice."

Art critics were scandalized, saying the drawings were about sex, but women seemed to like them. A lot of people were horrified that a schoolteacher nobody had ever heard of had her work on display in a gallery where Picassos and Cézannes had been shown.

"People are asking, 'Is it really art?'" Mr. Stieglitz explained, obviously enjoying the controversy. "And I think that's a triumph for abstract art."

When I felt strong enough, I painted. I was experimenting with very spare, simple lines, like Japanese calligraphy. First I did them in charcoal, then five or six times in black watercolor, and then—because I really couldn't do without color any longer—in blue. I made a whole series like that. I wasn't doing landscapes or anything representational. Everything I painted was abstract. By the time summer classes ended, I had completed almost fifty drawings and watercolors.

Late in August I went camping with friends in the Blue Ridge Mountains—the mountains where I had tramped with Arthur—and sat in the tent looking out at the deep velvet night. Here, in these mountains, I had first begun to believe that I loved Arthur, and that night, sitting under the stars, I believed I still did. He was affectionate when we'd said goodbye in New York, and his letters were tender and caring, but they were not passionate, and passion was what I wanted from him.

Later I painted the curves of the opening to the tent in black, blue, and light gray watercolor, simple shapes and wavy lines. I titled it *Tent Door at Night*.

I told the man in charge of the art program at the University of Virginia that I would not be coming back to teach summer school the following year. West Texas Normal School had offered me fifty dollars more to teach in their summer program, and I had agreed to do it.

Before I left Charlottesville, my sisters and I went for a walk out into the lush countryside. Claudie, seventeen, had just graduated from the high school where Ida was teaching. I had promised Mama that I would look after my youngest sister. It was the one thing I could do for Mama, and I believed it was the right thing for Claudie.

"I want you to come to Texas with me, Claudie," I said. "You can go to the college and study whatever you want. But it's your choice."

She didn't hesitate. "I want to be with you, Georgie," she said, and flung her arms around me.

"Why don't you come, too, Ida?" I asked. "Maybe we can persuade Auntie as well. The O'Keeffes will take over Texas."

Ida didn't hesitate either. "No. Auntie and I will stay right here. Charlottesville suits me, and Auntie is happy here, too. You may want to come back here someday. You never know."

But I did know, and when I left Charlottesville I felt sure it would be the last time.

PART VI

"Deep reds, delicate pinks,
rich ochers, orangey yellows.
This is something I could paint."

22

Canyon, Texas—Fall 1916

The dusty, windswept town of Canyon, Texas, was a quarter the size of Amarillo, with a population of some twenty-five hundred souls. It took its name from Palo Duro Canyon—Spanish for "hard wood"—a deep gash in the earth, about a dozen miles from town, that you couldn't see until you were at the very edge of it. Long lines of cattle, silhouetted like black lace against the sunset, were driven in from the range to be loaded onto trains. Not much else happened from one day to the next.

There is nothing here, I wrote to Anita, who was still in New York. But I was not complaining. That nothingness appealed to me.

In the middle of this nondescript town was the college, a huge, new, yellow brick building, replacing the old one that had burned down, and the pride of the citizens with its swimming pool and central heating system.

The administration had arranged for me to rent a room in a teacher's house, notable for the hideousness of the wallpaper, pink roses enclosed in dark green squares that covered all four walls. Roses bloomed even in the carpet. I moved out the following morning.

The next place I found was more suitable, but I kept my eye on a house being built for the physics teacher, Mr. Shirley, and his wife. When it was almost finished, I went to see about renting a room from them. I especially liked the attic room with dormer windows and a view of the endless prairie, and it would be big enough for both Claudie and me. Mrs. Shirley, a nervous little woman, was reluctant. They didn't have money to decorate it, she said. I tried to convince her that I didn't object to the absence of curtains and other decorations, because I wanted to fix it up to suit my own taste. I asked if I could paint the woodwork black.

Mrs. Shirley looked at me as if I were completely mad. "*Black?* You want to paint the room black?"

"Just the woodwork. I think the effect would be interesting."

"Yes, I suppose it would," she said, pursing her lips. "I'll speak to Mr. Shirley about it."

I wasn't surprised when Mr. Shirley said no to the black paint, and of course I had no choice but to do as they wished if I wanted the room. But that was not the end of it. Mrs. Shirley was a gossip, and in no time at all it seemed everyone in town had heard what I proposed to do. The story grew from black woodwork to a whole room painted black, even the ceiling, a rumor that earned me the reputation of being eccentric. After the last pieces of white furniture were carried in, I tried to minimize all that prettiness by hanging a long strip of black cloth down the middle of one wall.

Once I was settled at the Shirleys', I sent for Claudie. In October, she stepped off the train, just as wide-eyed as I'd been when I first arrived in the Panhandle. I enrolled her in the college, and we took our meals with Miss Hudspeth, the mathematics teacher, who ran a boarding house.

As long as the weather stayed hot in the Texas Panhandle, I wore my white skirt and white shirtwaists, and when the temperature dropped I switched to black. I must have been the only woman in town who wore black. It wasn't the fashion in Canyon. I certainly hadn't been seen as stylish in South Carolina among all the Southern girls in their pretty pastels and lace and ruffles, but they had been polite enough not to comment. Black hadn't been fashionable in New York either, but no one in a city as cosmopolitan as New York cared enough to comment. The way I wore my hair, pulled straight back, was also not the style, nor were the men's low-heeled shoes. I bought myself a man's hat and wore it almost all the time out of doors, to keep my white Irish skin from scorching.

If people thought I looked odd, I shrugged it off. I dressed only to please myself.

Eventually I became friendly with Leah Harris, a practical, forthright woman my own age who taught home economics. Many of her students took my morning class in clothing design, in which I taught how to make dress patterns and sew French seams, the way I made my own clothes. I rattled them by advocating simplicity and straight lines in place of ruffles and lace. What really floored the girls was my opposition to corsets.

"They're afraid they won't look like women if they follow your advice," Leah reported. "All of us have been brought up since we were twelve or thirteen to believe that a corset is an absolute necessity."

"But a straight line is so much more pleasing," I said. "And it's natural."

"They also worry about wearing black. Only people in mourning wear black."

"Black is so practical," I pointed out. "It's also an aesthetic choice."

I'd been trying to teach my students, both male and female, what I'd learned from Arthur Wesley Dow's theories: that every choice needed to be an aesthetic one—how you comb your hair, which teacup you choose, what you want your clothes to say about you.

"If you want to follow the fashion and look like everyone else, then you make one kind of choice," I told the girls in the design class. "But if your main goal is to please yourself, then you make another kind of choice and go your own way."

Straight lines and a minimum of decoration were my choices. But I knew the girls were startled when I showed them how my clothes were made—a shirtwaist with a plain collar and French seams, a wool skirt lined in patterned silk.

As head of the college art department, I was free to pick the books I wanted and decide how to teach. I taught five classes, including costume design and interior decoration, and I asked Anita Pollitzer to send me photographs of Egyptian art and Greek pottery. On my walks out on the prairie, I found the bleached bones of cattle and brought skulls and ribs into the classroom to show my students the beauty of those shapes. My goal was to teach them how to see. But I also taught them skills such as how to use blocks of wood and other carved surfaces to print on paper and cloth.

Claudie was a dozen years younger than I, but she turned out to be a fine companion. Every Sunday we went exploring. Our favorite place was Palo Duro. We'd get a ride out to the canyon and set up a camp near the rim. You couldn't see the bottom. The narrow paths worn by cattle were so steep that we hung on to tree roots or opposite ends of a stout stick, to keep from pitching over. We loved the challenge. I bought us each a shotgun and some bullets and taught Claudie to shoot—I'd learned how growing up in Sun Prairie. We bagged wild ducks and quail and roasted them over a campfire.

For months I had been drawing in charcoal the shapes I imagined inside my own head, but when I discovered the canyon and layer upon layer of rock, deep reds and delicate pinks, rich ochers and orangey yellows, I told Claudie, "This is something I could paint," and I did.

It wasn't only the canyon that was influencing my work—it was the great bowl of the sky with the moon rising and the zigzags of lightning and the storms I could see coming for a week before they arrived. I was also affected by what I could hear—mostly silence, but also the sharp calls of birds, the relentless scrape of the wind that rubbed my nerves raw, and the mournful lowing of cows that had been separated from their calves in the holding pens. It went on hour after hour, and it was especially haunting at night, sad enough to break my heart.

I showed one of my canyon paintings to Mrs. Shirley. "I don't understand this at all," she said, her brow furrowed. "I don't even know top from bottom. Seems to me you could hang it upside down and it wouldn't make one bit of difference."

"It isn't supposed to show what the canyon looks like," I said. "It shows how I feel about what I saw."

Mrs. Shirley let out a bark of laughter. "Must have had a stomachache when you painted it!"

Even the mathematics teacher, Miss Hudspeth, who claimed to be deeply interested in art and beauty in all of its forms, failed entirely to grasp what I intended. When I showed her my painting of a blazing sunset, she concluded that it was a watermelon and laughed heartily when I explained it.

At a party at the college president's house I met a local lawyer, Joe Sommer. Whenever I turned around, Joe seemed to be hovering there. Before I left the party, he asked if he could call on me. He hadn't made much of an impression, and I hesitated, until I saw his hangdog look and relented. After Joe's first visit, during which I had served him tea and we had discussed the election of President Wilson for a second term, Mrs. Shirley found out that I had entertained a gentleman in my room. The college had a rule against a student receiving male visitors in her private room, and Mrs. Shirley insisted that the rule applied to me as well.

There were plenty of rules in Canyon, Texas, both written and unwritten, and I was expected to observe them to the letter. Joe proposed that next time we take a moonlight drive in his auto. But according to the student handbook, there was a rule against that, too: *Auto rides at night are an unpardonable impropriety.* We decided to ignore that rule, but after I burst out laughing when he attempted to put his arm around me, Joe abandoned the courtship, if that was what it was, and I was not disappointed.

I continued to upset the good citizens of Canyon. For some reason, faculty members weren't supposed to socialize with students. I often spent time with my students, because I believed that some of the best teaching happened when we were out of the classroom and the art studio, just talking informally. One particularly hot day in Indian summer, I had been sitting on the front steps of the Shirleys' house, chatting with a group, and without giving it much thought I kicked off my shoes and peeled off my stockings, exposing my naked feet for all the world to see, and apparently to be shocked by. It became the talk of the town.

I thought often of Arthur, wishing he were there with me. After I'd finished teaching the summer course in Virginia and gone on a camping trip, I'd hoped he would come with me, but he had not. Then I allowed myself to hope that he would come to visit me in Texas, perhaps to stay for a while. *Arthur, it's great out here, it's like another world,* I wrote. I described the wind and the lowing cattle and the gorgeous colors of Palo Duro, but I didn't tell him about the paintings I was doing of the canyon and the sunsets, and only briefly mentioned the classes I was teaching. Although he replied to my letters, he never seemed much interested in my work. His interests were entirely academic.

In spite of his reticence, I still poured out my feelings in my letters, making no secret of my longing for him and wanting to tell him that I loved him. *Love is great to give,* I wrote. *You may give as little in return as you want to—or none at all.*

As much as I wished for a reply, there was none—and so I had my answer. Yet I clung stubbornly to the belief that I loved him and hoped, perhaps foolishly, that he would love me back.

At the same time, I was receiving a flood of letters—wonderful, amazing letters, sometimes four or five a week—from Mr. Stieglitz. I'd been sending him my drawings and watercolors, and he responded to them so passionately that I found it a little unsettling. I learned that he had hung some of them in a show with the work of artists like John Marin.

Every time I sent pictures to Mr. Stieglitz and read one of his letters, I felt as though I was betraying Arthur. How could I feel that way about one man and at the same time be drawn so strongly toward another?

My feelings frightened me. I didn't know what to do, and so for a long time I did nothing.

Late in the winter Mr. Stieglitz wrote that he was arranging a solo exhibition of my paintings of Palo Duro and the blue watercolors, along with a couple of oils and some charcoal drawings—one of a train as it rounded a curve, a great cloud of smoke billowing from the tiny locomotive. It was a train I saw every day from my classroom window. I sent Mr. Stieglitz the plaster figure of the grieving woman, the piece I'd done immediately after my mother's death—the only sculpture I'd ever done—and he promised to put that in the show, too. This would be the first solo exhibition of my work, and I was giddy with excitement.

The show opened on the third of April. Three days later, on April sixth, the United States declared war on Germany. To make the world safe for democracy, President Wilson said.

Suddenly the war was all anyone in Canyon was talking about. And it was what Mr. Stieglitz wrote about in his letters. Although he was born in the United States, his parents had emigrated from Germany, and he had spent most of his early years there as a student. He loved

Germany, he said, but he was also a loyal American. The mood of his letters became dark and gloomy. He no longer wanted to take photographs.

Mine would be the last exhibition at 291, he said. He was closing the gallery. The owner of the old mansion had plans to tear it down. He sounded so dispirited, so bleak, that I yearned to go to New York—to see my work displayed and to see *him*. It was a completely impractical idea—my classes did not end until the final day of the exhibit, and I would begin teaching summer classes three weeks later.

I asked Claudie her opinion. "The trip would cost two hundred dollars, and that's exactly the amount I have in the bank. What would you do?"

"If I felt like you, I'd go," she said.

But it was impossible. I was reconciled to that, and I tried to put thoughts of it out of my mind.

As the spring wore on, I taught my classes and flouted the rules of both college and landlord by going for long, unchaperoned walks—and drives, too—with a student named Ted Reid, a popular football player and the president of the drama club. I'd gotten to know him when we were building sets for a student play. Ted was a tall, lanky Texan with intense blue eyes and a disarming grin who'd grown up herding cattle. We were drawn together by our love for the landscape. As often as we could make time for it, we took long walks together, away from the town, the school, the prying eyes and gossips.

Although nearly ten years younger than I, Ted claimed he was in love with me. "Come away with me, Georgie!" he begged. "You must!"

Here was a man who was not afraid of his own feelings and not afraid to tell me how he felt. This was so unlike Arthur, who either could not or would not tell me he loved me, that I actually considered going away with Ted as soon as the term ended in June. But the more I pondered it, the more foolish it seemed, and when Ted pressed the issue I made a sensible decision and told him that I could not.

But two days after my last class, I made an impulsive decision—not a sensible one. I went to the home of the local bank manager on a Sunday afternoon, convinced him to open for me, and withdrew the two hundred dollars.

"I'm going," I told Claudie, and on Monday morning I boarded the train for New York.

23

New York—Summer 1917

I WENT STRAIGHT TO 291 FROM THE TRAIN STATION. Edward greeted me warmly, smiling as he opened the gate on the top floor. When I stepped out of the elevator, I saw that my work had been taken down. The walls were bare. Several people stood in the otherwise empty room, and Mr. Stieglitz, his back to me, was talking animatedly. He broke off in midsentence and turned.

"Mr. Stieglitz," I said.

"Miss O'Keeffe."

Time seemed to stop, both of us unable to say another word.

Mr. Stieglitz recovered first. "You must see your pictures," he said. "I'll hang them again."

His companions murmured goodbyes and left. Mr. Stieglitz opened the boxes stacked in a corner, unpacked the pictures and began to arrange them on the walls. "I want you to see them exactly as they were for the exhibit."

One of the paintings had been sold, the charcoal of the locomotive and the billowing cloud of smoke. "Two hundred dollars," Mr. Stieglitz said. "A gift for the collector's wife."

My first sale! Two hundred dollars! I wanted to put my arms around him, embrace him, even kiss him, but I stopped myself. He was a married man, much older than I, and it would not have been the right thing. "Thank you," I said, all I could think to say.

"It is only the beginning, Miss O'Keeffe."

When all of the pictures had been hung, Mr. Stieglitz set up his tripod and camera and insisted that I pose in front of my work. I did as he asked. After he had taken a half dozen photographs, he put away the camera. "Now we will go and have something to eat, and you will tell me everything," he said.

We talked and talked. So much to say, but we understood each other so well that much could be left unsaid. The connection between us was deep and strong and irresistible. Hours must have passed, but whether it was noon or night, I had no idea.

I'd wired my old friend Dorothy True when I left Canyon, and she invited me to stay with her in her tiny studio. I visited as many people as I could. Dear old fuddy-duddy Alon Bement had married an actress and seemed blissfully happy. Charles Martin, who had allowed Anita and Dorothy and me to arrange our own still lifes behind a curtain in his drawing class, confessed that he was disheartened and felt that the critics misunderstood his work.

I wanted to see Arthur. He had no idea I was coming—I told him I'd had no idea either, until I actually went—and he seemed glad enough to see me again. As I expected, he had a great deal to say about the war that America was now part of, but he had not gone to see the exhibit of my work at 291. The two evenings we spent together were unsatisfactory for us both. I confided to Dorothy how I felt.

"Oh, Georgie, I've always thought you were a poor match. Arthur is good-looking and intelligent, but he's terribly straight and prim and proper, and you don't give a fig what others think!"

I laughed, but of course Dorothy was right. Maybe Arthur and I had never had much in common.

Since the declaration of war on Germany, the pulse of New York was beating even faster. There were patriotic rallies and speeches and cheering crowds everywhere. A glaring Uncle Sam pointed a fierce finger from posters plastered on walls and fences and declared *I Want YOU for U.S. Army.* The wild enthusiasm for the war made me uneasy. We'd elected a president who promised peace, and the mood had now swung dramatically in the opposite direction. I'd learned from Ida that Alexius had gone to the officers' training camp in Fort Sheridan, Illinois, and was awaiting orders to be shipped out to France.

Mr. Stieglitz arranged a Decoration Day outing to Coney Island with two of his friends—an inventor named Henry Gaisman, who had developed a camera that allowed the photographer to make notes on the negative, and a *very* handsome young photographer, Paul Strand. We strolled the boardwalk, taking in the sights—all those people in black bathing suits, packed tight as grains of sand on the beach, and the midway jangling with player pianos and penny arcades and barkers luring customers to try the ring toss or the high striker to "win a Kewpie doll for the little lady!" All three of my companions were opposed to America's entry into the war, but there was no getting away from it. When we bought franks with sauerkraut from a cart, the owner complained bitterly that nobody wanted to eat German food and he would have to sell his cart.

Mr. Stieglitz thought Paul Strand was enormously talented, and after our Coney Island excursion he showed me some of Paul's photographs. Paul was interested in shapes and unexpected angles, and he'd taken extraordinary pictures of ordinary objects viewed from an unusual perspective—stacks of bowls, for instance, and chair rungs and things I'd never imagined could be the subject of such beautiful pictures. The last edition of Mr. Stieglitz's publication *291* was devoted entirely to Paul's work.

But there was more to it than just the striking pictures. I could not stop thinking about Paul. I saw that look in his eyes, and I knew what it meant. I had fallen for him almost instantly, and it was clear that he had fallen for me just as fast. The physical attraction was powerful—I wanted to touch him, to kiss him hard, to tell him exactly how I felt. But I did not. My head and my heart were roiling with confusing feelings, desire pulling me in first one direction and then another—to Ted Reid in Texas, who wanted me to go away with him (and I had nearly agreed!); to Arthur, who, for reasons that I could not explain, kept a strong hold on my emotions; to Mr. Stieglitz, who understood more than anyone what I was trying to accomplish with my art; and now to this handsome, charming, talented photographer, Paul Strand! It was exhilarating and exciting, having these four men drawn to me—and my being drawn, in different ways and for different reasons, to each of them.

After ten days in New York—I barely slept at all—I said goodbye to Paul and to Mr. Stieglitz. There was no further conversation with Arthur. I boarded the westbound train, grateful for the long journey across the country to give me time to refocus my thoughts where they belonged—on my art.

Before I left New York, I wired Alexius, who was stationed at Fort Sheridan, asking if he could meet my train in Chicago during the one-hour layover.

It was a shock to see him in his uniform, standing on the station platform, tall and fine-looking and beaming proudly. We found a lunchroom in Union Station and ordered pie and coffee. I could not get over how much he'd changed since I had last seen him, as he'd been leaving for Wisconsin to study engineering and I'd been leaving to teach in Amarillo. As a boy he had been lighthearted and fun-loving. He always seemed like a large wind when he entered the house, but now he was sober and serious as he talked about the war, and how important it was to fight it. We hardly knew each other.

"It's my duty to serve my country," Alexius said earnestly. "I hope to be among the first to sail for France, probably within a month."

"Alexius—" I began, but I could not continue.

"Georgie, I don't expect to come back. I'm prepared to die." He reached across the table, and I gripped his hand.

I stared at him with a lump in my throat that I could not swallow. I heard my train being announced; I let go of his hand and stood up to leave. He hugged me hard, and I rushed away with my eyes filled with tears.

As the train rumbled across the plains, I had another day and a night to think about this war. I had never been much interested in politics, but it was impossible—and immoral, I now saw—to ignore what was happening. I already knew where Anita Pollitzer stood on the subject: in her long letters she had written that she was a committed pacifist and was working hard for women's suffrage. *Once women have the right to vote,* she said, *they will also be opposed to war.*

Mr. Stieglitz had argued that the main reason for declaring war on Germany had less to do with saving democracy than with reaping big profits for big business. It was hard for him to see Germany headed in such a wrong direction. Paul Strand was also philosophically opposed to the war and undecided about whether to enlist.

After spending that hour with Alexius—so patriotic, so sure it was the right thing to do—I could see both sides. I thought it was necessary to choose one side or the other, but I wavered, unable to make up my mind as to where I stood. I agreed, intellectually, that fighting the aggressors was a necessity, but I couldn't square that need with basic Christian beliefs.

Back in Canyon, I saw no indecision or wavering: war fever had infected Texas. *Food will win the war*, President Wilson told the country, and to show their patriotism Texans planted war gardens and observed Meatless Mondays and Wheatless Wednesdays. As I understood it, we were to conserve food on the home front so that farmers could send more to the troops and our hungry allies overseas. It wasn't easy to grow anything in the Panhandle—this was ranching country, not farmland—but my friend Leah Harris, who taught home economics at the college, organized classes for housewives, to teach them how to can the beans and okra they'd grown in their war gardens. "If they don't do it right, they'll poison their whole family," she said.

The Texas heat was exhausting, but I taught my summer courses and continued working in watercolor, and in spite of everything I was more productive than I'd ever been. At the end of the summer I mailed off a bundle of my new paintings to Mr. Stieglitz. There were quite a lot of them, and I was sure they were the best work I had ever done. Even though 291 no longer existed and my paintings would not be shown, I needed his response to my work. And he gave it freely, writing to me almost daily. Those letters were a lifeline, my connection to the art world in New York.

Claudie had finished her first year at the college and was mad to get out of Canyon before she started the fall term. It was her idea to take a trip to the Rocky Mountains in Colorado, and I agreed. Just before we left, we learned that heavy rains had caused flooding—either there was not enough rain in the Southwest or there was too much—and railroad bridges had been washed out between Amarillo and Denver. We decided to go around the flooding, taking a train west to Albuquerque. Then we made our way north through New Mexico and Colorado, riding over rutted roads, sleeping in log cabins, tramping for miles every day. I painted watercolors of the snowcapped Sangre de Cristo Mountains and deep pine forests and a church bell in a small Colorado town.

On the way south again, we stopped in the quaint village of Santa Fe, with its fascinating mix of eccentric artists in cafés and Indians and local farmers and ranchers in the dusty streets. I fell in love with the houses built of adobe bricks that had been made of mud and straw and dried in the sun. It felt as strange and mysterious as a foreign country. We were there for only a few days, but that was long enough for the clear light and the landscape to leave their mark on me.

"I'm coming back here someday," I told Claudie as our train rumbled eastward toward the Panhandle. "I don't know when, but I know in my bones that I will."

24

Canyon, Texas—Fall 1917

THE JOB WAITED FOR ME IN CANYON WHEN
Claudie and I got back, but I felt I no longer belonged
there. Suddenly, Texas was the last place I wanted to be.
I had painted through the spring and summer, and I knew
that my work was better—bolder, more abstract—than
anything I'd done before. But now I felt off-center, mixed
up. For the three months of the fall I did no painting—the
longest time I had not worked in three or four years.

I'd come back to a pile of letters from Paul Strand.
He and I were writing often, and I confided to him how
I felt—unbalanced, unable to get my feet on the ground.
I told Paul, *I'm in the middle of a bad dream. There's
nobody I can talk to.*

It was not strictly true that I had no one to talk to.
There was Claudie, starting her second year in college,

but she seemed as caught up as everyone else in war fever. And Ted Reid was there, in his senior year, and although we no longer worked together on stage sets for the drama club, I saw him nearly every day. He claimed that he wanted to marry me. I laughed and told him it was impossible, but sometimes I did wonder what that might be like, living with somebody. He kept insisting, but I kept saying no.

Some of our boys from the college were enlisting. The administration promised students that if they weren't already called up by the draft—it had been instituted in May—they could skip the last months of the school year and still graduate.

I advised Ted and my other students to do just the opposite. "Finish out the school year and then enlist. The war will still be going on then."

I worried that they didn't know what they were getting into, and I suggested that the college offer a course on the political causes of the war, so that young men would understand why they were risking their lives. The boys in Canyon seemed to have romantic notions of war, notions uninformed by reports of mustard gas and trenches and bombs and landmines. Alexius had understood what it would be like—he knew that he might die—but he had wished to go, and he had gotten his wish. It sickened me to think of it, my brother in France.

The months of fall dragged by. The enthusiasm of the year before had evaporated. I couldn't paint, and I could barely find the energy to teach my classes. In December it got worse: Claudie left to do her required student teaching in the tiny town of Spur, one hundred fifty miles from Canyon over rough dirt roads. I missed her steady companionship more than I had imagined.

In the months since America had entered the war, hatred of all things German had been growing throughout Texas. Amarillo canceled a concert that included a Beethoven symphony. Professors were not allowed to assign Goethe's poetry or a Mozart sonata. Anyone with a German-sounding name was suspect, and there were plenty of them in towns like Boerne, New Braunfels, and Muenster, where hundreds of Germans had settled long before anyone in Canyon was born. There were stories of beatings and violence against the descendants of those early immigrants, and that disgusted me.

When I saw the display of Christmas cards with ugly, anti-German messages, I confronted the shopkeeper. "Those are such anti-Christian sentiments," I said. "Whatever happened to 'Peace on Earth'?"

The shopkeeper grew agitated. "Lady, I've heard about you," he sputtered. "I know all about your kind— sympathizing with the enemy! Telling our boys not to join up! Germany should be wiped off the face of the earth, and all those damned Germans with it!"

He wasn't just sputtering, he was roaring, and I left the shop. He kept selling those awful cards, and the pious souls who went to church every Sunday morning probably kept buying them. After that encounter, everyone in town knew that the art teacher was no patriot and might even be subversive. An editorial in the local newspaper reminded the people of Canyon that the Espionage Act, passed by Congress in June, made it a federal offense to be critical of the war.

I tried to ignore the ill feelings boiling up around me, but I didn't fit in, and we—my supporters as well as my enemies—all knew it.

By the beginning of 1918 I felt entirely depleted, barely able to get to my classes. The temperature in the Panhandle dropped below zero. A relentless wind tore through my clothes. Thanks to the war, there was a shortage of coal, and the college buildings were like ice-boxes. I stuffed newspaper in the front of my shirtwaist to block the wind.

Ted Reid, now halfway through his senior year, was the one bright spot in those dark days. He borrowed his older brother's auto, and we went on long drives together. Ted had matured in the past year, grown more serious, more focused. We still shared our love of the land, the wide-open spaces, but he no longer tried to convince me to go away with him.

One night when we were taking a walk—it was bitterly cold, but there was a beautiful moon—Ted told me the news: he and two other boys had signed up with the Air Service Signal Corps. He would not wait to get his degree before he left.

"I want to learn to fly," he told me. "I think this war is going to be fought in the air."

"You're making a mistake," I said, but there was no point in arguing with him. The deed was done.

Ted kissed me passionately when we got back to the Shirleys', and we said good night.

Over the next few days I heard nothing from him, which was unusual. I sent him a note, but he did not reply. Was he upset by what I'd said? There had been no sign of that; he'd kissed me as fervently as ever. I tried again—a message to his home—but again there was no reply. Finally I swallowed my pride and knocked on his door. No one answered, although I was sure I'd seen a curtain move a little, as though someone had peeked out.

It was not just Ted who vanished; it seemed that the entire community was no longer speaking to me. Patriotism had been at a fever pitch for months, and in the minds of many I was a traitor for advising Ted and other boys not to enlist before they had finished their education. It was from one of those boys—Johnny Miller—that I finally learned, several months later, what had happened.

Ted and I had been seen alone together, Johnny said, and although our behavior in public was proper, I was a teacher and Ted was a student, and faculty members were not permitted to socialize with their students—I'd been chastised for that the previous year. Even worse was that I was so much older: I had observed my thirtieth birthday in November, and Ted was only twenty-one. A delegation of faculty ladies had decided that I was an immoral woman, and they had taken it upon themselves to call on Ted and inform him that if he continued to see Miss O'Keeffe, he would not receive a diploma or a degree. And so Ted had dropped out of my life—to protect me, Johnny said.

I was shocked, nearly speechless. "But why didn't Ted tell me they made that threat?"

"Because he knew it would rile you," Johnny said. "He was afraid you'd give the ladies a piece of your mind, and probably get yourself thrown out of your job. And we had a pretty good idea they were mad at you for the other reason."

"The 'other reason'?"

"That you advised us not to run off and join up right away but to wait until the end of the term."

I was so angry and hurt and frustrated that I sat down and cried. Poor Johnny was so embarrassed that he probably wished he'd not only kept his mouth shut but avoided me altogether, like everyone else.

I fell ill with a throat infection, and the bitter weather and my feelings of isolation made it worse. Too sick to teach, I had to cancel my classes. When three weeks passed and my health hadn't improved, I asked the college to grant me a leave of absence and hire a replacement until I recovered. I had not felt so weak since the time I had nearly died from typhoid fever.

I described my misery in letters to Mr. Stieglitz and also to Paul, who sent me packet after packet of his photographs. I was strongly drawn to his art, so bold and original, with his use of geometric shapes and patterns to create abstract images. And the physical attraction I had felt when I met him in New York was still strong.

Mr. Stieglitz wrote nearly every day. Anxious in the beginning and then growing almost desperate, he ordered me to come to New York at once. He would see that I got proper care, which he was sure I would not receive in Texas.

I could see that he was deeply worried about me, and I appreciated his concern, but I had no thought of following his orders and going to New York. Being too ill to travel so far was only part of my hesitation. I knew Mr. Stieglitz well through our letters—we understood each other, we had the same vocabulary—but I recognized that these things were not the same as knowing someone in person and actually *talking*.

There were other factors, too. Mr. Stieglitz was old enough to be my father. And he was married.

I had been able to resist Mr. Stieglitz's entreaties, but then a letter came from his niece, Elizabeth, offering me the use of her New York studio, and I found myself considering the offer seriously. My life in Canyon had become almost unbearable. Unable to sleep one night, I climbed out of bed and wrote to Elizabeth. If she were in my shoes, I asked, would she leave these narrow-minded people, or would she stay and fight? She wrote back that of course it had to be my decision.

At the same time that Mr. Stieglitz was fretting about me, Paul was fretting about Mr. Stieglitz. *Our dear friend has become deeply depressed since the closing of 291,* Paul wrote. *It would be the best thing in the world for both of you if you came to New York.*

Still, I was unable to make any sort of decision. I couldn't teach, I couldn't paint, I couldn't think straight.

Help came from another, unexpected source: Leah Harris. One of my few close friends in Canyon, Leah had been diagnosed with consumption. She had resigned her position and gone home to Waring, Texas, not far from San Antonio, to rest and recover. When I wrote to her in a very dark mood, explaining that I had been ill and was having a devil of a time recovering, she responded immediately.

Why not come down to Waring and pay me a visit? I'm rattling around here alone at our old family farm. My brother, John, stops by every day to take care of the practical things. The weather is lovely, a sort of perpetual spring. The roses bloom all winter long, and the birds show up and wait expectantly for me to bring them a snack. Our pecan trees produced a bumper crop last fall, and I'm still shelling them. You can help! Your company would do me a world of good, and I'm sure your health will return speedily after a few weeks in the South Texas sun.

This was, I thought, exactly what I needed—to get away from Canyon and all the patriotic whooping and shouting. I wrote to Mr. Stieglitz, and also to Paul Strand, to let them know what I was going to do.

25

Waring, Texas—Winter 1918

I LEFT CANYON IN THE MIDDLE OF FEBRUARY ON A southbound train. With each mile I sensed the air growing softer, the temperature warmer, the scenery gentler. The browns and tans of the Panhandle landscape were replaced by greens. My eyes needed the change. So did my body, away from the tensions that had been tearing me apart.

Leah and her brother met me at the Waring depot in an old buckboard drawn by a horse named Molly, and off we trotted to the Harris family farm near the Guadalupe River.

The farmhouse was a plain sort of place—no wallpaper infested with pink roses, or dainty white furniture, or crocheted doilies. Unbleached muslin curtains hung at the windows. The floors were scrubbed pine with

Mexican rugs. The only decoration in my bedroom at the back of the house, next to Leah's, was a vase of wildflowers beside the narrow bed. Like a nun's cell, I thought, and much to my liking.

We sat on the front porch wrapped in quilts and rocked as the sun went down. When the air chilled, we went inside, started a little fire in the stove, and ate steaming bowls of vegetable soup. We didn't talk about the war. In fact, we didn't talk much about anything. It was so peaceful, not at all the way it had been in Canyon.

"I've been feeling so much better since I've come back here," Leah said. "And the doctor says my lungs are healing. I know you're going to feel better soon, too."

After a few days, once I'd rested up from the train ride, we began taking short walks along the river, stopping at a farm to buy fresh eggs. Leah's kitchen shelves were filled with colorful glass jars of luscious peaches and plums and tomatoes that she'd put up. We'd choose a couple of jars and fix a meal out of whatever was in them.

Reminders of the war were unavoidable. I wanted to forget about it, but even in tiny, remote Waring the posters had appeared with Uncle Sam's finger pointing at us. I was strong enough then to put what I was feeling on paper. I painted a watercolor of the flag—no stars or stripes, just a blood-red flag bleeding across a stormy, bruise-colored sky. It showed exactly how fearful I felt.

Anita Pollitzer, who had given up the idea of teaching and thrown herself into suffragist causes, wrote to me regularly. I waited anxiously for letters from Alexius, stationed somewhere in France, and worried when none came. There were frequent letters from Paul Strand, and at least one each day from Mr. Stieglitz. Nearly every morning Leah and I walked into town to pick up our mail at the general store, and Leah joked that I must single-handedly keep the U.S. Post Office in business.

Slowly my strength returned, although there were still days when I felt depleted, and I was often troubled by stomach pains. Once a week Leah's physician, Dr. Madison, drove out from Waring to examine Leah, to be sure that her early symptoms of consumption had not worsened. At the same time he also checked on me, prescribing a tonic that he believed would build my strength.

On a visit to the farm early in April, Dr. Madison pronounced that we were both doing nicely, but he warned us about the worrisome spread of a highly contagious disease he called "Spanish influenza." He'd heard about it at a meeting at a hospital in San Antonio. It was first diagnosed at an army base in Kansas, he said, and it was like nothing they'd seen before. Those who caught it became violently ill almost at once. "The first symptoms are extreme fatigue, fever, and headache," he told us, "and within hours, the victims start turning blue, and cough so hard that they tear the muscles in their stomach."

"What can be done?" Leah asked, alarmed.

"Nothing, once someone has contracted it," Dr. Madison said grimly. "Death comes quickly with this terrible disease. Our main worry now is how to keep it from spreading. My advice to you two ladies is to avoid going out in public."

The doctor put away his stethoscope and left us staring at each other uncomfortably.

"Well," I said with false cheer, "since we seldom go out in public in any case, we should be just fine."

Waring was a tiny community, with a population of about two hundred fifty souls, a tenth the size of Canyon, but it supported a corn and grist mill and a cotton gin, a stone quarry and a lumberyard, a boarding house called Oak Ranch that catered to consumptives, and a general store that also acted as a post office, pharmacy, and gathering place for local farmers. On our last trip to town I had bought a few yards of linen, some spools of thread, and a packet of needles so that I could stitch some new underthings for myself and for Leah, too. But now we felt that we had to avoid going there. Leah's brother came by the farm once a day to make sure we had whatever we needed. He brought our mail and kept us informed of the news from what we'd come to think of as "the outside world."

Although I wasn't completely over the illness that had brought me low in January, I was ready to start painting again. I'd felt compelled to do the flag painting as a statement of my fears about the war. Now I wanted to do something else. Because Leah and I had become quite comfortable around each other, I suggested that she pose for me.

"Of course, I will, Georgia!" she said. "What would you like me to wear?"

I decided to come right out with it. "I want to do some nude paintings in watercolor."

Her startled look bordered on shock. "Of me? Without clothes?" Her face pinked up, and she seemed flustered.

"Nudes are usually not wearing clothes."

"I'm not sure I can do that, Georgia. I think I'd be too embarrassed."

"I understand. A dozen years ago, in my first life drawing class, I was taken aback when the model turned out to be a muscular young man with only a scrap of cloth concealing his privates. He wasn't in the least uncomfortable being nearly naked in front of a class of young ladies; we were the ones who were uncomfortable. But we got over it. I promise that it will be an abstract rendering. No one will know it's you."

Leah hesitated for less than a minute. "All right then," she said. "Let's get on with it."

Lest she change her mind, I grabbed my watercolor box and brushes and paper. Leah undressed, and I sketched the basic outline of her body as she sat on a chair, one leg crossed over the other, one arm raised.

The sound of my voice kept her relaxed and compliant, and so I talked as I worked, telling her the story of the first time I met Mr. Stieglitz at his show of Rodin sketches. "I thought they were just scribbles. A lot of people agreed and said they were some kind of fraud being foisted on the public."

"What did you say?" Leah asked.

"I was too embarrassed to say a word," I admitted. "I didn't have the good sense to appreciate them at the time."

"You've made me blue," she said when I showed her the finished painting. "Except for that blotch of red on my shoulder. Is that supposed to be blood?"

"No. I just wanted some red there."

"What you said is true. No one would ever know it's me."

I did several more of her, rolled them up, and gave them to John to mail to Mr. Stieglitz the next time he went by the general store.

We passed the weeks of spring in enforced solitude because of the wildfire spread of the Spanish flu. We went for much longer walks along the river, and I painted and spent hours every day writing letters to Anita and Paul and Mr. Stieglitz and my sisters, and to Alexius, hoping they would reach him in France. I did not write to Francis, since my older brother and I no longer saw eye to eye on much of anything, or to Papa, who never wrote back.

My health improved, although there were occasional setbacks, but I was skeptical of what Dr. Madison had told us—that Leah's "tubercular condition," as he called it, was benign and that there was practically no chance of me catching it from her. He assured us both that she was getting better and that we shouldn't worry.

I was grateful to have a place to stay, and I liked Leah, but she had become clingy. She refused to go on walks alone and insisted that I go with her. When I was painting and the light seemed perfect and I wanted to keep on, she fretted over how late it was getting and said it was time to stop and eat. She was quite strict in her belief that we should eat our evening meal together at precisely the same time every day. I was growing restless.

It was early May, and I had been there for four months. On Dr. Madison's next visit, after he'd listened to my chest and assured me that my lungs were clear, I made an excuse to follow him outside. "Doctor, I want to visit San Antonio for a few days—just for a change, some fresh ideas for my work. Can you suggest a place I might stay, something inexpensive?"

He thought for a moment. "My sister Martha lives in San Antonio. I know she'd be pleased to have you as a guest. I'm going there tomorrow. When shall I tell her you'll arrive?"

"The day after tomorrow," I said, and prepared to break the news to Leah.

After we'd finished breakfast the next day, I said, rather abruptly, "I'm taking the train to San Antonio tomorrow. I want to do some painting there, before I go back to Canyon to teach the summer courses, and I'd best start now."

This was not the whole truth. I had not yet made up my mind to return to Canyon, and I was not even sure I'd be welcome there. But I had very little money, and I knew that I had to earn some, somehow.

Leah reacted with dismay. "You're going to San Antonio? Are you strong enough? You've lost so much weight, and you're so pale, Georgia!"

"I'm fine," I said. "Stop worrying about me."

I packed a few things, promising to be back in a week or two. Leah's brother drove me to the depot, where I caught the local train for the half-hour ride to San Antonio. I was relieved to get away.

26

San Antonio, Texas—Spring 1918

MISS MURIEL MADISON HAD A ROOM READY FOR me, in the back of a handsome old house on a quiet street. I immediately wrote to Paul and to Mr. Stieglitz, telling them that I had "escaped," and to send letters in care of Miss Madison.

I was waiting for a reply from my two faithful correspondents when a boy in a Western Union uniform arrived at Miss Madison's on a bicycle with a telegram:

STRAND ON TRAIN ARRIVE SAN ANTONIO MAY 12 HOTEL LANIER STOP STIEGLITZ

Paul was on his way!

My hostess had warned me not to go out walking around the city alone. Fort Sam Houston and Camp Bullis were nearby, and recruits being trained at the army base thronged the streets of downtown San Antonio. I ignored her warnings—I had spent too much time in cities like Chicago and New York to be put off by a group of rowdy young soldiers having as much fun as they could before being shipped off to fight a war. But it would be nice to have a man around, just in case.

The twelfth of May was a Sunday, and the streets of San Antonio were silent except for the sound of church bells. The morning was fresh and cool when I set out. I found the Hotel Lanier near a park close by the Alamo Mission. The pomegranate trees were covered in bright orangey-red blossoms. The desk clerk at the Lanier told me the train was due in at half past eleven. I left a note for Paul, telling him I would meet him by the bandstand in the park at one o'clock. That would give him time to rest a little after the long journey.

I found Paul waiting for me when I returned. He didn't kiss me, as I expected he might, but took my hands in both of his and held them while he looked into my eyes. Then, seeming to remember that we were in public, he let go of my hands and took my elbow instead. "You need to eat something," he said. "You're too thin. Come, we'll have lunch somewhere."

We found a little Mexican place by the river, Cafe Del Rio. Paul protested that he knew nothing about Mexican food. "But I do," I teased. "I've been in Texas for quite a while. I'm practically a Texan now."

I ordered enchiladas with fried eggs on top and pinto beans. While we waited for our lunch, we talked. The food came, and still we talked. There was so much to say about our work, the watercolors I'd been doing in the past weeks, the photographs Paul had been taking of New York street life. The waiter brought dessert, then coffee.

Almost a whole afternoon had gone by when I jumped up, grabbing Paul's hand. "Let's go exploring!"

Since my arrival in San Antonio two weeks earlier, I'd walked through the city every day until I was too tired to walk any farther. Now I wanted to show everything to Paul. He let me pull him along, laughing when I stopped to pick a flower from a pomegranate tree and pinned it to my dress. I knew that black showed off the red flower dramatically.

"I've never seen you so enthusiastic about anything!" Paul said.

"It's because I'm so happy to see you."

He hesitated and then plunged ahead. "Stieglitz wants to see you, Georgia."

"And I'd like to talk to him."

"Then perhaps you'll consider coming east?"

"I can't possibly do that. I'll be teaching summer courses at West Texas again this summer."

"Surely you could get out of that if you wanted."

"But I can't. I need the money. I have none, you see. I'm down to my last few dollars. And I'm worried about my sister. Claudie's finishing up her student teaching in some godforsaken little town, and then she'll be back in Canyon. I don't think she fits in very well there, and I should perhaps be there to guide her." I stopped and laughed at what I'd just said. "That's something of a joke, you know. I've never fit in there either, and I'm probably not the one to give her advice."

Later, I asked Paul how long he intended to stay in San Antonio, and he smiled and said, "I have no deadline. None at all."

It was evening when Paul took me to Miss Madison's, and I was so weary that I fell into bed without even bothering to fix myself supper.

For the next few days we went for more walks along the river, always ending back at the same table at the same Mexican restaurant. I introduced Paul to tacos and tamales and bowls of spicy chili.

We discovered a district of handsome old houses built nearly a century earlier by prosperous white merchants, and we explored a sprawling neighborhood where Mexicans who had come across the Rio Grande lived in simple adobe cottages with smoothly rounded corners and sensuous shapes. Donkeys plodded along dusty lanes, and chickens ran around; children played, shouting in Spanish, and women in embroidered shawls and long, bright skirts shopped at an open-air market.

I carried my paint box and brushes and paper with me, found a bench to sit on, and painted what I saw. People gathered around to watch me, their usually animated voices quieted. Paul set up his camera to take pictures—he'd become well known for his candid pictures of individuals caught unaware—but the people in that San Antonio neighborhood apparently didn't like to be photographed, and the streets were suddenly deserted.

One day he borrowed an auto, and we drove to Fredericksburg, a lovely town of old stone houses built by German immigrants nearly seventy-five years earlier. Given the anti-German sentiments I'd witnessed in Canyon, I wondered how the descendants of those long-ago immigrants were faring. Still, the place was appealing. I thought I'd like living there.

Paul moved out of the Hotel Lanier and into a boarding house a few blocks from Miss Madison's. We spent every afternoon and evening together. I painted, and he took pictures, many of them of me. After two weeks of exploring San Antonio with Paul, I left Miss Madison's and returned to Leah's farm. Paul began spending time with us in Waring and photographing Leah, too. She was not beautiful, but he'd come to appreciate the elegance of her long, slender body, pale skin, and raven-black hair.

Paul and I talked about everything—what he was trying to accomplish with his photographs and I with my paintings—but our conversations almost always turned back to Mr. Stieglitz.

"He's a deeply unhappy man," Paul said.

"I thought so," I agreed. "But I have no idea why he's so unhappy."

"He has been trapped in a loveless marriage for many years."

I knew that Mr. Stieglitz was married, but in all the time we'd spent together, and in all his letters, he'd never once mentioned his wife. I didn't even know her name.

"I've met her just once," Paul went on. "She's from a very wealthy family who owned a brewery. Her brother was a partner in Stieglitz's early business ventures, and she was very pretty and good company and it was expected that they would marry. There's one daughter, Kitty, who's off in college now. He's confided to me that they have absolutely nothing in common and that the marriage was a total failure from the beginning."

"But they've stayed married," I said.

"They have, but they no longer live together. He says he had to leave to preserve his sanity. The situation has been extremely depressing for him."

That was the only time we spoke of Mr. Stieglitz's marriage.

Leah and Paul and I had been getting along famously, but then the situation in Waring began to fray.

A farmer named Zeller who lived up the road had been giving Leah difficulties. One night soon after I'd arrived in January, someone had crept around the house with a lantern, shining a light into our bedrooms. Leah grabbed a pistol that she kept handy and yelled, "I've got a gun!" The man ran away.

Leah was sure it was Zeller, and she asked Paul to go and talk to him and make him promise to leave her alone.

"But this is none of my affair!" Paul said. "It's something that ought to be handled by a lawman. Isn't there a sheriff around here to take care of it? Or an order from a judge that he must stay away?"

"It isn't done that way in Texas," Leah insisted. "Here we take care of things like this in person. Mr. Zeller frightens me!"

I was annoyed at Leah for expecting Paul to solve her problem—just as she often seemed to be expecting *me* to solve her problems. But I did think it was ungentlemanly of Paul not to go to Zeller and settle the matter. That would have taken some pressure off me as well.

It turned into a comic opera: Paul finally went to see Zeller and convinced him to come and apologize. When Zeller did show up, Leah and I had gone for a walk. Paul kept him there, but when we didn't come back, Paul finally allowed him to leave if he promised to return. Zeller did return—this time with the sheriff and a warrant for Paul's arrest, charging him with "forced imprisonment." Leah and I arrived in time for her to explain the situation, and the sheriff, who must have struggled not to laugh, got everyone to apologize.

Paul was embarrassed and angry. Nerves were on edge. We were all irritating each other.

Occasionally Paul asked if I'd given any further thought to making a trip to New York. I said I had not, explaining again that I had no money, and that I was expected to teach summer courses in Canyon. Then one of us would change the subject.

Now he brought it up again. "Mr. Stieglitz is worried about you, Georgia. He wants you to come to New York so he can help you. His niece, Elizabeth, has a studio you could use, at least for a while, until you find something else."

"I know. She wrote to me before I left Canyon. It's very kind of her."

"Then why not accept the offer? Stieglitz is determined that you must be persuaded to come."

That was when I finally realized that Paul was there because Mr. Stieglitz had sent him. I had thought he'd come solely because he wanted to see me. But now I understood that he was pushing me away, and pushing me toward Mr. Stieglitz.

I knew it was time for me to leave Waring. Leah was weary of me, and I was of her, but I still could not decide what to do.

"My dear Georgia," Paul said tenderly, reaching for my hand. "You must know that I love you. You are very beautiful, and such a remarkable woman in every way. But you need someone to care for you. You know that, don't you?"

I nodded. "Yes, I do know." I felt drained. The fatigue and weakness had come back.

"Stieglitz has spent hours thinking about how to help you. He believes that you must come to New York."

"But is that what you want, Paul? For me to come to New York?"

He sighed, shaking his head. "Sometimes I don't know what I want. But you must decide what's right for *you*."

What *did* I want? I was strongly attracted to Paul, I was sure he was just as strongly attracted to me, but he was an artist and nearly as poor as I was. I was drawn to Mr. Stieglitz, who was remarkable in his constant and caring support from so far away. But I wondered if being in the same city and seeing so much of each other would destroy the bond that existed between us and had been made stronger through our letters. Maybe it would be better to remain far apart—better for him with a wife and daughter, and better for me as an artist.

Then a wire arrived, delivered by the telegraph operator, who brought it on horseback from the train depot.

GEORGIA YOU MUST COME SOONEST STOP STIEGLITZ

A decision could not be delayed any longer, and I made it.

I showed the wire to Paul. "Tell Mr. Stieglitz I'm coming," I said.

PART VII

"Success doesn't come with painting one picture. It is building step by step, against great odds."

27

New York—Summer 1918

MR. STIEGLITZ WAS WAITING ON THE PLATFORM when the train pulled into Penn Station. Although I'd thought I was better—had nearly recovered, in fact—I was so exhausted, so weak and feverish when we arrived that I could barely stand. Paul embraced Mr. Stieglitz, gave me a quick kiss, and disappeared into the crowd.

My benefactor, my guardian angel, or whatever role it was that Mr. Stieglitz had taken on, helped me to a taxicab and gave the driver the address of his niece's studio. He half carried me up three flights of stairs. One room of the tiny apartment was outfitted as a darkroom; the other, with windows and a skylight, was where I immediately collapsed onto the bed and closed my eyes.

For the next few weeks Mr. Stieglitz fussed over me constantly, nursing me patiently back to health. He came every day, bringing eggs that his friend Arthur Dove had sent from his chicken farm in Connecticut. "I gave Arthur his first show at 291," Mr. Stieglitz told me, carrying a tray with an egg he'd boiled perfectly and toast he'd buttered and kept warm under a napkin. "One of America's first abstract expressionists. You remember the little pastel that hung in my office?"

"I do." And Mr. Bement had shown me reproductions of Dove's work. "Please thank him for the eggs, and for his wonderful work. He and I see things very much the same way."

We talked as much as my strength would allow, continuing the intimate conversation—about art, about life—that we'd been having through our letters for more than a year.

I stopped calling him Mr. Stieglitz. From then on, it was simply Stieglitz; I never called him Alfred. We drew closer and closer, and within a month of my arrival in New York we had become lovers. He set up his camera, and I posed for him whenever he wanted. He moved into the studio with me. I began to paint again.

But the summer was passing, and I was expected back in Canyon at the end of August. Again I had to make a decision: to go or to stay.

Stieglitz asked, "What would you do if you could do absolutely anything you wanted for a year?"

I didn't hesitate. "I'd paint."

"I can make that possible for you," he said.

Stieglitz himself had very little money—his wife was the wealthy one—but he somehow persuaded his brother to lend him a thousand dollars.

"I love you," he told me after he'd made the arrangements. "This is your future as an artist."

He had given me an enormous gift: I would not have to teach. With Stieglitz's encouragement, I abandoned the idea of going back to Texas and resigned my position—probably to the relief of everyone in Canyon.

I wrote to Claudie, explaining that I was staying in New York, with whom, and why. She wrote back that she would stick it out in Canyon for another year, and then she planned to enroll at Columbia Teachers College and get a degree.

I remember when you took every cent of your savings to go to New York to see him, Claudie said. *I'm not at all surprised you're with him. Besides, it's your life, no one else's.*

Stieglitz was intense and eccentric, as one might guess from his wild hair and piercing dark eyes and excited way of talking. He could be incredibly stubborn about little things, like how long a soft-boiled egg should be boiled. He hated change—he wanted everything to remain the same, always. He was also passionate and tender and as energetic as a man half his age.

He adored me, and I was mad for him.

Naturally, people soon found out about Stieglitz and me. We made no secret of our relationship. Some were shocked and outspoken about their disapproval.

Although I was thirty years old and was used to living as I pleased, I felt guilty about living with a married man. Stieglitz's wife was furious. His daughter, Kitty, took her mother's side and was also furious. I hadn't had any contact with my brother Francis in years, but I imagined he would have been severely critical. Alexius was sternly condemning—not only because Stieglitz was a married man, but because he was a Jew; somewhere along the way my favorite brother had become anti-Semitic.

But not everyone disapproved: Stieglitz's mother insisted that he bring me to their summer home on Lake George, and from the start she welcomed me as part of the big extended Stieglitz family. It was a marvelously happy time for both of us. Stieglitz took photographs and developed them in an old greenhouse that he'd somehow made lightproof, and I painted and painted—abstract watercolors of trees, a forest fire, canna lilies. Every evening, after dinner with the raucous Stieglitz clan, he and I rowed out onto Lake George, where the only sound was the creak of the oars and the lap of water against the hull. We watched in blissful silence as the sun disappeared behind the mountains and twilight descended, and rowed back by moonlight.

The war in Europe raged on through the summer with no end in sight. The newspaper headlines delivered nothing but bad news. The former president Teddy Roosevelt's youngest son, Quentin, had been killed, along with thousands of our "doughboys." The Germans had crossed the Marne River, not far from Paris. I heard that Ted Reid was in the Signal Corps and still hoping he'd learn to fly. Alexius had been sent home on a stretcher from the war in France with lungs badly damaged by poison gas. Paul Strand came by to tell us that he'd enlisted in the army and thought he'd be assigned to the Medical Corps. Stieglitz could hardly bear to speak about the war.

Then the tide turned, and in November, just days before my thirty-first birthday, the Germans surrendered. The armistice was signed on November eleventh. The Great War was over. The city was a madhouse, the streets jammed with people screaming, cheering, and crying.

In the midst of all the joyful celebration, I received a telegram that my father had died.

Papa had been working as a carpenter at an army base in Virginia, and he'd fallen off a steep roof. We had once been a close family, but although we still cared about one another, we had scattered and had little contact. There was no funeral. Ida, who was in nursing school, arranged to have the body sent to Sun Prairie to be buried in the Catholic cemetery alongside Papa's parents and brothers. Mama's bones would remain with her family in the Episcopal cemetery in Madison.

I had not heard from my father in a very long time, but his death came as a great shock and affected me much more deeply than I had expected. I begged Stieglitz not to speak of it. I had to work through the loss alone.

Yet despite the pain of Papa's death and the corrosive gossip about my personal life, my work was getting better and better—watercolors of mountains and landscapes around Lake George, still life oil paintings when we were back in the city. I was painting what I wanted, and recognition of my work was growing. I was achieving everything I wanted as an artist.

And Stieglitz was wholly responsible for it—not only with the hundreds of letters he'd written and the financial support he'd given me, but with his belief in me as an artist. His contacts with art critics and collectors, too, were crucial. He seemed to know everyone of importance in the art world, and he had a great sense of timing. He had shown my first work in 1917, when I was in Canyon, but he would not mount another exhibit until he felt the time was right.

By 1923, I had done over a hundred pictures we both knew were worth showing.

28

New York—Fall 1924

STIEGLITZ'S WIFE FINALLY GRANTED HIM A DIVORCE, and he wanted to get married. I did not. I was almost thirty-seven, and Stieglitz would soon be sixty-one.

"I don't see any reason to marry," I told him. "We're fine the way we are." We had been together for six years.

"I'd be doing it for Kitty," he said. "She might feel differently about me if we're married and she sees there is no way her mother and I would be together again."

I didn't think that my marrying her father, or doing anything except disappear forever, would change Kitty's feelings, but I finally gave in and agreed to the marriage. He'd be doing it for Kitty, and I'd be doing it for Stieglitz. The one thing I would *not* give in on, though, was changing my name. I was born Georgia O'Keeffe, and I would remain Georgia O'Keeffe.

On a blustery December day a few months after his divorce became final, Stieglitz and I took the ferry from Manhattan to Cliffside, New Jersey, to meet our friend, the artist John Marin. John picked us up in his new auto and, with another friend, drove us to a justice of the peace.

After we'd repeated the necessary words and signed the required papers, John drove us back to the ferry. Stieglitz and I were in the back seat, and when John took his eyes off the road and turned to say something, he struck a grocery wagon and then ran into a lamppost. The wagon was demolished and the auto banged up. No one was hurt, but it seemed like an ill omen all the same.

A year after we were married, we moved out of the tiny studio and into an apartment on the thirtieth floor of the Shelton Hotel. I liked the simplicity of our life there: a room as bare as possible with gray walls, simple furniture draped in white linen, and nothing else. We lived without a kitchen and took our meals at inexpensive little cafés—I didn't want to spend my time and energy on cooking and housekeeping duties.

I painted the view from our windows high above the East River, especially the stark lines of the buildings at night. Stieglitz tried to talk me out of painting views of the city and wanted me to stay with landscapes and still lifes. "Nature is a more feminine subject," he said.

I ignored that advice. I didn't believe that art had a gender, and I hated being referred to as a "woman artist." Why must every art critic mention my sex? I could answer my own question: because the critics—all of them men—did not take women seriously as artists. When my paintings were shown at the Academy of Fine Arts in Philadelphia, it was over the objections of the men in charge who did not want to have a woman's paintings in the exhibit.

My watercolors and oil paintings attracted a lot of attention, not just for my skill as an artist but for the subject matter that people found "shocking"—my enormous flower paintings. When Stieglitz saw the first one, even *he* was shocked.

"I don't know how you're going to get away with anything like that. You aren't planning to show it, are you?"

Of course I was! If I painted a flower in its actual size, no one would pay attention to it and notice its beauty. But if I painted it in huge scale, people would be startled, they'd *have* to look at it, and then they'd see how beautiful it was.

But he could not tolerate change of any kind—and that extended to my work.

The same men who wouldn't take women seriously as artists decided that my paintings were erotic. They wrote that the flowers were renderings of the female genitals. That had not been in my mind when I painted them. Those men were writing about what was going on in their own heads and had nothing to do with what was going on in mine. I resented their assumption that my paintings were about sex. I got sick of hearing about it and being asked about it, and finally I refused to discuss it at all.

Stieglitz said I ought not complain; the pictures were fetching high prices.

I continued to experiment with subject and style—landscapes, still lifes, abstract shapes. When I finished a painting, I'd hand it over to Stieglitz. He knew art collectors who were willing to pay top dollar for a painting, and he'd decide which collector was worthy of owning my work. I did a series of six small flower paintings that were hung together at a show. A collector—one whom Stieglitz had not met before—saw them and wanted to buy all six. Stieglitz quoted him a price that was outrageously high, and the collector immediately agreed. But even that didn't satisfy Stieglitz, who lectured the buyer on the responsibility he would take on when entrusted with "one of the greatest works of our time." To my surprise, the sale went through.

I was now recognized as one of the most important abstract artists in the country, and my work was selling. Everyone assumed Stieglitz was wealthy, but money had always been a problem for him. He had not earned much from his photographs, and 291 lost more than it brought in. Fortunately for him, his former wife was from a rich family, and the other Stieglitzes were very well off, but it was always a struggle financially for the two of us.

We cared deeply for each other, but from the beginning there were tensions in our marriage. I wanted to go new places and explore new things. Stieglitz wanted only his familiar routines and surroundings. He detested the sort of changes I thrived on. I was tired of spending rainy, cloudy summers at Lake George with three generations of the large Stieglitz family, plus all the friends who came there for vacations—*their* vacations, not mine. During the six months at Lake George each year, it was my responsibility to keep the place running. I craved solitude, I needed it to paint, but Stieglitz couldn't bear to be alone. He had to have people around him.

One of our visitors was Rebecca Strand, called Beck, whom Paul had married in 1920. The Strands' marriage was turbulent. I liked Beck, but it was plain that Stieglitz liked her even more. Certainly he liked to photograph her, and she was not his only subject. Beautiful Katharine Rhoades was another Lake George guest who posed for him. I'd first seen Katharine's paintings at 291 with Anita Pollitzer and Dorothy True when I'd been a student in New York, and had not been impressed by them. I remembered when Dorothy had suggested—jokingly, I thought—that Stieglitz's interest in Katharine was more romantic than aesthetic. I tried to ignore his intense focus on these women and said nothing. It would not have changed anything.

In New York Stieglitz had rented a small, rather shabby space we called the Room, where he exhibited my work as well as paintings by John Marin and Arthur Dove, and Paul Strand's photographs as well as his own. We had been married less than a year when he met Dorothy Norman. She was twenty years old—forty years younger than my husband—and was married and the mother of a young child. She was also very rich. She began coming to the Room, and soon this foolish young woman had installed herself there to "help." I could see that Stieglitz had fallen in love with her, as he had once fallen in love with me. Although he vigorously denied it, it was obvious to everyone that they were having an affair.

The situation was very painful, and when it became too much to bear, I went alone to Maine to paint. I stayed there for months and came back refreshed. Somehow we carried on. For years Stieglitz had been central to my life, and still was, as I was to his, no matter how many flirtations and affairs he indulged in. His health was declining. He had countless ailments, including many that were imaginary. Then he had a heart attack. Now he needed my care far more than I needed his.

His obsession with Mrs. Norman went on for four years. We never spoke about it—not one word. We pretended that it did not exist. I wanted him to give her up. He would not. And I recognized, without the slightest doubt, that I would have to make my own life, a life that was separate from his.

I did not know how I would go about that—until one day, I did.

29

Taos, New Mexico—Spring 1929

HER NAME WAS MABEL GANSON EVANS DODGE Sterne Luhan, and she was a wealthy patron of the arts with an apartment on Fifth Avenue as well as a home in Taos, an artists' colony somewhere north of Santa Fe in New Mexico. Mabel was a gregarious woman who made a habit of surrounding herself with interesting, creative people, and when I met her in New York she immediately invited me to come out west to stay with her in Taos.

Mabel had been married four times, three of them to rich, successful men. Her third husband was an artist who had taken her to Santa Fe; she'd moved on to Taos, where she'd fallen in love with the landscape. When she also fell in love with a Taos Indian, she divorced Husband Number Three and married Tony Lujan. She changed the spelling of his last name to suit her and was now known as Mabel Dodge Luhan.

I'd often recalled the trip Claudie and I had made to New Mexico the summer of 1918, always believing that someday I would go back. Maybe the time had come to do exactly that.

I told Beck Strand about Mabel's invitation. Beck knew Mabel, too. In spite of her flirtation with Stieglitz, Beck and I had become close friends. She had just survived another of her epic battles with Paul, and she was looking for an escape, or at least a respite.

"Let's the two of us make a trip out there together," Beck proposed. "Mabel is very rich, and she's also very generous. I know she'd welcome us both."

Predictably, Stieglitz resisted when I told him I was going, one minute shouting at me angrily, other times swearing that he adored me and only me, weeping that he would be lost if I left. He never said a word about Mrs. Norman, and neither did I, but she was the main reason I wanted to go away. He must have known that.

I ignored his pleas and tantrums, and at the end of April Beck and I boarded a train and headed for New Mexico.

For the next four months we were Mabel's guests at Los Gallos in Taos. We shared a cottage known as Casa Rosita, and I had my own separate studio with a splendid view of the mountains. Mabel loved playing hostess and knew everybody who was anybody in Taos. Sooner or later they showed up at Mabel's Big House for dinner, dancing, and lively conversation. When Mabel left for her hometown—Buffalo, New York—to have an operation, the merry evenings were discontinued, but we behaved like children whose mother had gone away and left them unsupervised.

One day I came back from a walk on the prairie and found Mabel's husband, Tony, polishing her sporty Buick roadster by the shed where it was usually parked. The auto gleamed like a black diamond in the late-afternoon sun. It was a beautiful machine.

"Tony," I said, "I want to learn to drive."

He carefully put away the wax and polishing rag before he answered. "Get in," he said. "I will teach you."

I slid behind the wheel, and Tony patiently explained the throttle, the brake, the clutch, and the gears. It was more complicated than I expected, but I began to catch on and steered it slowly around Mabel's Big House, stalling out a few times until I got the hang of it.

"Let's take it out on the road."

"All right," Tony said.

I drove cautiously at first, navigating the rutted lane toward the plaza and turning on the road leading to the pueblo.

"Bridge ahead," Tony said. "Take it slow."

I was exhilarated when we arrived back at Los Gallos after that first triumphant lesson.

"Can we go again tomorrow?" I pleaded, and Tony nodded.

But the second lesson did not go as well—there was that business with the posts at either end—and I had to pay to have the dented fenders and sagging bumper repaired. Mabel never said a word about it. I doubt that Tony told her.

Two weeks after that unfortunate event, a former photography student of Paul Strand's who was a regular guest at Mabel's dinners mentioned that he was thinking of selling his Model A Ford before he went back to New York.

I didn't hesitate. I bought it.

Beck took over the driving lessons. She wasn't as patient as Tony, and she claimed that I didn't pay attention. Nevertheless, I learned. I loaded up my easel and canvases, paints and brushes, and drove all over, exploring the magnificent New Mexico countryside, going wherever I wanted to go, stopping wherever I felt like stopping. I turned the back of the Ford into a studio, and painted whatever I wanted to paint—cow skulls, mesas, and an old mission church outside of Taos.

I had made up my mind when I was a young girl, a student at Chatham, that I would live my life exactly as I pleased. It had been eleven years since I stepped off the train in New York and into Stieglitz's world, an important decision that took my life—and my art—in a new direction. Now I'd made another important choice. I had taken control. Whatever happened between Stieglitz and me, New Mexico was the place I would always come back to, where I was finally at home. I knew with absolute certainty that *here* was where I would do my best work.

Epilogue

New Mexico—1929–1986

GEORGIA O'KEEFFE WAS FORTY-TWO WHEN SHE staked her claim to New Mexico. She would call it home for another fifty-seven years.

In 1939 she bought an old adobe house on a dude ranch and began knocking out walls and enlarging windows, keeping the light-filled interior spare with a minimum of furniture. But life at remote Ghost Ranch was primitive, and in 1945 she found a near-ruin of a house owned by the Catholic Church in the tiny village of Abiquiú (pronounced *AB-ee-cue*), about halfway between Taos and Santa Fe. The door in a long adobe wall attracted her, and she convinced the Church to sell the house to her. She remade that place, too, and divided her time between the two.

O'Keeffe continued to live with the increasingly difficult Stieglitz in New York and to spend summers with him at Lake George, but she always returned alone to New Mexico. Although the marriage was over, somehow she and Stieglitz found a way to get along as friends and business partners until his death on July 13, 1946. That same year the Museum of Modern Art hung a retrospective of her paintings. It was the museum's first solo exhibit of the work of a woman artist, a label she hated.

Through the years Georgia experienced dark days that sometimes stretched into weeks when she was unable to paint. Her habit of concentrating single-mindedly for days and then not doing much of anything for long stretches had driven Stieglitz crazy. "I know what I'm going to do before I begin," she explained, "and if there's nothing in my head, I do nothing."

She worked methodically, making a drawing on a prepared canvas and studying color samples before mixing the pigments. Her goal was to finish a painting by the time the natural light had faded, stopping only long enough to grab something to eat. She claimed that her best pictures were the ones she'd painted the fastest. A fierce critic of her own work, she destroyed a batch of paintings she didn't think were good enough to keep.

"Of course I destroy my old paintings!" she snapped when someone protested. "Do you keep all your old hats?"

Georgia traveled widely—to Mexico and the Grand Canyon, through Europe, Asia, and the Middle East, and to South America—but always returned home to New

Mexico. Assisted by her staff, she grew herbs and vegetables, tended the orchard, baked bread, and cooked healthy meals for herself and her friends. Although she craved solitude and was something of a loner, famous people flocked to visit her through the years, the photographer Ansel Adams and the poet Allen Ginsberg among them.

O'Keeffe's reputation continued to grow. In 1970, when she was eighty-three, her first major solo show at the Whitney Museum opened in New York. In 1977 the Presidential Medal of Freedom, the highest honor given to American citizens, was presented to her by President Gerald Ford.

Within a year of the Whitney Museum triumph, however, she had begun to lose her eyesight. Most of her central vision had gone when a young man named Juan Hamilton came by the house in Abiquiú looking for work, and she hired him to take over a number of practical chores. In her advancing years, Georgia had become imperious, unpredictable, and difficult if she didn't have her own way. Juan Hamilton knew how to get along with her, and his role and influence expanded. He showed her how to make pots—he had studied sculpture in college—and suggested that she try sculpture again. She found that when she worked with clay, her sense of touch was even more important than her sight, but she complained, "The clay controls me. I can't control the clay."

Even with her eyesight failing, she began painting again, using watercolors. Juan made sure collectors knew about her new work, fulfilling the role Alfred Stieglitz had once played, and her paintings were again in high demand. Prices skyrocketed.

Not everyone trusted Hamilton. Many felt that he was keeping her friends away from her and controlling her for his own benefit. But Georgia trusted him, and she wrote in her will that she was leaving him many of her paintings and most of her property.

Georgia O'Keeffe often said she wanted to live to be a hundred. She had come close to her goal when she died on March 6, 1986, at the age of ninety-eight. Her body was cremated, and Juan Hamilton scattered her ashes from the flat top of Cerro Pedernal, Spanish for "flint hill," the mesa that she had painted over and over during her years in New Mexico.

Her story has been told in television productions, films, biographies, children's picture books, and a selection from the more than *five thousand letters* that she and Stieglitz exchanged over the years of their relationship. In 1997, when the Georgia O'Keeffe Museum opened in Santa Fe with 140 of her paintings on display, more than fifteen thousand people stood in line the first weekend to see her famous paintings. The museum is still a major attraction, with several new exhibits opening each year. The research center maintains a library and archives, and her Abiquiú home has a yearlong waiting list for visitors.

Georgia O'Keeffe may be best known for her paintings of flowers on a large scale, as though they were being viewed with a magnifying glass. There are more than two hundred flower paintings, about a quarter of her work; other subjects are cow skulls, landscapes, shells, and abstractions, all in her unique style. One of her best-known flower paintings, *Jimson Weed/White Flower No. 1*, painted in 1932, sold at auction in 2014 for more than forty-four million dollars. Her painting of a poppy was issued as a stamp by the U.S. Postal Service in 1996; *Black Mesa Landscape* was issued in 2014. The Tate Modern, in London, exhibited more than two hundred works, including *Jimson Weed*, in 2016, exactly a century after Alfred Stieglitz first showed her paintings at 291 in New York.

Georgia O'Keeffe's reputation as one of America's most important painters remains undiminished, her work among the most recognizable. But she would not have been happy to be referred to as "the *mother* of American Modernism." You can almost hear her insisting that her work had nothing to do with being a woman and everything to do with being an artist.

Alfred Stieglitz's photograph of Georgia O'Keeffe
a few years before their marriage

Author's Note

I ARRIVED IN NEW MEXICO, AT AN ARTISTS' COLONY in Taos, in the late 1970s, intending to stay for a month, but the stunning beauty of the place had much the same effect on me that it must have had on Georgia O'Keeffe. I managed to stretch one month into nine, at the end of which the director informed me that it was definitely time for me to leave. I returned to Pennsylvania just long enough to pack my belongings and drove a U-Haul trailer across the country to Santa Fe. There I discovered O'Keeffe's work—flower paintings, cow skulls, majestic Pedernal—on posters and prints on the walls of corner coffee shops and high-end tourist hotels.

I met a man named Ben who claimed to be a great friend of Miss O'Keeffe and promised to take me to meet her in Abiquiú. That never happened, but a few years later I was invited to Ghost Ranch to teach a writing course, and I drove to nearby Abiquiú, a small village perched on a mesa, to look for her house. I had parked in front of St. Thomas the Apostle when a man with an enormous mustache, driving a pickup truck, chased me away. "This village is private property," he growled. "And you are trespassing."

Years passed before I began to write a novel focusing on Georgia's early years. While I was in the beginning research stage, I met Deborah Blanche, an actor and storyteller, who had developed a program on O'Keeffe that she presents to audiences in public venues around the country. In her one-woman performance, Deb transforms herself into Georgia with words, voice, dress, and mannerisms. Deb suggested a reading list of biographies from which I gained an understanding of the important events of Georgia's life.

Continuing the research, I pored over large-format art books featuring her best-known paintings, cookbooks with her favorite recipes, and a small book with some of the spare drawings and charcoal sketches she made while she was teaching in South Carolina. Deb also referred me to the research center, housed separately from the Georgia O'Keeffe Museum in Santa Fe. I watched videos, as Deb had, to get a feel for the sound of Georgia's voice.

I had lunch with my friend Consuelo, who has spent her life in northern New Mexico and was once offered a job as an assistant to Miss O'Keeffe in Abiquiú. "I turned it down," Consuelo said. "She was very imperious. She would have been much too difficult to work for."

When I write historical fiction, I don't change historical facts, but I do invent fictional people and places to create an engaging narrative. And I spend a lot of time online searching for the bits and pieces to make daily life come alive for the reader. When Georgia made herself clothes, how would she have sewn the seams so the skirt and jacket could have been worn inside out? What did Amitola look like, and how long would it take to row across Lake George? When she left Leah's farm in Waring, Texas, to go to San Antonio, how did she get there? If she went to an art exhibit in New York City, what would she have seen?

In the process of my sleuthing, I found a major error in the biographies. Georgia fell ill in Texas in January 1918; her condition was serious enough that she took a leave of absence from teaching, and she remained sick throughout the spring. Her biographers called the debilitating illness "influenza," which they said was sweeping the country. In fact, "Spanish influenza"—the flu—was first diagnosed in April of 1918 at an army base in Kansas, and it killed its sufferers in a matter of days, if not hours. Georgia had some sort of throat infection, but it was not influenza.

I am often asked about my research methods, and I wish I could say that I approach it in an orderly manner—but I don't. I read enough to figure out what direction the story will take, and I begin to write. The writing and the research proceed in tandem; there's always something I want to look up, another layer I want to uncover, and that often leads to something else, and so on. The research is finished when the book is finished and the story has been told as fully as I can tell it.

Carolyn Meyer

Albuquerque, New Mexico

To View Georgia O'Keeffe's Works

The Georgia O'Keeffe Museum Collections Online
cdm16622.contentdm.oclc.org/cdm/search/collection/
  gokfa

**A List of the Top Five U.S. Museums
with O'Keeffe's Work**
theculturetrip.com/north-america/usa/articles/
  the-5-best-places-to-see-georgia-o-keeffe-s-art/

Carolyn Meyer's
Other Calkins Creek Titles

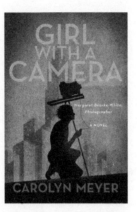

HC: 978-1-62979-584-3
eBook: 978-1-62979-800-4

HC: 978-1-62091-652-0
eBook: 978-1-62979-059-6

Picture Credits

Georgia O'Keeffe Museum, Santa Fe / Art Resource,
NY: 2, 312